The Intersection

Brad Windhauser

Black Rose writing™

First printing

ISBN: 978-1-61296-751-6
PUBLISHED BY BLACK ROSE WRITING
www.blackrosewriting.com

Printed in the United States of America
Suggested retail price $16.95

The Intersection is printed in Minion Pro

For Jared

The Intersection

1

On that Monday morning, Rose had been smoking outside the Laundromat. As usual, when the whirl of dryers and the thumping of the spin-cycling washers had overwhelmed her, she checked her watch. The children were about to occupy the soccer field across the street, so she left the office, checked the loose lock, clutched her single cigarette and lighter, determined that their two customers wouldn't need her attention, and pushed through the store's front door. There, by the corner, far enough from the entrance so her smoke didn't sneak inside the Laundromat, she lit her morning cigarette. Slightly impeded by a cloud of smoke, her eyes followed the little legs chasing after that white and black ball. She leaned towards the sounds of their shrieks of joy that cut as deeply as they soothed. Closing her eyes for a moment, she could feel her Charlie, hear him stomping through their front door, chasing his dreams into their kitchen.

Then, when it happened, she flinched.

She had thought all the dryers in the place had screeched, so she turned towards the store. But then the sound sunk in and she looked the opposite way, and peering up the street to the intersection, she saw the mess. She had recognized, she later understood, the sound of tires yelping, of metal meeting metal, of pain. Then a scream. Later, perhaps years later, she would never understand how she mistook all of that for the sound of dryers. But in that moment, she was afraid for reasons she could not yet comprehend. Everything stilled. That little girl shrieked. Or maybe she screamed before Rose had turned. The moment enveloped her, movement frozen, air vacant, sound thinned, like when the doctor tells you the cancer has taken your husband or the soldier walking to your door is about to tell you war has claimed your only son.

She stared at the intersection.

Fumbling with her glasses, "My lord, my lord," she repeated, her heart clenching. By the time her glasses were useful, that boy was motionless in the street; his dreads resting in the blood fleeing his body. The driver eased from his car, dazed. He turned towards Rose who snatching in her breath, almost hiccupped. One of their best customers, one of those people you never see on the news, the ones wearing their plain polo shirts and cuffed shorts; nice, close cropped hair. Then he started shaking, in a way she'd never seen a white person do in this neighborhood.

Folks started gathering at the corners of that intersection, and then she turned and shuffled towards the store. Lillian wouldn't understand watching trouble come together. Rose pictured that dark grey lock box on the office floor, the one that she avoided when she was in the office. She knew all too well that guns were nothing but napping snakes waiting to be aroused. She second guessed her decision, holding the door handle—should she? Imagining that she'd be of no real use, she opened the door.

Back inside, in the office, Rose slid the glass window open. With the remote, she raised the volume on the TVs. A woman dragging her children entered the store. She smacked one on the forearm, scowled up at the TV, and then shoved the children towards the washers in back. She yanked her laundry bag behind her. Rose resisted looking out the window, fearing what was collecting on that corner. She knew an ambulance would be there soon—and if she scrunched her ears she thought she heard a dull siren—but she feared what would happen to that white driver. Then she pictured that black boy's body sprawled in the street. A fire truck sailed past her window and turned down the street. Once all the official folks got things in order, could she be useful to the crowd? Who knew how her neighborhood would treat that white driver once the law left. Something had been set into motion that wasn't about to be easily undone. One of the dryers sounded, and she encouraged herself to stand. She needed to fold those clothes before the wrinkles set in, given Lillian's drop off service prices.

She shuffled towards the far wall, opened the dryer, and extracted the hot load of clothes into a basket-on-wheels. She eased the cart towards a table and pulled out the first shirt. On her third attempt, she was able to get the limp shirt folded. She set it down and scratched her scalp. A police car raced past the front window and turned down the street. Through her graying dreads, her short fingernails found skin, and she worked what she could. When the itch kept on, she let it be. With her restless hands, she jostled the change stuffed in her apron's front pocket. She would've whistled if she'd known how, but as soon as she thought about forming her mouth the way she'd seen folks do, she felt some heads turn in her direction, as if they thought she was studying them. She shuffled to the front and peered out the window. Still nothing to see. She leaned her ear against the glass. *Nothing.* She picked up some crumpled paper—looked like a receipt—and then returned to her folding table in the back of the store. *That nice white man. Oh lord, why did these things always happen to the good ones?* Of course, she was thinking of that poor black man, but the doctors would tend to him, and when he came home, folks would help him. That white man, given the way things were in this neighborhood, he'd be alone, most likely. She knew how a person needed people when your mind was in trouble, and seeing him shake the way he did, she knew he needed a hand from at least one person. She turned towards the TVs—yep, they were far too loud—so she reached through the office window, grabbed the remote, and turned them down.

Back at her folding table, when Rose had reached her fourth shirt, the young woman who had just entered stepped to her.

"The dryer ate my money." The woman, whose hand was thrust towards Rose, wouldn't meet her eyes. Her kids were busy opening empty dryers, sticking their heads in, screaming, and then slamming the door shut. Her hand, with those callused fingers and grimy fingernails, twitched a bit. Then, one of the children decided to chase the other around the middle island of washers and dryers. This woman's eyes were tired with shame. Those brand new machines had yet to eat one of Rose's quarters, of which Lillian had provided her 12 extra just in case. Seeing this woman's world in shambles in those cold eyes, Rose thought of the neighbors who brought food when her heart wouldn't let her cook in the house after Charlie and then Edgar.

Rose draped the shirt over the already-folded ones. "Which one, baby?"

The woman's eyes drifted to the side and down. "That one." She pointed over her shoulder.

"Momma, get me a soda." Her little boy jerked her sleeve. His eyes were great big moons.

"How many quarters did you put in, baby?"

She held up three fingers. The boy looked at Rose with those vacant eyes

Charlie used when she couldn't afford the toy in his hand. The woman's other boy was fussing with the broken sink faucet in the corner. Rose handed over three quarters. The woman turned and then dragged the boy behind her. He looked at Rose over his little shoulder. Her stomach got real tight. She turned and counted the full dryers—she'd have her hands full with five loads to fold. Would this occupy her mind long enough to forget about what she knew was happening in that intersection? She walked towards the front door but stopped half-way. *Don't get involved, don't get involved.* So knew something was gathering outside those walls—she could almost see the fire being built. She knew people were standing by with their kindling, waiting for sparks, and imagining that anger clouding those eyes, she flinched.

Back at the folding table, Rose lifted the next shirt and thought she saw a blotch. Clothes sometimes got tagged with bleach, seeing as how some folks didn't realize that their sloppiness with dropping bleach in at the wrong time could affect others. But Rose always sniffed before a load. She couldn't afford to wonder if Lillian would make her pay for ruining a customer's shirt. She held it up to the light. She could practically see right through those red threads. Her eyes roamed. The neckline was all stretched out. What a shame, though she was relieved.

The little boy by the sink darted over to his mother and brother. Before he said a word, the woman turned from the load of laundry she was busy over-stuffing into a dryer. "No, now quit." She held his eyes until he turned, slump-shouldered, and sulked to a chair. She looked at Rose, who turned away.

By the front window, trash blew past. Rose searched the floor. How many times would she have to scrub the floor to get those black scuff marks up? The ambulance whizzed past the window. She imagined that white driver would soon be alone, feeling a bunch of strangers' eyes on him.

He was a Thursday man, in the afternoon, right between pushes. After walking in, he'd set his baskets—one stacked on top of another—on a counter and then turn to set his car alarm. In those white and blue plastic baskets, his four loads already separated. His nice work shirts and pants sat on top of his whites in one basket; shorts, t-shirts and polos bunched on top of his towels and bed sheets in the other. Once he got his washers going, he mouthed "hello." From time to time, while he waited on his wash cycle, she'd mention a new show she wanted to see at the Academy of Music or the heat driving her crazy. But he never came over to begin a conversation. She couldn't tell if he maybe didn't want to disturb her while she folded. The better dressed white customers tended to do the same thing. With their eyes, they apologized for using the drop-off service for the armfuls of mingled white and colored clothes. Some clothes spilled every which way. Some of these folks you helped, if they apologized in that warm way that suggested they didn't expect you to (which some did).

That young man's words were warm, gentle. He seemed to bring a little sunshine with him every time, too. Once he showed for his fifth week in a row, Rose approached him while he was loading his wash. Before he had fed the last quarter, Rose touched his shoulder real soft so he wouldn't jump. "Baby, now let me show you something. Go ahead and deposit that last quarter." He smiled real shy and did as Rose told him. She lifted the detergent lid on the top of the machine. "These past few weeks, I seen you dump your detergent in all at once. You gotta split it up. Now, get on your tip toes a bit. See where it says 'pre-wash'? Now, you dip a little detergent in like this." She took his measured cap and poured some out. "In about seven minutes, this light will go off. You see here?" She pointed to the "wash" light. "When that lights up, you pour the rest of this here in there. That gives your clothes a nice, good wash." His eyes shone like he'd found a couple folded dollars in his pocket.

"Thank you very much." Though warm and full, his brown eyes were almost painful to stare at too long. So full with life. *Like Charlie's brown eyes.*

She patted him on the shoulder. "You call me Ms. Rose. You need anything, you find me." She felt like a shepherd welcoming a new sheep into the flock. She'd heard the whispers from a few black customers, that she was too nice to all these white folks coming in and taking over, but—and this was more than just her job, to make people feel welcome—she was wise enough to recognize that these folks were coming, whether you liked it or not, so might as well make them a part of what's already here rather than keep them apart and encourage them to start something new.

He'd check his dryers after 15 minutes, yank out a sweater or nice shirt, pat it down, and then sling them over the side of one of his baskets before he started the dryer again. When his loads were done, he folded his shirts in threes. His pants, he smoothed out the legs before bringing the ends together and folded them in half. People like him respected other things, Rose thought. Places, people. His socks, he tucked together. None of that turning them all into one another to make sure they stuck together. His underwear, stacked neatly. When he was done folding, he'd left no speck of lint, no trace of himself behind. But she hadn't seen that wide smile in four weeks. He'd been coming in with less clothes, loads all mingled. His face droopy, he'd been avoiding eye contact. He'd lean against the wall, staring at the dryer. His arms folded. There were times Rose wanted to sit down beside him, put her hand on his shoulder, like she used to do for all kinds of folks on the block when they came around worrying about some man problems, losing their job, their kids messing up again. Now, she wished she'd gone to him, maybe put an arm across his shoulders and rock him a bit, just like she used to Charlie when he'd come home from school. But then that young man would just scurry out of the store with his dry clothes all in an unfolded heap.

She knew without being told that he was a neighbor; people didn't come to this place unless they lived close. Instantly, she recognized her duty to welcome him.

She'd had high hopes for the Laundromat, studying the flyer in the window announcing the opening weeks before the washers and dryers had been delivered. The place was big, bright, clean, and all shiny new—finally, a respectable place to clean their clothes. She hoped that people would respect it. And she needed a job. A few people had traipsed through the door ahead of her—the first day the place had been open for business—and they left without a job as if life had wronged them again. Perhaps they should have worn an ironed shirt or slacks instead of jeans. When Rose entered—after lunch time, for Edgar had always told her people negotiated better on a full stomach—she collected a newspaper from the floor, balled it up, and dropped it in the trash before approaching Lillian, who had her eye on Rose the moment she'd crossed the threshold.

"Hello, are you the owner?" Rose had asked in her firm, professional tone Edgar had taught her. Command attention, he'd always coached her.

Lillian nodded. "Yes."

"I would like to apply for a job here."

Lillian's eyes floated to the trashcan Rose had just used. "Not enough work to hire someone. Bunch of people already ask." Her eyes looked over Rose's shoulders to some commotion. Rose turned. A man was banging on the dryer.

"Young man." The banging continued. Rose walked to him and placed a hand on his shoulder. "Young man, you got to respect these machines. Now what's the problem?"

"It didn't register my quarter."

Rose eyed the machine. At the coin return, a quarter rested. "This one?" She pointed to it.

"Oh." He grabbed the quarter and shoved it back into the machine.

Rose walked back to Lillian, whose mouth had lifted at the corners. "Maybe I see if we can find something for you. Leave me name and number and I call you."

Rose had Lillian's keys and her 12 quarters the next week. On her first afternoon, when someone walked in with an armful of dirty clothes, looking for drop off service, she said, "Put them on the ground there, baby. I'll get to them." She was surprised when the first face she encountered that day was white, and she smiled, although she had to admit it made her a bit uneasy, in part because she knew how her neighbors weren't looking for the change such folks tend to bring.

• • •

Four more baskets of clothes, folded and bagged; the folding tables, cleaned of dirt and lint; the trash, gathered and taken outside; the dryer lint traps, mostly emptied. With every task Lillian had set for her complete, Rose ached for her afternoon cigarette, although she wasn't yet ready for what she would or wouldn't see at that intersection. Still, she walked to the front door and stood.

"They chasing everyone out," a man who appeared next to her barked. He smelled of bad whiskey and cheap cigars. Was he talking to her? She turned. *Willis.* Crumbs dropped from his mouth as he spoke. She could tell by his stained teeth that he drank too much coffee. She wished he'd put on clean clothes rather than those dirty contractor overalls he was always wearing. "Coming in, buying up all our property, getting rid of us. Don't you agree?" His raised voice as much as his bitter words made her joints hurt. Yet she couldn't move. This day had awoken something in her, and she felt it her duty to monitor all chatter.

A couple weeks ago, he'd struck up a similar conversation. His eyes had been glued to that nice young man, watching as Lillian said hello and handed him a fabric softener sample. That nice man smiled, nodded, and then looked at the sample like he didn't know what it was. Lillian darted back to the office. Shaking his head at the same time, Willis couldn't have chewed that toothpick in his mouth harder. Willis had coughed. "Hmmf," he snorted, as if he held a lottery ticket and watched someone else's numbers drop.

Last week, he'd pestered people with, "you hear about how the city putting through that soda tax? Man, if that ain't the biggest piece of bullshit. How they expect people to live if they keep coming for us like this?" The lady he was next to shoved her stuff in a cart and found the farthest free table. When a man filled in the space a few moments later, Willis continued. "You hear how they're writing people tickets for being on a bike and running a stop sign. How do these people expect us to get around if they always on us?"

"Man, I heard that shit," the man said. Willis' face stiffened, like he was digging in for a full blown venting.

Now, at the front window, he slouched towards her, like a motivated salesman. He put a greasy hand on the glass she'd just cleaned. She had half a mind to simply walk away. Instead, before she could stop the words from leaping from her mouth, she heard herself say, "Don't want to sell, don't sell." She sucked in her breath—you never knew when you kicked a hornet's nest whether it was empty or not. She'd surprised herself with the antagonism in her voice—where had that come from? He eyed her like she'd just tossed a cigarette butt in his change cup. She organized the bags of folded clothes by the day they were due to be picked up. Willis fled to a plastic seat in the back of the store, by the woman whose kids were still running around like unleashed dogs. She may not have agreed with his anger, but she understood part of it.

When the first white face reappeared in the streets six years ago, escorted by realtors in suits carrying clipboards, they pointed out crooked windows, chipped paint, cracked sidewalks, and boarded-up shells like they were at a museum. The wave of change swelled, and as she looked at the bars on the windows, the ones she'd stopped noticing long ago, she didn't care if it crashed down, just as long as it scrubbed these streets. True, less leaves packed in the streets' gutters, more flowers in front of houses, but a lot more than trash was getting swept away. So she understood how people went from fighting their day-to-day struggles to now fighting for the roofs over their heads in a different way, as if the teacher had now returned to the room and they needed to behave, or else. Now this accident. If people lost their heads over it, they might thwart this change, but at what cost?

Then through the front window, Rose saw *her*. There, strutting outside that window, poking her head every which way. That Mexican gal caught

Lillian by the arm when she could, whispered, looked in Rose's direction every so often. She didn't have the decency to meet Rose's eyes as she snaked her way home. Rose knew which cards she was playing. She may not have been the quickest hands Lillian could have in that place, but Rose knew how to treat clothes. But did Lillian value her? That Mexican saw Rose, then scurried away like a little cockroach. She'd return.

Maybe Rose needed to trust Lillian, but anxiety raised would not be easily dispelled. She thought about how some customers rolled their eyes at Lillian, believing she was stupid because her English was kinda broken. They talked down her prices before Rose pointed to the price sheet posted by the office window. Rose couldn't imagine that Mexican having any luck with that. After one of those episodes, when someone huffed out of there, Lillian nodded and smiled at Rose. Were they a team? Still, Lillian kept the detergent and dryer sheets under lock and key in that cabinet by the office window. Lillian liked money more than she liked people, and Rose noticed her avoiding her more and more each time that Mexican appeared.

Rose felt the urge to speak to Lillian, like a sneeze gathering in her head, but Edgar taught her to keep her mouth shut when it came to work stuff. "Mouths make targets," he used to say. "Let someone else bring the fight, then slide right on through with the changes they bring." That philosophy kept him employed at the factory for 36 years. He may not have made it to the top, but he made day shift manager, and that was good enough. She had a feeling she shouldn't trust that all her hard work was being noticed. But should you have to convince someone that you're worthy? Maybe she was too old for this fight. Once, she would have left it in God's hands. If her hard work wasn't enough to keep her job, she would have to accept that. Of course, she'd surrendered Charlie's fate to Him, and look where that got her.

"Hey Miss Rose," Brenda yelled as she entered. Sometimes Rose would watch her boys when Brenda was in a pinch. She had her two full baskets with her. Rose opened a dryer and searched for any stray piece of paper or lint left behind.

"Hey baby, how you been?"

Good thing Brenda had missed that Mexican, for a couple of them had gotten her fired from a house cleaning job a few months ago. Whispering about her in Spanish, they were the ones who probably said she wasn't working hard enough. "If I could do it over, I would knock one of them bitches out for yapping about me, I tell you what," Brenda had said, shaking a bit.

"Let it go," Rose had said. On probation for her temper, Brenda'd come close to prison after she wrecked her baby's daddy's car with a hammer when he came round the block with a new woman. If Brenda went away for a stretch, Rose didn't have the energy to care for her babies. If Rose looked in the mirror right then, would she have seen that same look Brenda had on her face, as she was nibbling her finger nails, her jaw all tense? She should probably not mention that Mexican.

"Better than some folks. You hear how that white man hit that brother on the bike today? Bet you that motherfucker ain't going to do no time neither. Fucking white people moving into this neighborhood, just running people the fuck over like they just ain't nothing."

Rose stuck her head deep into another opened dryer. If she had had two hungry mouths to feed and no man to help, maybe Rose would find something to lash out at, too. She wanted to stick up for that nice young man, yet she knew how much Brenda's anger meant to her. Plus, since she'd said it loud enough to invite a conversation, one Rose knew was bound to happen, Willis would make his way over.

"No Lillian today?"

"No, not yet." Rose pulled her head out.

"Good." She jerked her clothes out of her baskets. "Can't stand that bitch."

"Where would you do your laundry if she hadn't opened this place?"

"I hate the way she always making eye contact and smiling fake. I get enough of that from the new neighbors. There's this white chick who jogs with her dog around the block, sometimes in the morning, sometimes in the evening. She always smiles when she passes, like we're friends. Two years ago, you never would've seen that shit." Brenda's tone tightened. "It's like that bitch and every other one of 'em is above us or something because she has the time and energy to bounce down the pavement like that without caring about anything." Rose was two moments from placing a hand on her shoulder. "It's as if whites are coming back to fuck with the community again after they bailed on this city decades ago. I don't trust nobody that don't look me in the eye. Fuck that."

"Don't you just love watching that bitch run away like that?" Willis appeared next to her, like one of those little devils on someone's shoulders in the movies. Brenda moved half a step away. "Doesn't even bother to learn to speak fucking English."

"Who you mean?" Brenda opened her wallet and pulled out some dollar bills. "Ms. Rose, the change machine working today?" She walked towards it.

A heavy-set woman plopped down on a plastic chair, dropped her McDonald's on the empty seat next to her, and rustled the wrappers. From halfway across the store those French fries reeked. Rose nodded at her. She smirked back and turned the music on her cell phone loud enough for the people outside to hear. She chomped that burger, sucking in air through her nose as she stuffed her mouth. Ketchup spurted on to her shirt. She rubbed it in. Before she was finished chewing she had a cigarette lit. Rose eyed Willis like he was a dog hovering by a plate of food. "Yes, it's working, baby."

"That Asian woman who run this place. Always scurrying to the office when too many of *us* is in here." Willis looked at Rose as he spoke.

"I know that's right." Brenda fed the machine.

"What'd you hear about the accident today?" Using his elbows, Willis rested on the table. Rose took her time cleaning a lint trap.

"Same as you, that the man driving didn't get taken away, that he'll be strutting around here, free as a bird. Ain't no shit going to happen to him, no how." The machine coughed up quarters like a slot machine. She gathered the quarters. Since they'd been so busy, Rose wondered how many were left.

"Say, I tell you about that white couple that moved next door, what a pain in the ass they turned out to be?" Willis leaned closer to Brenda's washer.

Brenda half rolled her eyes as she plunked the quarters in the machine. "Yeah, what they doing that's pissing you off?"

"Well, I should've known, they're dog people. You know, those white folks getting down real close to them, rubbing them behind the ears, shaking their fur, talking to 'em like they kids or something. They probably have that animal on their couch, snuggling up with them in bed." Rose scanned the room. Every washing machine lid was raised and only two dryers were spinning. She wondered how much time was left on it.

Brenda loaded her wash. Willis eyed each batch that dropped. "So anyway, last Saturday night, we were playing music—might've been a bit loud—kids were doing their thing in the basement, and we get this banging on the front door. It's a cop, talking how 'a neighbor' complained about our noise. I knew who it was, so I said to the cop as nice as I could, 'Go talk to them; them folks is the ones creating the problems. It's Saturday night, they should go out, leave their homes. I got kids, what their excuse?' But the cop wasn't hearing none of that, told us to turn it down."

"That the house with the tall flowers planted in the new window flower boxes?"

Rose coughed. "Now Brenda, did you check to see you ain't mixing no delicates in there? You know some clothes can't take the hot water. Take your time, get it done right." Willis eyed Rose, like she was swooping in on his commission. They all three just kept looking at each other.

A dryer sounded.

"That's me. I am going to dump that in the basket and head out. You take care, Brenda." Willis shuffled away. Brenda shook her head. Rose felt a hollowness open in her, like she was soil that had just had plant roots ripped from it.

Rose needed a walk, maybe a high-ball before heading home. This uneasiness building inside her, crouched and hissing like a hungry, mangy alley cat in her gut, would not be discouraged. She needed to pass the intersection on her way, but what troubled her wasn't what she would see but what she wouldn't. Too many times in her life, misery had blindsided her, but this time, she would see the warning signs, and if one didn't jump at her, she'd look harder. Something wicked was brewing. Her neighborhood needed her—whatever that might mean—and not just that white driver, whose name she didn't even know yet. But, if she tried, she was sure she could find someone who did.

2

A week before the accident, the line had gone dead; Carol had heard the click, then a brief moment of silence, soon eclipsed by droning. Against her ear the cold phone rested. Geoffrey had provided details of his classes that week, evasive answers about his dating life, and something about his hopes for the upcoming neighborhood association meeting. During this particular weekly chat, he felt the need to obsess about this new park in his neighborhood, as well as a few shells that had been sold and extensive rehabbing undertaken—*had she ever known three-story houses on her old block?* he'd wondered, in his naively hopeful voice. Why in the world did people like her son romanticize those filthy, dangerous streets? Lord knew, growing up, she hadn't seen a spec of which to be proud in that neighborhood. Hadn't they given him enough money to live more sensibly? A vague, bad premonition nipped at her, not unlike the vexing feeling when, sitting in a court room, she'd nailed closing arguments, but then the judge walked in, scowling in her direction. There, in her kitchen, standing on bare feet, she noticed that the lush forest green marble tile (which she'd bought against Mason's protests) felt colder than she'd ever noticed. Her eyes focused on a fly fluttering against the sparkling glass of their sliding door, and then she heard the lawnmower's buzzing, which threatened to engulf her kitchen. The appalling noise machine turned at the edge of their deck and clattered towards the back wall. *Had she told her son that she loved him?* She set the phone down.

Across their lawn, the mower chugged, leaving an erratic line in its wake. Far too close to their stone back wall, the mower turned and plodded towards her.

She jostled her head like she'd just awoken from a nap, and walked to the bay window. There, with the back of her hand, she nudged aside Mason's new bonsai tree, which he had insisted could not catch the right amount of light anywhere else. Why she thought this small window would afford her a better view than the glass door, she wasn't sure—perhaps less by which she could be distracted? Watching the gardener slow, make a circle, then double back towards their wall—and, this time, far too close to the flower bed Geoffrey had helped her plant—she wondered what type of insurance this new company carried. The first half of their lawn had been shorn evenly, appropriately; but this second half was apparently more challenging, for certain patches gave this section the slight appearance of rolling hills. So much for Russell and Stephanie's recommendation. The cheery white couple next door would undoubtedly ask how *their man* had taken care of them, so what would she say? On a chaise lounge on the deck, Mason rested, a copy of the *New York Times* propped on his chest. His eyes followed their mower like a gambler tracking his horse. She walked to the sliding glass door and opened it.

Mason's gaze never wavered from their help. Not when she eased into the unoccupied chaise, not when she cleared her throat, especially not when the gardener slowed the mower, hopped off it, and crouched in order to inspect the side. He wiggled something with his filthy hand and then shook the fallout from his fingers onto their grass.

"I'm worried about Geoffrey, Mason."

"Hmm." His eyes narrowed. She wondered if he wished he'd had his opera glasses close.

"I'm serious, Mason. Listening to him prattle on about his plans for his eventual degree. I wondered if we shouldn't have discouraged him pursuing that urban planning program with a little more effort."

"He's an adult now, Carol, and about time he made his own mistakes." The gardener inspected the machine's other side and then cut the engine.

Mason's face tensed, drawing her attention to his ears and to the long, curled graying hairs protruding from them. She wished she could yank those unsightly hairs with her fingertips. Why, why hadn't she forbidden Geoffrey from living in that awful, trash-strewn neighborhood? Why hadn't her husband supported her reservations when they'd discussed it?

"How much latitude do you plan on providing this one?" she asked, as the man wiped his hands on his shabby jeans and returned to the mower's seat and started the engine.

"A few more attempts." He snapped the paper as if he'd be able to concentrate on one single article when the mower resumed its zigzagging away from them.

• • •

The following Sunday night, she dreamed of a capsizing cruise ship—that Alaskan cruise had been on her mind, hadn't it? This dream was then followed by one in which she was hopscotching with an old friend on a cracked sidewalk. The brilliant yellow of the chalk caked to the bottom of their shoes. Her mother reprimanded her for tracking it into the house, up the stairs, and all over her parents' bed comforter.

She woke exhausted.

Replaying these two dreams, Carol breezed into the downtown Philadelphia courthouse building. She smiled at the handsome gentleman who had held the door for her. As she strode towards the elevator, she used the hand not occupied with her briefcase to button her suit jacket. She pushed the "up" button on the granite wall. *Darnell better have worn that suit.* Should she have reminded him to press it? Judge Williams had a thing about proper attire. If today ran smoothly, she could accommodate Geoffrey's small window between classes, even though he'd been evasive when she'd texted the suggestion. She entered the elevator and fanned herself as it lifted.

At the fifth floor, she exited, turned right, and then paused at Room 3's door. She would get her client custody. That child needed a good, stable home. Her heart galloped.

Already at the conference table sat Darnell. She cringed at the suit drooping off his shoulders and took the chair next to him.

"Darnell, how are you?"

He turned, and the cheap cologne leapt off him. "Do you really think this is going to swing our way today? What if the judge sides with her? What then?"

She checked her watch. They had eight minutes. She wondered what response would quell his anxiety and at the same time discourage small talk that might involve his neighborhood. She'd almost recognized the address he'd provided on the community center form he'd completed, but, as with every case she'd taken on as part of her once-a-month pro-bono work downtown, she tried not to picture those blocks she'd grown up on. Sure, these people needed help, but from a reasonable distance—a safe distance. Why couldn't Geoffrey understand this? "Darnell, your case against your ex is fairly solid. We have her recent stint in rehab on our side. The judge likely won't grant her a fourth chance. Relax, if you can." She crossed her legs. As she did so, she noticed a stray thread at her skirt's hem. *Hmm.* "May I have your lighter, Darnell?"

"My what?"

"Your cigarette lighter, Darnell, may I borrow it for a moment?" She extended a hand while fingering the fraying hemline with fingers from the other. Another article to be donated.

"How do you know I smoke?" He sounded like a child who had eaten the last cookie.

"Darnell, if you don't want people to know you smoke cigarettes, you should realize that no amount of cologne disguises that smell for long." Grudgingly, he placed the grimy lighter in her hand, and, quickly, she singed the thread. After she returned the lighter, she wished she'd bought that bottle of Purell on her way home yesterday, the one that occurred to her as she passed the drug store parking lot.

The door opened and a court reporter entered, followed by the judge, who clutched a folder and notepad. Darnell bolted up while Carol eased from her chair. She whispered to her client, "Relax." He nodded.

The judge settled at the head of the table, while the court reporter set up the stenography machine across from them. "Good morning, counsel. Please take your seats." He opened the folder and plopped a pen on his notepad. "Counselor, I have reviewed your petition and now you may make your client's case, as to why I should grant this custody petition."

Straightening her back, Carol placed her hands on the table and cleared her throat. "Your honor, my client's child is currently under the custody of her mother, who, unfortunately, has fallen into drug addiction, placing this child in harm's way every moment she lives under that roof. We ask that you grant the custody petition for the sake of the child, to come live with her father, who is more than prepared to care for her wellbeing."

"Your petition states that the mother is in treatment currently."

"She is in a six-week in-patient facility. Though this is her third time through and we have little confidence in her ability to remain sober."

"And in whose care is the child currently?"

"The grandfather."

His pen whipped across his page, his brow creasing. He lifted his head and studied Darnell. His eyes shifted to the drooping jacket.

"The petition does not mention why your client was not awarded rights before. Why wait until now?"

"My client was without gainful employment, a situation remedied five months ago." She cleared her throat. "Together with a strong community, he is now in a position to care for his daughter." She hoped the line had carried the whiff of truth she needed it to, though she'd struggled with the statement's validity when watching herself practice it in her mirror.

"What kind of drugs are we dealing with?"

"Crack. Crystal meth. Oxycontins."

He scribbled. "Was he aware of the mother's drug use?"

"He suspected, but lacked confirmation." He crossed his arms and cocked his head. She continued. "There was a restraining order, which limited his ability to ascertain the situation's severity. When he received a phone call from the child's aunt, he took the necessary steps to protect his child." Slowly his arms dropped, like they were parts of a draw bridge she'd been waiting to cross.

He fiddled with the pen, perhaps waiting for the right words to cross his mind, and then the pen dashed on that pad. Her heart thumped at a comfortable, measured pace. Out of the corner of her eye, she saw sweat trickling behind Darnell's ear and into his collar. "Okay, counselor, I will review all of this information, taking into account what you have added here. You will be paged when I am ready with my decision."

• • •

Later than she had wanted, she learned she had won her client's case. Resting on her chaise lounge, the cool air kissed her ear lobes. The light traffic on her drive home had softened her disappointment over missing Geoffrey. And as she had reached her highway exit, she questioned why she had been so determined to try and meet him for coffee, which they hadn't found time for in months. Surprisingly, the lawn looked meticulously groomed. Staring at the cropped blades of grass—perhaps the days since it had been cut had encouraged it all to fill out appropriately?—she wondered if Mason had landed in Hong Kong yet. His frustratingly packed itinerary was difficult to manage, though she was sure he'd already taken off. Hadn't he? The chilled glass of a wonderful Chenin Blanc perspired on her hands and, for some reason, she did not mind.

She sipped her wine, and then set her glass on the side table. The envelope was waiting but she had needed the wine to tickle her finger tips first. Correspondence from Sherri required that little lift. With her fingernail, which she was having done tomorrow anyway, she slashed the top of the tea green envelope. At least her taste in stationary had, apparently, improved, though those new envelopes were far too thick. She extracted a bulky folded paper and something dropped into her lap.

A newspaper clipping. She considered it like it were an annoying ladybug that had just landed on her, one which she would have simply shooed away had she not allowed it to linger a moment longer, hoping it would fly off on its own. Reluctantly, she unfolded the paper and angled it towards the patio light. Near the top, in Sherri's scratch-like cursive, she'd dated the article. On a small fluorescent blue post-it, a note: "I'd set this aside for you a while ago; just found it." A two-year old article. On the accompanying stationary: "Hope you're well, S." Carol sighed and shook her head.

"Graduate Hospital, Philly's Next Real Estate Hot Spot." Carol rolled her eyes. Amidst the text, a map of the area, which Sherri'd outlined. A thick scribbled red arrow pointed to their parents' former block, as if she could have forgotten that house. She folded the article and, after lifting her glass, placed it on the envelope and note. At least she now didn't need to fetch a coaster. *Sherri, Sherri, Sherri. Always with one foot in the past.*

Her attention turned to the bushes and then to their stone wall comprised of the river rocks Carol had sourced from a quarry in western Pennsylvania. Even from where she sat, she appreciated how the variations in color complemented one another well. Then she leaned forward: *what is that roundish object in the grass?* She squinted. It wasn't moving, whatever it was, so she stood, and then fetched a flashlight from the kitchen and crossed her yard. Half way, she turned on her light. Approaching the wall, she slowed and the light revealed a basketball. *Those neighbor kids again.* Through the bushes that divided their two yards, she eyed their basketball court. She retrieved the ball, realizing too late as she handled it, that it had dirtied her blouse. She had almost foisted the ball through the bushes when she stopped. How many times had they been told to control their balls? They'd pester her about the ball tomorrow.

In the house, she crossed the kitchen and opened the basement door. Descending the stairs, she guided herself with the wall. At the bottom, she groped for the light, which she was sure was in reach. Finding the cord, she pulled and could finally see. To her right, she walked to the sturdy clear plastic bins shelved. *Why wasn't some of this stuff in the attic?* she thought, as she surveyed their contents. On the middle shelf, there'd be room among their strings of summer lawn lights. Into that bin she stuffed the basketball and returned the bin. She blew dust from the tip of her nose, and then walked upstairs and back outside.

Settled on her lounge, she fanned herself. When she felt sufficiently cooled, she reached for her glass and plucked the now damp article from underneath. She sipped, rolled the wine around her tongue, and then swallowed slowly. There in the moonlight, she felt, as her grandmother would say, right as rain.

Grandmother. She could still hear the musicality in that strong, though overly optimistic woman's cadence.

"Always believe in the good of people, Carol." Her words coasted on the buoyancy of a full holiday belly, even on those days when she would learn that her vacationing neighbor's copper piping had been cut out by thieves who walked it out the front door. Yet while Carol was growing up in that filthy pocket of Philadelphia, which white flight had left pocked with crime, violence, and sadness, she used to immerse herself in television shows. Seeing on a nightly basis all that she didn't have, Carol failed to understand from where her grandmother's hope had originated.

As that child, she could have never imagined that her life would have turned out like it had, although she'd dreamed it would. Her law school parachute had opened on the first try; her marriage anchored her; the suburbs had insulated her; and like the others who had managed to flee, she'd never looked back, only tethered to that life by the family who'd remained behind. Now, she would tell her grandmother, she'd learned you didn't have to believe in people as much as understand them. And that neighborhood had taught her plenty.

• • •

Later that night, at her kitchen table, she thumbed through a Pottery Barn catalog. The phone rang. She couldn't know that when the voice on the other end finally finished, she'd be fumbling for her car keys, nearly slip in the garage getting into her Lexus coupe, curse the front gate for inching open, honk her way through the sparse traffic on the Schuylkill Expressway, berate the hospital clerk for his ineptitude until a doctor calmed her down with the details: her son had been in a bad bike accident and his prognosis was grim. Watching the phone ring that night all she could think about was how, time and time again, those persistent telemarketers just didn't get the hint that she couldn't be less interested.

3

Almost two years before the accident, Michael was desperate to own a home. Constrained by a modest salary and little to put down, he took a chance on an "up-and-coming" neighborhood. Convinced the time window within which he'd be able to still afford this "great opportunity" was diminishing, he'd scoured the MLS database, emailed potential properties to his realtor, and showed up for the scheduled appointments. To his dismay, more than one owner had allowed their property to fall into disrepair, and although these homes might have been a "good buy," he was no miracle worker. Still, he'd wanted to grab a rag, a duster, a paint brush, hedge clippers, and perhaps a bottle of bleach and contribute a little love before moving on. Bolstering his anxiety, he was maintaining his high spirits for two, for his boyfriend Aiden was doing everything he could to sabotage their—okay, *his*—quest, and he was exhausted. So with his enthusiasm flagging, he stood on the first floor of house number 13, for which Walter had graciously scheduled a showing. He was imagining how he could make this one work, if for no other reason than to put this whole excruciating process to bed. His armpits sweat in ways he hoped didn't show. Biting his lip, he watched Aiden pull a marble from his pocket, crouch, and ease his hand towards the hardwood floor like he was approaching a ticking bomb. Michael winced when he eyed Walter, who, having ushered them through this latest reject, had yet to apply any pressure. *Just how much patience did the promise of a future commission buy?*

Aiden lined up his marble along some imaginary line. Annoyed that Aiden kept belittling the options their budget could afford, he wondered what it would take for him to accept that new construction wasn't in their cards. Who needed 90-degreed corners, flush floor grooves, bathroom fixtures still cellophane-wrapped, the warranty information dangling from the refrigerator, when you could finally achieve the security of owning your own property? Aiden let go.

The marble rolled between the wood planks and then curved towards the baseboard, which it tapped before retreating. It stopped. Sauntering towards the marble, and using only two of his boney fingers, he plucked it like it was a flower. Michael wanted to apologize to Walter, thank him for wasting his time, but the moment had been lost when Aiden smirked. No one likes a smug asshole.

"How about we give the rest of the house a good walk-through?" Walter motioned towards the stairs and moved over the black scorch mark in the floor's center that hopefully Aiden hadn't noticed. Sure, the house needed some extra love, but there was so much space—three stories—and so much potential.

"Pretend nothing is the way it is, imagine everything it could be," Walter said as the stairs creaked with each step. The hand rail wiggled underneath his fingers. "You buy on the future, not the present," he encouraged. Was he hoping this time the advice would stick? When they hit the spongey second floor landing, Michael avoided Aiden's eye contact.

Walter sniffed and seemed to be searching the air for something. He looked at his feet. "As you can see, the owners have Berber carpet down. It was a rental, and it's good for high traffic, but you could probably pull it up if you want to go with the floors underneath." Michael had to resist yanking up a corner to peek. He'd made that mistake at the last property.

"A really great supermarket that was just overhauled is five blocks up. Also, two really cool coffee shops opened recently in the area. One's on 22nd, between Pine and Spruce, and the other is over on Catherine, at 20th, I think." His voice sounded hollow in that used car salesman way, a point that Aiden would mention. "You gotta see the cabinets they put in the remodeled kitchen on this floor."

In the second floor kitchen, Michael followed Walter's eye to a haphazardly discolored spot in the ceiling. At least the window was clean. Their shoes squeaked on the cheap linoleum that was curled at the corners. At that moment, he was trying not to think about why there was a second kitchen upstairs.

Aiden tilted his head slightly at the cabinets. "They're up there straight, it's just the walls that are a bit off." Walter nearly choked on the words, but

Michael understood. This neighborhood had just moved off the low-income census tract and deals were as good as they were going to get. Michael wondered if Walter could see the desperation that floated in his eyes. "You look like a shelter dog," Aiden had told him. He wanted to retort, "Look, I, *we*, need this to happen," but why bother? Aiden would appreciate it down the road, he was sure of it.

Then they reached the bathroom and the pink tile. *That could be replaced easily, right?* "Oh, there'll be no showering in here," Aiden announced as he surveyed the tub in desperate need of caulking. They coasted towards the front bedroom, where the easiest thing to process was the single-pane, non-double hung windows. He was losing track of just how much cash they would need to bring this place up to snuff. Aiden flicked the glass with his finger. "Are they still offering tax credit for upgrading to energy efficient windows?" He wondered if he sounded like Rudy in that football movie wanting to play the last set of downs.

"Yes, but you have to lay out the cash first." Now Walter avoided eye contact.

Michael turned his head back to the open area just before the bedroom, the area they zoomed past. They could fit a couch there and maybe have built-in bookcases built cheaply enough. He'd even be able to stain them to a nice walnut. That he was sure he could handle.

"There'd be too much natural light in this room. Can you imagine what the mornings would be like?"

Aiden was close enough to the window to squish his face against the glass. Walking over, Michael reached for his hand. Instead of accepting the gesture, Aiden walked to the center of the room. "I bet the wiring is awful behind those outlets. Look how old they are." Aiden shook his head as he gazed near the floorboards.

But look at this amazingly intricate crown molding, he'd wanted to stay, but he knew Aiden would only notice the stains in the grooves then bitch about the bubbling wallpaper—which, admittedly, was hideous, but would hopefully peel right off, given the condition.

On the third floor, they didn't know how they felt about the drop ceiling either. Was it really in all three of the bedrooms? Aiden chuckled as he used the sole chair in the room—where did that even come from?—to peer up there.

"Could we get the tiles to match the grid?" Walter followed Michael's eyes to the sun-bleached tiles held aloft by the grimy metal frame.

"Ah, probably."

They trotted downstairs. So maybe this house wouldn't work, but looking at the awesome, dark wood of the front door, he couldn't help clinging to the idea of: *well, maybe*. After all, people had been living here for years, right?

In a tone often used by toll collectors wishing you a good day, Walter went through the motions of saying, "So, what do we think?" They stood in the foyer, the breeze floating through the opened front door, the one kept ajar by Aiden's restless foot. Walter's nostrils flared as he took a deep breath and turned his back towards the door. "Michael, you should really spend a few days and walk these blocks, get a feel for the neighborhood's energy. No more houses for now. But, given what I know about your finances, it would be remiss of me not to say you will be priced out of this market sooner than later, so if you're really serious about buying here, you're going to have to bite on something, and soon."

Aiden whistled the *Star Wars* Imperial theme and Walter closed his eyes, ran his tongue along the ridge of his top teeth, then looked at his shoes.

"Yeah, that would be a good idea." Aiden tapped on the door with his nails. "Shall we?" Michael motioned towards the front door.

"I have to tend to the backyard a bit. I'll talk to you soon." He extended his right hand.

Before Aiden stepped completely outside, Michael offered. "Need help?"

Walter cocked an eyebrow. "Not necessary, but, if you have nothing better to do at the moment, I could give you a lift home when we're done."

"Aiden, if you want to head out, I will hang a bit."

"Have fun." He vanished, and when the front door closed a breeze whistled through the mail slot.

"Do yourself a favor, give the place another walk-through. Since I'm the listing agent on this house, I can tell you, without a conflict of interest, that the seller is motivated. When you're done, meet me out back." Michael took a deep breath. He felt freer with Aiden gone but he'd be lying if he didn't feel like he was cheating. Even worse, he could tell Walter was waiting to pity him, so he turned his head.

He revisited every floor of that house, and as he did he noticed more flaking plaster this time around but minded less the slight slant in the second floor wood flooring; paid closer attention to the kitchen window that didn't quite close but fiddled with the pink bathroom tile and realized how easy the demo would be. *Could I really pull this off?* Could he ignore the cosmetic imperfections until he could afford to address them in his own time? Upstairs, he stared out the window in what could be the master bedroom. Would this be his morning view? Had fate really shown him the article that touted how Graduate Hospital was the next real estate hot spot?

He trotted down the stairs two at a time, ignoring the creaking.

Michael met Walter outside, and as he did, he hoped he'd given the house a respectable amount of time. Fifteen minutes was plenty to decide that he could make the house work, right? Walter was sizing up a tree. Or maybe it was a weed. Whatever it was, it was about five feet tall, thick enough to take both hands to grab, and branches with leaves. "This has got to go," he informed Michael.

Michael eyed the Charlie Brown Christmas tree looking weed, if weeds had limbs that looked like a tree. If he was going to buy this house, shouldn't he have a say in it staying or not?

"My guys were supposed to get rid of this but it must have slipped their mind. You think we can yank this out?"

Michael shrugged. Could they? *Should* they? What, exactly, was the problem? Michael kept looking at it, as if it were going to answer him.

"These invasive weeds are the scourge of many residents, especially when they explode in size, at which point, they overtake these access alleys." Walter motioned to the area beyond the chain link fence, as if Michael didn't know what an access alley was. "You got to catch these things before the roots dig deep and wreak havoc on the backyard's concrete."

Michael looked at the six limp branches looming over the fence, picturing them thickening and maybe sprouting something. Walter shook it like it was a gift-wrapped box. That base was in there solid. He shook it again, as if he hadn't done a good enough job the first time. This produced the same dejected expression on his face.

"I guess you don't have any tools for this task?"

"Like a shovel?" Walter asked.

"I guess."

"Nope."

Walter tilted his head and kicked the base of the tree once more. Though the limbs shook, the trunk didn't budge. Clearly, the tree/weed was being a pain in the ass.

"Should we give it a few tugs and see what we're working with?"

"Sounds good." Walter rolled up his sleeves while Michael waited.

Walter put his foot to the side of the tree and applied pressure with his hands. Then he pulled them away, inspected them, flicked dirt from his palm with his thumb, and then gripped again. He nudged it. Dirt from the overhead branches landed on his head. He brushed himself off and then lowered his grip. The bark/skin oozed pale green. "Might gloves be a good idea?"

"Got any?"

Michael shook his head, and felt like an idiot for suggesting it. "What should I be doing?"

"Um, nothing yet."

Walter hunched over and wrapped his hands around the tree. As he continued to muscle the trunk from side to side, the dry ground eventually gave. Roots snapped but the base held. *Progress.*

"Come on, you." Walter gritted his teeth in a way that looked painful. "Okay, why don't you grab here, and when I say go, pull hard."

Michael set his hand below Walter's grip. "Okay, now."

They pulled, and the trunk gave. Most of the base, however, was stuck in the ground. Michael let go. Walter hoisted the majority of the tree over the fence to the access alley. When some limbs snagged the chain link, he yanked the branches free, and dusted off his hands. "No one goes in the access alley anyway," he said. If this were true, what was the big deal with them being "compromised"?

Michael looked to the clear blue sky. A little bird landed onto a branch of the burly tree growing over the neighbor's fence. The bird chirped a happy melody. They stared at the fragile bird, which had no care in the world. "You know, Michael, it's not my business, but I will say, because you look like you can use some sage advice: Don't be afraid to jump on one of these house on your own. This one might not be the best bet to take it solo, but there will be one that is." He put a hand on his shoulder. "It's going to be okay, with or without Aiden." Michael could not take his eyes off that happy-as-hell bird.

Five houses and four months later, Michael found his home—two-story, two-bedroom, one bath house, all renovated, central air. It was two blocks south of where he'd seen himself—them—living, but the numbers worked well and it felt right. At the closing, Walter reassured, "You bought the right house, Michael." He hadn't bothered to ask why Aiden hadn't showed. Why hadn't Michael insisted?

A week after that, Walter sent a pricey mail-order steaks selection. The accompanying card read: "Congrats on your new home. I thought you'd get the wrong idea if I sent a fruit basket."

Now, the night of the accident, two months since Aiden had left him, *them*, this *home*, for that piece of shit, back-stabbing friend of theirs… he still had half those steaks left. Damn you, Aiden. Damn *him*. Damn this house, damn everything. What a fucking mess life was at the moment. He was cursed, that was it, and that poor guy, whose body he kept seeing every time he blinked, was screwed because of him, too. The moment he'd gotten home from the accident, he had closed the blinds in the front room as tightly as the wand would turn. A headache was coming and he had little time left. He'd swallowed three ibuprofens and counted the seconds. After soaking a washcloth in scalding hot water, he had eased onto the sofa and closed his eyes. That guy kept coming, over and over, and over and over. His head turned on the pillow, and then he caught a whiff of Aiden and he scrunched his eyelids tight. *Why me?*

The minutes ticked by, and with no peace in sight and the washcloth growing more useless on his eyes by the moment, he sighed a pity-me sigh. *Was Elizabeth back from Italy yet?* Of course, she'd screen his call. The last time they met for drinks, she looked exhausted sitting across from him, listening to him. "Here," she'd said in a voice people use when grudgingly handing a homeless person a few dollars, "this might help." Across their small table she slid a standard envelope that contained a small bump. As he stared at it, she said, "It's a seed. Pot it. It will soothe you to have something small to nurture." Had there been a sadder parting gift? When she walked away from their hug, down the block towards her car, he knew he'd lost her, at least in the short term. Who was left? Now, just when he'd reached a plateau with Aiden leaving and accepting that he'd screwed himself with this house and there was not a thing he could do about it yet, *this* had to happen. If only he weren't *anchored* here. Sure, he had *some* equity, but he hadn't been here long *enough*. At least he didn't have to feel guilty anymore about all the equity being only his. God, he hoped that guy on the bike was okay. It would be wrong of him to call the hospital, right? Of course, he was probably going to be sued on top of everything.

You know your life has bottomed out when all you can do is obsess about money. He walked to the dining room. There on the table, the empty pot, a small bag of potting soil, and the envelope that contained the seed. Sure, he'd gone to Target to buy these things, pretend he was going through with it, but yet there they sat, untouched. *It will do you some good to nurture something,* she'd said. What's the worst thing that could happen? He grabbed the pot, the soil, and the envelope, and walked to the kitchen, where into the sink he placed his burden. He tore open the bag and then filled the pot about ¾ of the way with dirt. Was that enough? Too much? He added more. Then, after setting the bag down, he picked up the envelope, tore free a corner, then coaxed out the contents. The tiny seed felt weightless. He dropped it into the center of the dirt, pressed it down with his finger, and then added more dirt. After tapping it down, he added water from the faucet. Should he add more water? How easy was it to kill a seed? He stood back. Staring at the mound of dirt, he wondered how long this would take, to find out if he'd failed at this too. Maybe he should suck it up, admit defeat, and sell. Another fucking move wouldn't be the worst thing in the world. It was, after all, in his DNA.

As a kid, he'd logged his fifteenth address by his fourteenth birthday. Dad had made moving seem effortless. They'd occupied various parts of the Philadelphia suburbs as well as the northeast part of the city. His dad had a habit of changing jobs when he got bored—or pissed off the wrong person in upper management. This meant the family had to downsize. Or Dad would score a deal on a house and they would move so they could own again (only to sell when the enticing-though-challenging payments weren't so attractive any longer). It got to be fun—his father had successfully convinced him—switching schools occasionally, making new friends when the old ones were farther than a bike ride away. Plus he got to reinvent his room often.

When he was eight years old, though, he'd been told that they were fixed this time. And so he removed all his Star Wars figures from their carrying case and arrayed them on the built-in bookshelves in his new room. His father knocked three times on the open door.

"Hey buddy, you settling in okay?"

Michael had just placed Jabba the Hutt, on his long bed-like throne, against the right wall. Princess Leia, in her slave garb, was sitting, her legs straight because she didn't have knees, which sort of annoyed Michael, because he wanted things to look just like the film. So Michael made do and pretended she was kneeling, watching Luke Skywalker, in his black Jedi outfit, walk into the palace from the left side of the bookshelf. Michael loved that his shelves were painted with thick paint and was a bit sticky—with what his mother would later tell him was a disgusting layer of grime—so that his figures stayed put until he chose to move them. Without looking up from the Gammorrean Guard in his hand, which he couldn't decide to put in the scene's background or foreground, he said, "Sure."

Dad guided the folded sheets aside and dropped onto the corner of the unmade bed. "You like your new room?"

Turning, he met his father's gaze. Sure, he liked the blue carpet—he hadn't even known it *came* in blue—and his closet had *two* bars for his clothes. He couldn't wait to fill them with hangers. "Sure."

His father cleared his throat. "I really mean it, kid; this time, we're staying put."

"Okay." He eyed the other three empty shelves and marveled at how well he would be able to spread out his collection.

But within the year, the boxes were out, as they were every year until he graduated high school. He'd learned to keep less—throwing out posters after a year and donating books as soon as he finished them. *The less you have, the less you have to carry.*

Now, though, he owned his security. *I never have to move again if I don't want to*, he'd told himself the moment he walked into his home. But now, as he walked back to the front room and dared to lower one of the blinds, he didn't feel so secure. Where were all those happy faces he'd scoped out while people-watching in this neighborhood that day two years ago from the coffee shop? He wondered about his neighbors, most of whom he'd never met, never even seen, more or less, and whether or not they knew about the accident. Although he'd neglected to mention all the antagonism about gentrification he'd read right alongside the Graduate Hospital hotspot article, he was no idiot. He knew he was a symbol. How long before the pitchforks and torches came out? Without acknowledging that he was thinking like Aiden—who had never given this neighborhood, their home a chance—he wondered who among these neighbors would he be able to turn to and say, you know me, you know it was an accident? This seemed like the wrong time to begin a meet-and-greet campaign. He released the blind. At least his headache was gone. For now.

He walked into the kitchen, lifted the pot from the sink, allowed it to drip a little, and then wiped the bottom with his hand—which he dried on his pants. On the dining room windowsill, he made room for the freshly-potted dirt.

4

Rose had tempered her expectations for Lillian's reaction about the accident. But, given how she and her family had struggled to adjust to this country, Rose recoiled at the woman's complete indifference, as if she'd been told there'd been no mail that day. Maybe that was just her people's way, but Rose mentioned twice that the driver was a customer. Had she asked what they could have done, Rose would have understood that she was right to come up with some plan to help that nice young man. But now, she wasn't sure again. She felt the air thickening around her as she walked home, and at the intersection's corner, she stopped, and for the first time that day, she took a good look at the asphalt, searching for some sign. In the dark stain near the center, her eyes settled. Next to it, short skid marks. A few shards of glass glistened in the sun's light. How many people had come here to look for themselves? She imagined the panic in that driver's eyes, the helplessness that would soon find him. She imagined the cluster of people tending to the broken man lying in the street. Had anyone tended to the driver? Was this her job?

Instead of heading home, she turned up the street, for now she realized that a nice drink might uncloud her mind, and as she walked, she felt her stride quicken, for she could taste the smoky bourbon on her lips, feel its warmth on her tongue, in her throat; hear the soothing music massaging her ears as she would sip. In the trees above her head, a bird stutter-chirped. Rose stopped, peered at the bird's shimmery blue and black coat. She smiled. It was all alone on a stark branch, whose bumps would be replaced by buds soon. The bird quieted and eyed her. *Yes, baby, keep singing for the both of us.*

She thought of her Edgar and what his advice would be. She imagined his wonderfully wrinkled face near the end: puffy eyes, grey whiskers jutting every which way. Those eyes valued restraint, patience. Studying the first shiny, undented new car parked on their block, which, on that day, might have been the first time they hadn't been able to park their car in front of their own home, he'd muttered, "Nothing stays the same for very long." He'd lifted his daily black coffee to his lips and blew. Joining him on their front steps, holding her hot tea, Rose followed his eyes as they took in the contractors tossing old plaster from the Johnson's second story window into a large dumpster across the street. Just days before he left her, he set his coffee down, took her chin in his hand, and gave her a good look.

"What?" she whispered, hoping he wouldn't move his warm fingers.

"Nothing, just nothing." Then he kissed her forehead and returned to his coffee.

Her Edgar had loved this neighborhood of theirs. They may not have had much, but when a neighbor needed a little bread, can of corn to tide him over until payday, they shared what they could. Then, when a strike or work stoppage delayed paychecks, they returned the favor. These new folks setting down stakes—white or black—didn't even look people in the eye. Their slouched shoulders made Rose think that they were protecting themselves from a cold that hadn't even come yet, saying 'I may live here, but I am not one of you.' She pictured him taking these folks by the shoulders, looking them right in the face, saying, "Now, look here..." When she closed her eyes she could still hear his thick voice.

"Hey Miss Rose." Even from a block away, Miss Marcy's haggard voice could not be ignored. Miss Marcy hobbled towards her. *Hmm, if anyone knew where that nice young man lived, it'd be her.* Miss Marcy clutched the butt of an already-smoked cigarette.

"How you feeling this day?" A rush of vodka erupted from her breath.

"I'm well, Marcy, how're you?" She inched her head back.

"You know. You hear what went down earlier?" Miss Marcy didn't have her teeth in.

Rose hesitated. "If you mean that accident, yes, I heard." Miss Marcy didn't have much use for the truth.

"Didn't I tell you, all them white people looking to get rid of us one way or another."

"Maybe. Say, Miss Marcy, you know where that man who was driving live?"

She scrunched up her forehead, pulling her dark skin over her frail face, looking like a rug sucked up by a vacuum cleaner. "Sure do. He live over on Carpenter Street." She turned and waved her hand behind her, like Rose wouldn't know the street. "You know who know him, Miss Wanda. She heard about what car was driving and she knew exactly who it belong to. Nice BWM. *Real nice* BWM."

"Hmm." Rose tilted her head.

"She seen the accident too. Way they tell it, he jumped out of his car looking all disgusted, like some animal had hurt his car."

Rose searched her eyes for some break in the anger swimming there. "I got to be getting on, Miss Marcy. You take care." Rose stepped around her.

"You be well, Miss Rose. Say, you gotta cigarette?" Miss Marcy put her hand on Rose's shoulder, the hand still holding the smoked cigarette butt.

"Sorry, baby, I'm running low." Rose moved casually from under the skeletal hand. She would walk down Carpenter after her drink, or two. She was sure she had to find that man before Wanda started spreading her nonsense to more people. Though what she would say to him, she was not yet sure. She turned right at the intersection, and then crossed the street. She looked over her shoulder. No Miss Marcy.

She kept walking. Eventually, she reached the bar's front door, and she reached for the handle that, apparently, had been moved. Her heart started thumping. She wondered what else the new owners had changed, for she hadn't been inside since they'd re-opened. She pushed the door. Inside, a few folks sat on stools at the bar's far end. Mostly, she'd have the place to herself, which was the way she wanted it, for now. Her eyes settled on the long wood bar, which, as she surveyed the new tables and chairs that seemed to be cluttering the floor, seemed to be the only thing they'd kept. She couldn't wait to sidle up to it, to place her fingers on its worn, dark grooves.

That night Edgar died, that wood had soothed her weary eyes. Sipping her bourbon, she'd waited for the pain to strangle her. Walking in, neighborhood folks said hello, nodded, then shared a silent drink with her. Reggie didn't have a tab for her that night. Her eyes never left the dark, dull wood, which reminded her of Edgar. Resting her fingers on that wood's notches made her feel all warm inside.

Reggie's Place might have been four smoke-stained walls and the need for a sign telling all them thugs not to bother selling their drugs inside, but there, the neighborhood folks weren't reminded of what they didn't have. At the bar, people understood your work problems, were cutting corners on meat at the market too, and had just as much trouble affording their car repairs. Tending bar, Reggie re-told off-color Redd Foxx jokes. In that casual tone of someone who had just spent his last dollar and didn't care, he made them sound like his.

"Hey Rose, you heard this one?" Without waiting for an answer: "Do you know the difference between a pickpocket and a peeping tom? A pickpocket snatches watches." Maybe ten, fifteen minutes later, once you finished your first drink, someone new would sit down. "Hey Tony, you know the difference between a pickpocket and a peeping tom?"

At the bar, Tasha's toothless smile warmed Rose, because if there was sadness in her words, there was light in her grin. Smoking cigarettes, they would listen to Miles Davis, and Rose would run up a tab for $13.00 for three good bourbons. Lillian's Laundromat may have given her steady work after Edgar passed but she still minded her prices. But mind you, she was not poor, she was limited. Reggie's Place was her place, and there she was safe.

So when the neighborhood change found that corner, she'd felt empty.

But now standing at that threshold, the taste of bourbon smoky on her lips, overwhelmed by all the fancy fixtures and bright paint, she questioned her decision to stay. Those folks opened up the kitchen, added windows in the front area. As her eyes adjusted to the light, she noticed how shiny the old bar now was. *Why did they have to go and do that to that beautiful wood?* The lacquer did make the grooves shine though.

She sat at the opposite end of the bar from the couple of white kids with shaggy hair, ratty t-shirts that needed a good wash, and thick black glasses. Angry rock music floated. The bottles behind the bar were too clean. Against the wall, candles flickered next to a chalk board that listed a bunch of strange beers. She touched the bar and stopped when she realized she could no longer feel those grooves.

"Hello."

Why would a nice-looking white girl litter her arms with all of those tattoos? There was sweet honey in that voice though. Rose's nerves calmed. "Hello, baby. I'll have a bourbon, neat."

"Do you have a bourbon preference?"

Rose doubted she could afford the bulky bottles lined behind the woman. "The well brand will be fine."

The woman nodded. Rose sized up a black and white photo of that intersection's street signs, framed on the wall. The photographer was proud of that place in ways Rose had never seen someone be. Outside, one of the staff cleaned the chairs and set an ashtray on each table. A couple people drank and ate, taking turns eyeing that other dilapidated Laundromat across the street, with its barbed wire lining the roof and all. *So this is the neighborhood's future?* Would Edgar have sat in here, laughing when asked to put out his cigarette, then march right on home? Or would he have nodded, happy that everything was moving up?

That young man. That little girl's scream. That man on that ground. That blood. The palpable anxiety, anger swelling. What should she be doing to help? *Where was the bartender?* She almost felt Edgar's hand cover hers; she almost heard him whisper, "Relax." Rose took a deep breath.

Maybe she should consider her cousin Velma's offer of moving down to DC. After Edgar had passed, she'd been tempted, but she couldn't imagine being away from his memory. But now, maybe the time had come to walk away, leave this place to the young folks. But what in the world would occupy her time in DC? Not her ghosts on every block, that's for sure. She caressed the bar. If only she could peel back the lacquer and touch the grooves.

She wondered if that nice young man frequented this bar. She could picture this being his kind of fancy place. Charlie would have liked it here. She imagined him and that nice young man sitting next to her at the bar, enjoying a drink together, being friends. Why, oh why did she let Charlie enlist? Was there anything she could have even done to stop it?

She remembered that day Charlie stood in their front room and announced his plans.

"It's the right thing to do, for me." His shoulders back, his chin raised, his eyes firm. Don't you dare go, she'd wanted to scream, but she heard her husband's voice in her head: Let things happen the way they will. So she did.

She touched the empty stool next to her and the wood felt cold. *Not again.* Why couldn't she see how to help that nice young man? She remembered those long-gone warm Sundays, when, as a family, they put on their best outfits and basked in God's love. How certain life seemed reading the good Lord's book, hearing the preacher guide them through a life lesson; how simple life could be. Trust in me, she'd been taught. Then she trusted he would take care of her Charlie. She hadn't stepped foot in church since. But was she being called now?

She heard a thud and then the bartender rose from the basement stairs behind the bar. She was empty handed. As she closed the door, she said, "I'm sorry, we're out of the well bourbon. I even checked downstairs. Can I get you something else? A different bourbon?"

Rose could taste the sweet, smoky flavor on her lips. She tried to recall how much cash she had in her wallet. The woman's eyes waited. If I have just one, Rose thought, I can have whatever I want. "I'll have that one on the back right, the second one in."

"The Woodford Reserve?"

"Yes, that'll do fine." Rose moved her ring finger in small circles on the bar. The woman filled a high ball then set it on a coaster. "Thank you." It looked so calm, shimmering there in the light, settling like Jell-O in the glass.

"Sure." She walked off.

In the bar's mirror, her reflection haunted her. Had Edgar ever seen her look this exhausted? *There were too many damn mirrors in this place.* She clutched her drink a little tighter. Raising the glass, she inhaled the smoky fumes. The smell warmed her throat. She sipped. Her throat burned a bit as she swallowed a tight gulp. *That's nice.* A couple trickled through the door. The white man, wearing a sports coat, sat at the bar next to the dark-complected woman. Her high heels dangled right above the foot-rest as she climbed onto the chair. The slit on her lush red dress revealed too much thigh. They were laughing at the tail end of a story that began outside. Their smiles stung.

This was theirs now. All of it. Everything passes from one person to another at some point. Rose sipped again and closed her eyes as she swallowed. Where did she fit in with this new neighborhood? Another well-dressed couple walked in, followed by a cool breeze. The woman's perfume smelled sweet. The man brushed the hair away from his eyes after he took off his hat. He looked like that nice young man.

"You see that eye-sore of a house down the street is finally for sale?"

The woman shrugged.

The men in the kitchen were yelling at each other about something.

In a little while she would walk home to an empty, cold house. Tomorrow, her day off, she would clean that house. In the drying rack by the sink, her single plate and glass would sit. Every day, the same plate, the same glass. In the dining room, where'd she'd read her paper, the same lonely chair. Why had she allowed herself to become so shut off? What would a change bring her, and if she sold her house, what could she get for it? Did she owe it to the house to let new people fill it with fresh memories and love? Could those walls convince people that they could protect them from the outside world? Could it again be a house that anchored a block, a community?

Three young men pushed through the door, their voices spilling ahead of them. She caught her breath. The resemblance to Charlie made her eyes twitch. She blinked a few times and then reached for her glasses. "My word," she whispered. It had been a number of years, but she knew him: Her nephew Curtis. Could he really have grown into a man like that, those broad shoulders? And so put together, with that respectable haircut, collared shirt tucked into his jeans. What was he doing in Philadelphia? A server directed them to an open table. Rose reached for her bourbon. She hadn't spoken to Donald since Charlie died. She hadn't appreciated his perspective on what she did or didn't do regarding her son's enlistment. But she still sent Curtis a card every year, even though he'd never responded. But her heart fluttered thinking of how she'd always doted on Curtis when they visited. The way he used to devour books warmed her heart. If only Charlie had been a reader, she'd thought every time his eyes bulged when unwrapping a present. What had his father told him about her absence? She felt a warmth beside her. She blinked.

"Aunt Rose?" Before she could respond, he enveloped her with his strong arms. She felt warm.

"My word, baby. Curtis, what are you doing in Philadelphia?" Last she heard, Donald and Regina we're living in Virginia. She didn't realize until that moment just how much she'd missed their chatty Christmas cards. She'd lost one boy; how in the world could she have let this one slip away as well? She pictured them playing ping pong at their summer BBQs.

"I'm going to Temple next year for Pharmacy school and was checking out apartments. Apparently this area is really booming." One of her kin, a doctor, or whatever it was when you were a pharmacist. Her heart swelled at the sight of his gleaming, straight white teeth. Would Charlie have become a professional something one day?

"Look at you, going to graduate school. You be proud of yourself, young man."

"Just trying to make something happen, Aunt Rose."

"Well, how long you in town? Where you staying? Your folks with you?" This last question tensed her. What if they were and hadn't said something?

In fact, why hadn't Curtis called, said he was coming? The more she thought about it, the more she accepted why.

"I'm crashing with friends." He motioned to the two boys sitting at the table. "We're in this together. We're driving home Wednesday or Thursday."

"Okay, baby, but if you can make time to stay for dinner, Wednesday would do just fine. I'd love to have you." She wrote out her address for him on one of the Laundromat's business cards and made sure she told him how to find it.

"Okay, Aunt Rose, we'll try."

Rose waved to the other boys, who waved back, and gave Curtis another big hug. She had to tell herself to let go. He smiled and rejoined his friends. She shook her head. Her nephew Curtis. They beamed with life at their table, those three young men. Charlie would have been right at home among them. She looked away. Had they noticed she'd been staring? She closed her eyes and relived Curtis' arms around her. *We're up here looking at apartments.* She had three bedrooms in her house. *Hmm, could she be happy in DC?* She had to be careful, for she knew better than to get an idea running. It might just wear you out and then disappear. Tanya and Carl had rented out their home last year, let other folks pay their mortgage while they traveled in a Winnebago.

Three more white people entered. The air thickened. Rose thought about that Mexican. She would be back, hunting for that job. She knew all too well that the hunger in those eyes would not die and she steeled herself for a fight. As her shoulders tensed, she wondered if maybe she was gearing up for the wrong fight. She turned her head slightly, taking in the laughter from Curtis and his friend's table. She sipped her bourbon. This would be her last drink here. When her bill arrived, she would commit to this notion. She needed to let these things happen, for her energy could be better spent elsewhere. Like a plant, she needed fresh soil. Her eyes settled on the wood bar. In vain, she tried one last time to feel those grooves.

Sometime later, she emptied her glass and set it down. She pushed her chair back and stood. She studied her fingers on the wood bar until they dropped.

At the entrance, when she placed her hand on the piece of glass that made up most of the door, her stomach rumbled, like it had on Charlie's first day of school. He'd be fine; she'd taught him to raise his hand when he had a question. The school was a few blocks from their house and she could stop by at recess to watch him play on the jungle gym. She hoped he would do well, prayed he would return home safe, the way young parents do when they count the seconds their child is first out in the world on his own. *Did I teach him everything he needed to know in order to behave?* she thought, as he waved to her before he dashed off to his classmates who were standing in line, waiting to go inside. In the end, maybe they hadn't taught him enough?

Still at the front door, she looked at all the people enjoying this new space. She hoped, in her heart of hearts, that the boy who got hit would wake up and cool the neighborhood off, for she would have hated for things to get ugly all on account of an accident. The chatter she'd already heard planted doubts, for she knew how people like Willis and Wanda enjoyed stirring the pot. One spark of violence in the streets and that bar would be lost, in more ways than one. But was this situation too delicate to gamble on someone else taking care of this? What if fate decided to take that black man's life? In that moment, she realized that that feeling she'd felt tugging at her was a call to action: that young man, these streets, needed her. How could she put out this fire? She studied all the people in their little groups at their isolated little tables and she wanted to walk to each one and tap the folks on the shoulder, tell them to reach across the empty space next to them and speak to their neighbors. Then it hit her. That's what she could do. How could she bring these folks together, teach them to be a strong neighborhood? She wondered if the sweet, smoky taste in her mouth would soon turn bitter. She opened the door and the wind swept her face. She pictured that Mexican gal and wondered how she would handle her. Yes, she was tired of allowing life *to* happen to her.

In ten minutes or so, drifting into her home, she would set her keys on the table by her stairs, and her eyes would find the flyer she had saved from the day's mail: a community meeting on Wednesday night, at the community center, starting at 7. Something had told her to save the information she would have ignored weeks ago. She hadn't seen the need to go since Edgar had died, but holding that paper, she felt she might discover how she could help.

Then the phone rang. "I talked to my friends Aunt Rose, and we all agreed, we'd love to come over for dinner Friday. We can put off leaving until

Saturday. That is if the offer is still open."

"Oh yes, baby, it is." She smiled with all the strength she had. She thought about what she had in her kitchen and made a list for the market. She repeated the address she'd already given him.

"So we'll come by around 6?"

"Six would be fine, baby."

"Can we bring anything? Wine, something?"

"No, Curtis, just yourselves. That will do just fine." She pictured all four of them sitting at her table, she, her nephew, and two strangers, and she allowed herself joy for the first time in a long while. This felt right, damn right.

5

Years before the accident stood to derail his rental properties, Milton was being yanked into the adult world before his time. His father's suitcase was set by the front door. Dad hadn't mentioned a business trip. Nor had Mom, who had left for work at her usual time, crunching the pieces of broken dishes littering the kitchen floor in order to kiss his forehead on her way out. Dad leaned against the kitchen entryway and stared out the window as Mom left, as if he'd been watching a TV show. After a few painful minutes, he pulled Nathan into the dining room.

There, at Grandma's dining room table, they sat. "Now, son, I'm going to teach you something that my father taught me." From the deck of cards, he whipped off the plastic and it coasted towards the carpet. After extracting the deck, he shuffled it, the cards thwacking together. "This is poker, son, and, as a man, you need to learn. You can do it for fun, for money; these cards can teach you how and when to take chances in life. But first, you gotta learn the rules." Shuffling the cards twice, he cracked the cards hard, like they were wet flippers. Dad slammed the deck on the table and held it there with a finger. "Cut 'em."

Milton glanced at the bag by the front door and then back at the deck.

"Worry about that later, son. Cut this deck."

His hand trembling, Milton divided the pile. His father stacked the bottom half on top and then picked up the cards. He smacked the edges together and eyed Milton. "Pay attention to what I'm about to tell you, son. Now, look at the dealer when he deals the cards, not the other players, not the table, not your hands. The dealer. And never trust a dealer who looks anywhere besides the cards he's dealing." Milton hid his hands in his armpits and nodded. His father dealt a hand to each of them. "Now, always be the first one to look at your cards. Once you see what you got, you can study everybody else."

Milton checked his cards while his father waited. Two face cards and three low cards, no matching suits.

"Control your face, son. You smirked the moment you saw your cards, like you were annoyed. You gotta learn to bluff, son. Keep your best two cards, preferably face cards, toss the other three." Milton kept the Jack and the Queen. Dad pulled two cards from the top of his hand, then swept the discards away with the edge of his hand and tossed Milton three, himself two. Milton took his cards: an ace and two 3's. He smiled a little, but stopped once he felt his mouth move.

"You caught yourself. Never smile until everyone is done betting, son. A pair won't win you much either." Milton cocked his head. "If you'd had more, your smile would have been bigger." Dad flipped his hand over. A low straight, starting at 4. "Listen, this would win most hands, but just cause I got lucky with this, don't mean I will always get this hand. You have to learn to manage your luck, son, know when to discard, know when to up the bet, know when to fold. You do that, life will be good to you. Got it?"

Milton nodded, though he was sure he'd have no use for any of it. He looked at the suitcase by the door. In a bit, Dad would walk out the door and eventually board a train to Chicago. In five years, Milton would see his father again, though the visit would be like old friends who had come together to wallow in how much they'd changed in the intervening time. Milton rubbed the goose bumps from his arms. From this day forward, when he heard the sound of slapping cards he thought of Dad. This sound surfaced at odd moments, like when asking a girl on a date, brushing his teeth at night, watching a father-son bonding show on TV, and when entering a house, newly listed on the market, that some would have called unsellable but he would describe as a diamond in the rough, one just waiting to join the other three he owned.

• • •

Over the years, Milton had always done his due diligence when it came to his finances; studying trends, scooping up investment properties when it made sense to, putting just enough money into them to entice renters, drawing on his equity when he could to expand his share of the pie while trying to do right by his mother, and give back to his community—he turned blight into opportunities. He'd also accepted that he was making the most of the cards life had dealt him. With his mother's ailing health, he'd moved back to this community to care for her but he didn't have to feel cheated. Not anymore, anyway. One day, his houses would allow him to write his own ticket. If in the process he set a good example of what a little faith in yourself and hard work can do for you, then maybe his neighbors might learn something and pitch in. *Work the change from within and you won't have to worry about it coming at you from without.* But at the moment, standing in front of one of his vacant properties, he really wished that tree would stop dumping those damn budding flowers all over his sidewalk. Nothing discouraged a prospective tenant quite like seeing how much work was in their future. And since the accident, he couldn't afford to take chances with any little detail.

For every bud collected, he dropped two. He should have used both hands. This would have been easier if he'd brought the one broom and dustpan he owned. On his cracked-skin fingers, pollen mingled with drywall dust. Packed under his finger nails, sawdust. Did he have any good soap or paper towels inside? In seven minutes, prospective tenants would show, hopefully possessing a credit score over 600. If only his construction company hadn't been priced out of so many jobs recently, he could let some of these details worry him less, but things were getting too tight.

His hand full, he stretched out his tightening lower back. He then kicked whatever else was still on the concrete into the gutter. *Good enough.* Back in the house, the breeze had cooled the dining room. He crossed into the kitchen and emptied his hand into the trash can. At the sink, he knocked the faucet handle with his wrist. With his nails he scrubbed the mess layered in the grooves of his fingerprints. After a few minutes, he shut off the water. He rubbed his hands on his jeans a couple times, and then checked his watch. He went to the front window and parted the blinds. *No cars.*

His cell phone vibrated.

The vacant voice on the line said that he'd be passing, found something else. Thanks anyway. *Damn.* Milton closed his phone. They would have been good too—a young couple, looking to plant roots for a bit, based on their SUV and iPhones. Now, his third cancellation or no-show in two days. *That damn accident.* He'd brought the paper with him but this wasn't the time to read their take on that nonsense he was increasingly more aware of being unable to avoid. He tucked it under his arm.

His eyes swept the kitchen he'd rehabbed himself. The grouting on the tile looked a little more uneven than he had realized. He turned and noted where he'd patched the stained section in the ceiling—you had to squint to tell, even in this light. Should he open the blinds wider or close them tighter? He checked his watch again. The mail would arrive soon, and with it, maybe another bank notice. He didn't want to deal with Mom asking about the mortgage he'd taken out on his (their) house, so he headed home.

• • •

Sitting in his kitchen chair, anxious, he faced the open front door and freshly painted black bars on the security gate. *5:45, and no mailman.* He unfolded the newspaper and tapped his fingers on the newsprint while he sipped the last drop of his lukewarm coffee. Should he go for a third cup? He sighed. Lifting the paper close to his weary eyes, he scanned for headlines. Nothing for the Graduate Hospital neighborhood ever made the front section. Passing news of protests in the Middle East, grim news on the housing market, and budget cuts for the Philadelphia school district—there, on page 13—he stopped.

A man suffered severe injuries Monday afternoon after being struck by a car, police said.

The accident occurred at 1:35 p.m. at the intersection of Carpenter and 18th street. The bicyclist, a 20-something African American male, suffered severe trauma to the head and back. He was not wearing a helmet. The driver, a white male in his late 20s, was treated for cuts at the scene and released.

The bicyclist is listed in critical condition at Graduate Hospital in the trauma unit.

Police investigated the accident, though no charges against the driver were filed.

Residents of the southwest portion of the city, some of whom claim to have been witnesses to the accident, claim that the driver ran the stop sign. They indicated that the driver's race is the reason no charges have been filed against him. One witness, however, indicated that it is the bicyclist who ran the stop sign. The police report indicated no evidence that the driver ran the stop sign.

Residents have called for action from the police department, whom, they claim, have turned a blind eye to the African American population in that section of the city, which has seen an influx of more affluent residents in the past few years.

In a part of the city plagued with issues of racial unrest, residents are uneasy. "They need to stop protecting all these white people moving into this neighborhood," one woman, who declined to be identified, said.

When asked, Police and City Hall officials had no comment.

Typical nonsense that was going to go a long way to get people bent out of shape. There are plenty more effective—and legal—ways to be racist than mowing someone down in the street. People need to get off their asses and position themselves so that their race didn't matter. Thinking of his three vacant properties, he checked his watch. Where was that damn mailman? He folded the newspaper and tossed it next to his empty coffee cup.

Upstairs, Mom shuffled down the hall. He heard some twigs cracking outside. He rose and went to the door. Just a woman walking her pit-bull past his front steps. He returned to the kitchen table.

"Milton, honey, can you make me some tea?"

"Yeah, Mom, I got ya."

Filling the kettle, he then set it on a burner. After three attempts at twisting the knob back and forth, the pilot lit. He sighed, wishing there was something else he could do in the three minutes he had until the water boiled. Man, the soft 2008 market allowed him to feel like a kid playing Monopoly, snatching good properties left and right. Was he getting bargain basement deals? No, but good enough, and with what he could get for rent he'd be able to cover his expenses and generate a little cash to keep the ball rolling. How could he lose? he thought as he'd signed those mortgage papers on this house, cashing the check that day to finance his buying streak. The incoming rent covered his notes while he sat back and let equity accrue. He'd bought well, smart; safe. But that shifty couple left him holding the bag on the Bainbridge house, even after he said he'd work with them. Then that skinny white dude left mid-month. Who knew finding tenants mid-summer would be so hard? Then the maintenance. His own work on projects meant he had to hire someone to recoat one roof, patching the stucco around the front windows for another—ascetically, he should have stuck with the brick, but stucco seemed a better, smarter treatment. Until you had to maintain it. Some months, he barely broke even. But once someone was late on their responsibility, he got smacked. Now, he wondered if he needed to do the smart thing and unload a property. Given how he'd been drawing on his equity, would he break even? More than anything, he needed cash.

The metal of the kettle creaked and he sat. Once he settled, the mail clunked on the hard wood floor. Springing towards the door like he'd been shot out of his chair, he snatched the batch. He sifted through the shiny, colorful postcard for the new show at the Arden Theater, a cable TV mailer—no, he didn't want to upgrade to any pay channels—solicitation for AT&T, Sixers season tickets info—complete with some star dunking, probably one of his only good plays from the previous year—and then his water bill. He exhaled. Behind him, the kettle whistled.

"Bring me some cream and sugar when you come up, dear." As he walked to the kitchen, his foot found the soft spot in the linoleum. So much for the teal blue tile he'd had his eye on buying this coming summer.

"Yeah, Mom, I got ya." He poured the steaming water. *Mom had to have some money stashed, right?* But then, what his mother didn't know wouldn't hurt her. He had to make sure she never did. The mail better be on-time tomorrow, he thought, as he set the steaming mug on a tray, plucked sugar from the cupboard and cream from the fridge. In the mug, Earl Grey clouded the water. He lifted the tray and mounted the stairs. In the middle room of the second floor, she was watching TV.

"Milton, you heading to that meeting?"

"Yeah, soon. You need something?"

She squinted, like she'd lost track of a word. "Stop and get me more cough drops." Her voice was scratchy like someone who'd been screaming for days. Doctors couldn't figure what was wrong with her vocal cords.

"The lemon ones?" Had she blown through those bags he grabbed last Wednesday?

"Those would be fine." Her tone had softened. "You need money?"

"No, I'm good. He set the tray on the small end table near her Lazy-Boy. "You need anything else?" As she inventoried the tray, the loose skin on her neck wobbled. Was she losing more weight? "No, this is fine."

When he kissed the top of her grey wig, he wished she'd tossed that thing. Though still presentable after all these years, the mustiness wouldn't leave. He trotted down the stairs, and on his way out the door, after grabbing a light jacket, he snatched his keys.

• • •

Outside, in the early evening air lingered something that he couldn't identify. The guy who always parked his Honda's bumper on Milton's used, though-still-well-maintained Lexus walked towards him; Milton nodded as they passed and the jerk avoided eye contact. *So much for "brothers" at least pretending to be tight with one another.* This type of behavior reinforced his negative impressions of this new breed in the neighborhood. Sure, you live in the city, so bumpers get scuffed; however, inconsiderate people like him dumped his trash at the curb first thing Sunday morning, giving the bums incentive to linger. Before reaching the corner, Milton crossed the street.

Nearing the community center, he jiggled the keys in his jeans. With the tip of his finger, he probed the hole forming under the pocket. A headache threatened. *Not now, not now.* At the next corner, a driver waved him across even though Milton didn't have the light. Milton stood his ground. The car sped past and he crossed. He watched it race to the next red light. Maybe the accident was charging the air. Or maybe just his?

He forgot how much he missed that charge in the air, though he remembered when it meant something different. As the third relay leg in high school, during races, watching the race unfold from over his shoulder, he'd felt this same charge. The early leg bolted around the bend. Milton focused on the air moving in and out of his nostrils in measured bursts; in his fingertips, his blood pulsed like it was being squeezed tight. The second leg chugged in that boring straight line and then Milton tensed. When his teammate entered the passing box, the seconds stretched out as the air quieted. In his ears, he felt his heart thumping, his adrenaline bursting. In those moments he prayed that the baton would land squarely in his hand as the teammates matched speeds. With that hot metal in his palm, he launched into a dead sprint, hoping that his sweat wouldn't slip the baton from his grasp. He pounded through that last turn of the track, the other teams nipping at his heels, his breath galloping out of his chest, his eyes finding his waiting teammate who would bring them home.

Now, as he surveyed his neighborhood, everyone seemed to be on a different pace. Next to the crooked windows and rotted window frames, new windows with plastic strips to mimic genuine divided panes. Beside houses with freshly painted windows, bars installed and security system signs mounted next to realty for-sale signs, wooden benches chained to basement window bars; front marble slab steps so worn, rain water puddled. Were homes batons to be passed from poor people to richer people, by way of developers? After nearly tripping over a dug-up chunk of sidewalk, he stopped to regain his balance. He was bringing change from within, right? So what if most of his renters were new to the area? He should've grabbed Ibuprofen before he left.

"You check your paper like I told ya to?" Out of nowhere, Miss Marcy appeared in his path. Menthol cigarettes stench wafted off her, and he pulled back. This smell reminded him of sitting in Reggie's Place.

"Miss Marcy, how are you this evening?" Milton watched his words. You never knew what kind of information an old head was likely to fetch.

"I'm fine, thank you kindly. Now, you check what I told you to? Was I right?" She got right up in his face and he was engulfed with a nose full of gin.

"I did read the article, yes." He took a half step back.

She folded her arms. "That white boy that done it live right on your block," she said, eyeing the street, like she was worried someone was coming for her.

She settled her eyes on him, and then her composure changed, like a dog waiting patiently for a treat. Milton despised this m.o. On her daily rounds, she'd stop at various houses, relying on people's manners to offer her food, a drink.

Milton's mother had scolded, "I don't need that busy body of a woman sitting in my kitchen, drinking my coffee, sucking up my oxygen, needing to be told to get on." At 11, Milton had made the mistake of inviting Miss Marcy in, in part because he'd seen Mom do it.

"You got a smoke on you?"

"You know I don't smoke, Miss Marcy." Milton checked his watch. He needed these 15 minutes before the meeting's start for small talk to discover what people were saying about the accident. He might also get a line on people looking for a place to rent.

"Oh, that's right." She scratched her forearms and scanned around again. "Anyway, you hear me, son, that white man live on your block." What was her angle here?

Of course she was talking about Michael, who surely hadn't hit that kid on purpose. Good people—the neighbors you want—didn't pull shit like that. He'd seen Michael move Ms. Williams' empty garbage can after the trash truck had been by. The guy was solid. "If he did it, Miss Marcy, I'm sure he didn't mean to." Though Michael *had* seemed skittish the past couple days. He'd almost asked how he was doing, but he wasn't picking a side until he had to.

"Uh-huh, white people don't never mean to do nothing, it just happen, and it just happen to us." The wrinkled skin on her cheeks sagged as she scowled.

"You take care, Miss Marcy. I have to get to the Community Center for the meeting." She stepped aside and Milton passed.

"You tell that mother of yours I said hello," she yelled when he'd made it half a block.

• • •

Six steps up the Community Center stairs, the swell of strained, annoyed voices slowed him. Too many heads, too much friction. This was why you prayed for heavy rain or snow if you had a license or permit hearing before the board. His neck tightened.

At the last meeting he'd attended, mostly old timers had shouted down a third story add-on here, a roof deck there. One old woman cried about how folks were looking in her window at night, watching her get undressed. "Not you," he'd wanted to shout, but he held his tongue, for her shoulders were pushed back and her chin raised as she spoke into the microphone. "If you don't like what's going on around you, pick up and leave," he mumbled. He'd chewed on a straw to keep his mouth shut for the rest of it. Just because you own a house don't mean you can control progress. That night, he'd needed a multi-use permit on one of his properties. Getting it through got him afloat again, though not exactly caught up. That was six months ago.

Tonight, board member seats were up for a vote. Since Sarah and Fred pushed projects through, he wanted to see them get re-elected. Reaching the second floor landing, he joined the line snaking out of the auditorium door. Among the frustrated faces and people fanning themselves with pieces of paper, he waited, jiggling his keys. Up near the front of the line, Willis stood. Milton nodded. When Willis smirked back, he knew disaster loomed.

The line moved. Near the entrance, he heard, "Sorry, we don't have your name, sir. We have lost a lot of our records due to poor record keeping." Milton closed his eyes and thought of the smell of fresh paint, the feel of raw drywall. His neck muscles eased.

Someone behind him chirped, "What did they say?" He turned. He didn't recognize her, but wished he knew someone as striking as her, with that illustrious caramel skin. She was whispering to the white guy holding her hand. He turned before he stared too much. At least people were more stressed than he was. Finally, he reached the welcome desk.

"Hi, are you registered?" the woman asked, with all the enthusiasm of a Black Friday clerk. Her ear lobes were stretched like taffy pulled thin. Maybe the community organization manned the desk with any black old head willing to volunteer.

"Milton Roberts."

Her finger combed the list of names on her sheet. She highlighted his name and handed him papers.

And into the chaos he stepped. Crammed on top of one another, people struggled to set up folding chairs; others pulled single chairs from closets, leaving whatever mess they'd made in the process. Those chairs plopped down whether they were part of an existing row or not.

"How is this possible? How could you have lost my information? I have registered on three different occasions!" some guy shouted. This was clearly the gravest injustice to ever strike his white life, as he snatched a registration packet out of the volunteer's hand. He had no idea what it meant to have his "voice silenced." Sure, things would be much more organized with a computer system, but who was gonna pay someone to get that together? Look around you, we're in a run-down community center with bars on the window, Milton wanted to point out to him. He would add: You think the people sitting their butts in those plastic chairs are here because this is what they do for a living? No, they get done what they can so people like you have somewhere to come and shout. Sure, it sucks that some might have gotten shut out, but if you want to see things change, volunteer. He pitied the two women manning the front table.

From some of the roving volunteers, Milton took handouts. Board candidates had typed up their credentials, though, by the looks of it, with varying success. Some offered a paragraph, some presented their CV; one woman had a bunch of bullet points about how being "green" would enhance the board. *Poor proofreading, though.* Milton was sure she didn't mean to say that she was looking to make the "area surfer for residents." No Sarah, no Fred. *Hmm.*

At the table against the back wall, Milton poked the donuts to see which was the freshest. He picked up a powdered one stuffed with red jelly then an empty coffee cup. Some heavy-set white guy who'd spent too much on a polo that didn't do a good enough job covering his gut brushed next to him. Milton moved. Smiling to be polite, Milton studied the guy. Why didn't people wear socks with loafers? The guy surveyed the table like it was a sidewalk sale. "No Splenda?" Was he talking to Milton? He plowed through the sugar packet basket, sending most of the packets to the table.

"What do you mean you don't have my name?" a woman asked, her arms crossed, at the front table.

Without moving his hand from the sugar basket, Tubby offered: "Makes you wish that driver had run over some of these people instead, yeah?" Without waiting for an answer, he stomped off, leaving a steaming cup of coffee on the table. Milton flicked his two sugar packets and then tore them. Along with Tubby's abandoned coffee, he dumped the packets in the trash.

"Milton."

Milton froze. He hadn't spoken to Dylan since he'd left that crew to start his own thing. "Dylan, how are you?" Milton stuck out his hand, but Dylan was occupied with the donuts.

"Anything good here?"

Milton retracted his hand slowly. "Ah, I grabbed a jelly one. Looked fresh."

"Yeah, well, sometimes things look a little fresher than they turn out to be, right?" He grabbed a glazed donut with a napkin.

"I guess. So how's business been for you?"

He coughed. "You take care, Milton."

There were days when Milton regretted striking out on his own, after Dylan had taken a chance on him and showed him the ropes, but he needed to do more than float through his finances. Had he made the right decision gambling on himself? Why was it so easy to take the home his mother had entrusted to him—the one owned free and clear—and turn it into an ATM?

Watching Dylan cleave the crowd, he wished he hadn't have burned that bridge. He had a few concerns he would have liked to run by him. Milton shuddered. Grabbing his coffee, he shook his head and leaned his back against the table and sipped. Willis waved him over.

Pushing through people who were glued to their phones, he finally reached him. "Hey, man," Milton said, taking a free chair.

"Milton, good to see you." Willis scanned the crowd. "Perhaps now we'll get a piece of sanity up in here." His deep rasp discouraged people from asking him something twice.

"That bad, eh? I caught the tail end of some nonsense on the way in." Milton sipped his coffee. Thank god it was hot.

"Folks is all kinds of bent out of shape, though, clearly, it ain't "us." These white folks is pissed, as if they here now, things is going to go the way they say they are. Martha, she said she didn't have the patience for this." He would have liked to have said hello to her.

Milton nodded to a couple people milling behind them. Weren't they a new couple who'd moved a block over from him, on Montrose Street? His eyes bounced. More white than black faces. Ten years ago, they'd almost all be black, though they'd only draw half the crowd. The room was getting claustrophobic.

"Anyone worth looking at on the ballot?" As Milton flipped the pages, hoping a different sheet would contain Fred and/or Sarah, or, at this point, any familiar name.

Willis watched Milton. "Don't know none of 'em. Not like that matters all that much." Milton threw Willis a look. "No one's speaking tonight; another reason why everyone is all kinds of pissed. Like I'm supposed to figure someone out by what's written on a piece of paper." He dug dirt from under his finger nail, then bit a cuticle and spit it out. Someone with a clean front-of-the-house, that's someone to listen to, Willis would say. But it seemed like the community looked up one day and those folks were gone or no longer interested. Milton doubted he would have believed any of the fresh faces anyway.

Agitated, murmuring voices circling them spiked. These meetings didn't generally get bent out of shape, especially not even before they began. Board seats didn't present a glamorous job when your neighborhood only recently escaped the low-income census tract, so now maybe their increased tax base might earn them better city services. Perhaps City Hall would finally provide shovels and trash bags to the person who bothered to organize a street cleaning. Clearly, gone were the days when this was their biggest issue. These people, with their expensive watches and starched collars, would lobby for Washington Avenue to get overhauled with nice trees in the center divider; maybe bubble out the corners to allow residents to cross the street better, and then ask where the money was without pitching in. A lot of heart only gets things done in the movies.

A middle-aged white woman in a shapeless, unflattering dress tapped the microphone. Grey streaked hair tied back, glasses drooped on her nose.

Cathy? In the organization for decades, she looked like she'd been snacking a bit much lately. She used to be the one to quell any conversation that veered off track when Milton was more involved. But with it looking like she had little help, maybe she was doing less steering and more herding. No one noticed her either. Throwing her shoulders back and saying something sharp would help. Willis eyed her like he was watching a late-quarter Eagles playoff game, just waiting to be disappointed. She'd been instrumental in getting him voted off the board four years ago. The dirt he'd dug from his shoe soles he flicked to the floor.

While working a chunk out of the tread in his heel, he said, "By the way, was meaning to ask you, what'd you think about that white man running over that black kid?"

"That *accident*, you mean?" Milton couldn't read Willis' eyes but his paranoid tone was in full swing.

This one time, his mail hadn't shown and he came around when Milton had been installing an address plate on the house.

"Milton, my man, got a minute?"

"Willis." They shook hands once Milton descended his step-ladder. "What's up?"

"Man, you heard? The post office is going to start charging us a monthly fee, on top of stamps."

"Yeah, where'd you hear that?"

"Around. I also heard the postal workers going to strike until it gets pushed through. Man, I tell you, I am sick of this city."

"Strike?"

"Yeah, and I didn't get my mail today either. Seems curious, don't you think?"

"Willis, it's Veteran's Day. No one gets mail today."

Willis stewed. "Well, I'm just saying, brother, you keep an eye out."

In the Community Center, as he thought back to that moment, Milton resisted chuckling. But Willis could stir the pot and the fewer mouths talking up the accident the better.

"Yeah, accident." Willis' eyes danced a bit when he spit back Milton's challenge. Willis needed something real to sink his anger into since the neighborhood changes hadn't, apparently, invited him to the party. Like the new restaurant on his corner with outdoor tables, the one that served delicious food he'd rather not eat, with names too long for him to learn.

"Come on now, Willis, just 'cause he's white doesn't mean he's out mowing people down with his car. Way I heard it, that bike blew right through the stop sign. How's a driver supposed to drive on the road if the other people don't obey the traffic laws?" Willis half chuckled and crossed his arms. Milton continued: "Look around, my friend; these are our neighbors now, not the enemy. These folks want a piece of it like the rest of us. Doesn't matter what color they are." But Willis was from the south, Deep South, where history looked different. When ideas reached up from the ground, like ivy that clung to the side of a house, they clutched tight. This was the hate that Willis grew up with, those vines. He quieted. Did he think Milton had sold out by not feeling him?

Though probably a bad idea, he asked, "You know anyone looking to rent a place?"

Willis raised an eyebrow. "Maybe, though depends what you're asking."

"I got two places. Best deal I got right now is $1600 for a two bedroom, one bath. Nice outdoor space in back."

Willis frowned and turned his head forward. "I don't know no one who's looking to spend that kinda money living in this neighborhood."

Milton took a deep breath and eyed the stage. "Hello," Cathy, still occupying the stage, chirped. Milton cringed, like watching some bad grade school recital. A few people stopped talking and focused their attention. "Listen, folks, people are still trying to make their way in to the room, but the center wants us out of here by 8:30." She eyed the wall clock. "That gives us about 55 minutes to complete our agenda, which Richard is going to read through, if you all would please quiet down a minute."

Rumbling eased as a guy in a well-worn sports coat stepped to the side of the room. With glasses a bit too big for his face, he looked like Milton's junior high science teacher. Another new face. How many meetings had he skipped? Standing underneath poster board tacked to the wall, the man fidgeted. His voice squeaked when he said, "The first measure is to vote whether or not we should amend our bylaws so that we can vote tonight to replace the vacant board seats." Milton raised an eye brow. "Can I get a show of hands of all those in favor?"

Behind Milton, a black guy in a sweater vest muttered, "Well, not everyone gets to vote."

"Shh," some people said. He waved them off. A smattering of hands rose and Cathy counted.

Milton looked forward. "The second measure speaks to whether or not we should replace all 15 board positions or only the seven vacant seats." People exchanged looks. Dwayne, one of the only other members Milton still knew, shifted anxiously in the back of the room.

"Does everyone get to vote who's here or only the people who are registered?" A 30-ish white guy with wavy hair and John Lennon-type glasses barked from a corner of the room. Some shh-ed, some rolled their eyes. "You shh," he responded, "Why should I let anyone else be heard if I can't be heard?" People standing close to him moved. From the stage Cathy cleared her throat as her scrawny finger counted the raised hands. She avoided the man's general direction.

"Okay, then, we will be voting to fill seven seats tonight. Each of you has a ballot with all the candidates' names. Check a yes or a no next to each candidate you would like to vote for. Before we do that, I will announce each candidate and ask him or her to stand so that you can attach a face to the name. We will, however, not have any time for questions or speeches."

"Wait a minute," a man shouted. Then an old head, who most of the neighborhood kids avoided on their walk home from school, stood. He lived on Grey's Ferry and sat in front of his house on a beach chair, yelling at people to not let their dogs pee on his sidewalk. "Now, aren't we going to talk about how this organization's mismanagement lost its charter with the city?"

A handful of people looked at Willis, whose name had surfaced in the embezzlement discussion four years back, the first step in the neighborhood organization finally losing its city charter.

"Now, sir, this is neither the time nor the place for such a discussion. We have to get through the items we have scheduled tonight. If you'll please take your seat, we can make that happen. Now, again, if everyone would take their ballot, we can move on."

Grumblings from the back of the room surged forward. Outside these walls, did people know what was happening on their behalf? Would they care? At the microphone Cathy scanned the crowd. She looked like she was annoyed to be getting home to a late dinner, like maybe her only worry was whether the corner trashcan got emptied.

Milton wondered which of the people on that ballot might okay his zoning change to convert a single family home into a duplex, allow him to get that roof-deck on his Catherine street property next year, once he scraped enough money together. Those rough-looking "resumes" didn't offer much.

He wanted more than a paragraph from the beauty shop owner, and slightly more impressive credentials than being a contractor from this other guy. For all Milton knew he was angling for an inside track on development projects. *Competition.* Sure, more businesses would be a plus in the area, as one guy thought, but those wouldn't last if residents didn't have a dime to spend there. What if the people who could afford it were afraid to get their groceries after a hard day's work? He thought about the accident. Was he being naïve, too cautious? Maybe the area was ready for a couple more coffee shops and a place to buy pastries that was not owned by Starbucks or Dunkin' Donuts. Who would encourage the kind of change he was bringing: from within? Could any of those candidates make that happen? Milton scratched his nose. Hearing the names called, he watched people stand. Really, not *one* black person in the whole lot? He was feeling the walls close in on him, maybe fed by the anger in the air.

"Who you backing?" Willis' eyes danced with fire as he glared at the white people—none of whom he recognized—who flanked Cathy on the stage like security guards.

Milton's throat was drying. "Not sure I can hang for this much longer."

By the looks of things, the people in charge couldn't have cared less about people making an informed decision; as long as votes got cast, job done. When she folded her arms on that stage, the murmuring quieted and people took up their pencils and started marking their forms. Behind Milton, a woman asked, "Are we really not going to be able to hear what any of them have to say, ask them any questions?"

"Willis, I gotta get out of here." As Willis nodded, Milton stood and pushed through the crowd. He walked right past Dylan, who followed him with his eyes.

Outside, his anxiety ebbed the moment he crossed the threshold. Still, Milton felt like the city was waiting to sneeze. He wondered who was going to provide the Kleenex.

"Milton, that you, baby?" He paused. Something told him to keep walking, as if he hadn't heard his name, but then he recognized that slight rasp. *Charlie's Mom.*

"Ms. Rose, how are you?"

"Getting by." She eyed him as if he were a ghost. He flinched, for their friends had always joked how much he and Charlie had looked like brothers. The years had apparently not dulled her pain. She patted his arm and wrapped her fingers around his bicep as if she were worried he were going to fall into traffic. He knew he should have dropped by her house since he'd moved back but one year became two and he felt the opportunity slip away. There were a lot of memories for him to avoid there too.

"You still over on Mildred?" Even he couldn't help the crack in his voice.

She cleared her throat. "Your mama still over there on Carpenter Street?"

"Yes, Ma'am."

"You back there with her?"

"Yes, Ms. Rose, I moved back five years ago to help her out, you know, with her health being what it is. I've kept a kinda low profile though." She nodded and he braced for a dressing down, for she'd always been the neighborhood mom to scold you about your homework, your manners at the dinner table when she had you over. Every moment there introduced guilt he hadn't realized had been buried. Why hadn't he taken better care of the relationship they'd had, if for no other reason than Charlie? Her eyes were lost in a memory and a little life colored her cheeks. "Mind if I ask what you came to see. I've been to a lot of these meetings and never seen you here before." Her smile dipped.

Her eyes focused on him and she struggled to regain her smile. "I hoped I would figure it out when I entered the room. But I didn't belong, not even welcome to the conversation. I'd listened to the noisy crowd and, baby, my heart grew weary, as if I'd been staring at a bill I couldn't pay. So I came out front, smoked two cigarettes, waited to see if maybe I should try again." Her voice deflated and she maneuvered her jaw. Milton tensed, for she was choosing her words too carefully. "But, now that I've finished my cigarettes, and, based on your appearance here, there's no reason to return inside, so I guess I'll go on home. You headed that way?"

"I am."

"Mind some company?"

Although this was exactly what he needed to avoid at the moment, he nodded. She tossed her cigarette, stepped it dead, and then kicked it towards the gutter. They walked, and although she let him set the pace, he could tell she was moving quicker than made her comfortable, in part because she was clinging to his arm.

"I'm glad you're back here, baby. This neighborhood needs good people like you."

"Thank you, Ms. Rose." She was making his presence sound so final. This sense of the future made him sad, like he was settling and watching his big dreams of having his own flourishing construction company in a different city disappear. Though in that moment, he couldn't remember why it was so important for him to leave these streets. Had it been his father who had planted the seed in him, the one that suggested staying meant failure? Didn't he have it pretty good here now, given all the opportunities at his fingertips? Then he thought of Willis recoiling at his mention of his rent. Did he not have a right to make things happen here? If people wanted a piece of the action, they should step up. Of course, he was choosing to ignore the very real fact that most of his neighbors in this neighborhood who were renting, the very ones who would be priced out of all this change, lacked his same financial resources to take advantage of all these "opportunities."

"Not like they used to be, when everyone was of a like mind, is it? You know," Subtly, her weight slowed them. "I often wonder, when I allow myself the luxury, how Charlie would have liked these changes." His throat constricted. She stopped and lit a cigarette. "You know, baby, I have to admit something. Part of why I came there tonight was to find out what folks thought about the accident, see if anyone knew about that driver." She slowed here and looked at Milton. "I heard he live on Carpenter. Your block by any chance?"

Why would she ask about Michael? Did she know the guy who got hit?

Ever since that one night he'd heard him cussing outside, he'd felt protective of him. Milton had stepped outside to Michael swearing at the cement and then stomping into the street, craning his head a few different ways, then searching behind him.

"You okay, Mike?" He wasn't bleeding; couldn't have been too bad, whatever it was.

"Yeah, I... Hey, Milton. Someone swiped my tree, that one I put out a few weeks ago."

Glancing at the house, he had recalled a nice new ceramic pot by the basement window. He had meant to tell him to weigh it down, but maybe he wanted to test how much things had really changed. "Yeah, that happened once to us. That's why we got a real big pot for this plant here. Loaded it down with rocks." He nudged the pot with his foot. "Anyone tries to steal it, he'll throw his back out."

Michael walked towards his house, looked once more into the vacant street. *You can buy another tree,* Milton had wanted to tell him. But Michael's eyes were sad, scared and mad all at the same time. "Yeah, guess I'll know better next time. Have a good night, Milton." He sulked into his house and killed the light he usually left on. He never did put another tree out there. On trash days, Milton didn't see that big can Michael used to drag from his back yard, just a couple trash bags piled on the curb.

That was six months ago. Trying to make someone feel more settled in the neighborhood soothed Milton. Like he was needed. And if a missing tree was where they were, they weren't doing too badly. Besides, he was sure that Michael now had more on his mind, to the point where he wished a missing tree was all he had to stress.

Rose and Milton resumed walking. "No. I think I've seen him around though."

"Hmm." She kept her eyes forward. Maybe she didn't want to see the lie in Milton's eyes that she'd heard in his words. "Do you think this change will swallow people like me up, Milton?"

He searched for the right answer but only shrugged. He thought of the new folks who had moved in, especially the ones who had mingled at the summer block parties, relaxing at least a few of the longtime people. But lately, the change had been such a jolt; construction on nearly every block; nails in the street, puncturing kids' bike tires, not to mention the cars'. Would everyone be able to—or even want to—blend? Too much on either side, you create groups, not a community, and without a community, would people want to rent—or even continue to buy—on these blocks? His stomach soured.

Looking away from her, he was reluctant to feel her pain. He was partly responsible for the change, and it had enhanced his life, to a degree. But not all change brought out the best in people. Milton's old neighbors, Mr. and Mrs. Jones, their two girls, they'd changed—or at least one had. The girls were older, but they were as close to friends as Milton had on the block then. He had loved to chase Sherri, who was five years older than he. Carol, her older sister, didn't have the time for him. When Sherri got married, she moved down south. She knocked on Milton's door when she brought her children for Christmas. Carol, after her law degree, married a businessman, and bolted to the Main Line. When she and her husband visited, back when her mother was still alive, the husband, with his long coat and tight, shiny leather gloves, tapped his car alarm twice. Standing in his doorway, Milton shook his head. You don't have to be afraid of me, brother, he wanted to shout. But the guy barely nodded before ducking in the Jones' door. That look of suspicion in his eyes said, I hope you are not looking too hard at my property. No one was surprised that by the time Mrs. Jones passed, they unloaded the house fast.

He hadn't thought of them in forever. Milton turned up the collar on his coat when the wind stung his neck. From the corner of his eye, he could see Rose staring at three leaves blowing down the curb. He'd never seen someone smoke with such despair before. They resumed walking.

When they reached the next corner, he realized he'd forgotten his mother's cough drops. The Rite Aid on Walnut was open 24 hours. He checked his watch. He could still get home in time to have a good meal before crashing. Rose's house was close enough that he could accompany her. At the next block, they made a right.

When they reached Rose's block, she turned, gave him a good, tight hug, then stood back. "You take care, now, baby. Tell your mother I said hello. And Milton," she stared deep into his eyes, "I want to help that white driver. People like him need our help, so when you see him, extend a hand." She waved as she shuffled away. Turning in the direction of the drug store, he felt stung.

When his phone vibrated, he stopped and checked the text. *Hello. Saw your craigslist ad for the apartment on Fitzwater. Can I come check it out?*

Milton typed back: *Tomorrow at 11? Name?*

Milton took a deep breath, like he was waiting for someone to say yes or no to a date. A car zoomed by blaring music. The exhaust blew into him. His phone vibrated. *Cool. Name's Tom. See you at 11.*

He took a deep breath.

• • •

When Milton came home later, his mother's TV was on upstairs. Something in him tightened, and he couldn't figure out why. Stress, he guessed. Then the Post-it on the envelope on the dining room table caught his eye. A bank envelope, ripped along the top—jagged, like the paper had put up a fight. By the address, a torn tag for registered mail. *A different mailman.* Milton crept towards the table.

This came yesterday. You might want to call and clear up this mistake, Milton. Mom.

Upstairs, the TV went off, followed by the light.

6

The nurse had just left, and with his departure, Carol's heart groped for the sense of life he had taken with him. Though Mason sat in the uncomfortable chair by Geoffrey's still body in the guard-railed bed, Carol was as alone as she had been when she was a girl. A shiver rippled up her exposed arms. She walked to the room's doorway, peered into the hallway—was someone else coming to tend to her son?—and then turned around.

Mason was grinding his teeth. Two fingers pressed against his cheek bones while two bent fingers covered his lips.

"We should begin marshalling our options," he half mumbled.

She watched her son's chest inflate and then fall. Revenge was very far from her mind. She looked again at her husband, whose tired eyes seemed to be cracking in the early morning light filtering through the spotless hospital window, and she felt a shift in her, in her life, beyond the damage done by that awful phone call. Was this the same man who had held her gaze and probed her mind for every percolating idea; the same man who would decline a steak were it not the rib-eye he craved? How could that man consider a lawsuit to compensate for their boy? She bristled. She resented the notion that she was understood to be of his same mind.

"At the very least, I guess, we should request copies of the police reports." She turned to the wall and hoped she'd checked her tone as carefully as she'd wanted. The last thing she needed was a protracted conversation about this idea.

He nodded.

She stepped to the window that was far larger than it needed to be. Outside, the dirty streets were choked with traffic, not to mention honking and, in the distance, the sounds of construction work. From this fourth floor view, she saw across the rows of flat roofs, all crammed one right next to another, of this vile neighborhood that had burrowed its claws into her son. A dullness in her metastasized. She needed air. "I would like to head to the house, clean up a little. I trust you will be fine here."

"Yes," he croaked, and in that moment she relived the last moments she had shared with her father-in-law, who had passed some years earlier from emphysema. She reached for her coat, and soon after, grabbed her purse, and was well on her way to the elevator before that image could take further hold.

Exiting the hospital's parking garage, she looked to her left and her right. A man in a wheel chair, whom she guessed to be in his 50s, was dragging along, dressed in a tattered pair of slacks and a greased stained jacket. Although the sun was tucked behind cloud cover, she flipped her visor down and swung it towards the driver's side window. Once she made the expressway's on-ramp, she allowed herself a full breath.

• • •

Finally safe in her living room, she slumped to her favorite wingback chair, an antique Mason had bought for her years ago and had reupholstered with a pattern she'd remarked, in passing, liking. In that chair, she'd read countless books (she was in need of an invigorating biography), thumbed through magazines (though she'd tired of the *New Yorker* of late), and composed letters to cousins she hadn't seen in years (perhaps she should relegate their correspondence to holiday cards). Now, as she sat back, hoping to find her spirit warmed in the silence around her, she realized how unforgiving the cushioned back felt, as if it were encouraging her forward. Outside, a squirrel traversed the lawn. It leapt into a pile of leaves, poked its head up, and then dashed to the far tree, which it scaled in seconds. She thought of her husband's face—that cold, tight scowl he wore—and she wondered if that was really the face she'd seen for the past 27 years; or was it slipped in recently, an unordered appetizer on a restaurant bill; or had the accident created this? She wasn't sure which of these answers would soothe her, for one might mean she'd just woken up to a life she hadn't realized she'd been living or another signaling the start of a life about to begin. Were the two mutually exclusive?

She walked to the kitchen and fetched club soda from the refrigerator. She gulped the chilled beverage and contemplated, for a moment, hurtling the solid tumbler across the room, just to see in to how many pieces the glass might shatter. In what state would it leave the wall? She walked to the sink. Through the kitchen window, she saw in the distance, the neighbor boys throwing a football. She watched one chase after the ball and catch it without looking over his shoulder. With a confident grin, he turned and hurled the ball back to his brother, who fell short of the toss. She placed the glass in the sink.

She walked to the bookshelf in the family room, where, from the bottom shelf, she extracted a plush photo album. On the couch, she settled the bulky binder on her legs and thumbed through Geoffrey's first Halloween, his graduations, his prom, his first dog, his first science fair award, his bike after he'd removed the training wheels on his own. Among these unorganized memories, trips to the Caribbean, Canada, Hawaii, the summer they spent traipsing around Europe before Geoffrey entered high school.

Subconsciously, she'd been searching for evidence of her childhood. Had she been so successful at burying her memories of the home that now seemed so warm, lovely? The one she'd made it her mission to unload, against, naturally, her sister's short-sighted wishes.

Of course, Carol had had to make the arrangements. She had convinced a friend of theirs—an agent who typically only handled properties on the Main Line—to list it for her, one who, when told where the house was, paused before asking the zip code. "Hmm," he said, as if she'd suggested their families buy McDonald's for a picnic in, of all places, Fairmount Park. But he agreed to meet her there the next day.

That day, while she counted the minutes he had been late, she shifted her weight on the worn sofa in her parents' front room, and in so doing, released the scent of a stagnant life that threatened to seize her had she not bolted from the cushions and paced the worn carpet.

The dull beige paint on the wall leading up the stairs begged for a fresh coat, and she wondered if the painters whom they'd hired in the past would work in the city—specifically *that* part of the city. She grinded her teeth.

Around the room, the corners did not align; the roof likely needed a new coat; the bathtub, caulking; the basement floor, sealing. *Why invest another cent into this property?* She wondered if the realtor would recommend an "As Is" clause in the listing. For a strange moment, she wondered if this was what it felt like to offer your child for adoption. And for a reason she didn't care to touch, a pang of sadness found her.

The doorbell rang. Her heart twisted. *This is just a house, just a house.* She buttoned her blouse's top button.

Standing on the front step, he wore a tucked-in button-down and slacks, both immaculately pressed. His professionalism encouraged her. "Thomas, come in."

Before crossing the threshold, he surveyed the street as if he were worried about being assailed at any moment. She wanted to laugh at the action, much in the way she'd chastised Geoffrey years ago for taking the tip money he thought they'd left on the table by accident.

"Can't wait to hear how you came to own this house, Carol." He chuckled in that men-on-the-golf course way and she flinched. She closed the stubborn security gate and shut the door. "You know, you hear things in certain circles…" He had walked into the middle of the front room and the ceiling drew his gaze. "You know, about how the city is just ripe for a housing boom, that people will descend in droves upon the '*opportunities*'"—using his fingers to cradle his word—"here. And then you visit and you look around and wonder what it is, exactly, that these people see." He looked as if he'd been asked to admire a drawing done by a preschooler, the parents of whom he did not particularly respect.

She was, however, happy that he'd brought a fresh pad of paper, though if this signaled that he anticipated making all sorts of notes—beyond the standard ones on an initial evaluation—she ignored it. Plus, there was something amusing in the camera swinging by its strap around his wrist: he resembled a tacky tourist.

"What should I do?" This whole experience could not end soon enough.

"I'll ask you questions, take measurements, snap a few pictures, jot down notes, and then get everything together at my office. I'll run the comps for houses with the same, uh, features." He paused to take in the room in which they stood. "See what they're selling for, and then set a selling price that makes sense." His smile resembled a setting sun and she knew Sherri would be quite disappointed with his final figure.

He watched where he stepped too much. The moment she braced for him to check his shoe, she realized the tsunami of memories threatening to assault her.

Her tongue swelled, like she was addressing a police officer. "The home has been in my family for decades."

His pen froze for a moment; he cleared his throat, then he scribbled something. "Do you know the age of the home?"

"Not sure; over a hundred, I believe." He scribbled.

"Okay, let's measure this front room. Can you hold this end?" He walked the floor. "Okay, now this wall." He directed her to the front window. "Okay, 13 by 15. Good. Do you know what's under this carpet?" He tapped his feet and cocked his head. Her family had celebrated her high school graduation party here.

"You mean, besides the floor?" He scratched his nose. In this moment, he thought her simple. She grinded her teeth.

"No, I mean whether or not the original hardwood floors are underneath." His tone softened, like he was asking a child what kind of ice cream she wanted.

Sifting through years, she couldn't remember anything but that brown, worn carpet. Her father liked it because he said you couldn't tell when the kids spilled soda. "I have no idea."

"All right, let's check out the dining room."

He felt the grooves in the wood paneling on the wall. She couldn't see his face. Turning, he eyed the mirrors that ran the length of the opposite wall. Her grandmother used to tape Christmas cards there. Carol had held the Scotch tape. His eyes frowned when they hit the popcorn ceiling. In that room for the first time, she was embarrassed. "Grab this end, if you would, and let's see what we got in here." She had to steady her fingers.

Done measuring, they moved into the kitchen. He toggled the lights twice. "Okay." He drew that word out. "So, a little need of up....dating." He opened the cabinets, evaluated the dishes (which had been a wedding present) and ran his hand along the edge. As he inspected the oven, she imagined her mother retrieving a steaming apple pie from the top rack. Carol could taste that flaky crust. He peeked behind the refrigerator, then scanned the front. He scribbled. At the sink window, he glanced outside. "Let's head out there for a sec, get a feel for it." She tensed because she knew that the moment she stepped outside with him, she'd scrutinize things she'd never considered. How he accomplished this without saying a word unsettled her.

When the door creaked, he scribbled. He kicked dirt from a crack in the concrete. "Hmm." He scribbled. The plastic sheets against the neighbor's side of the chain link fence crackled in the breeze. "How attached are you to that tree?" He eyed the maple tree her uncle had planted with her father when she was a child. With his eyes he traced it, following the bend by the second story and the branches that shaded the roof. Why hadn't she hired someone to gather those leaves?

"It provides good shade."

"You want to trim it back some. See how it looms over everything, makes this area seem small?" She nodded. "What shape is the roof in?"

"I'm not sure. It doesn't leak." She could hear her mother whisper that it didn't leak much. She'd believed that something only leaks when you can't stop the water from running, not when things get a little damp. She imagined this being said at a family gathering, with her aunt adding: "White people, they don't suffer anything entering their home that they didn't invite." She could feel the collective laughter inflate that room. If you want to handle the leak, that's what buckets are for. When she thought this, she caught herself, dazed that she could ever think such a thing with a phone book within reach.

"When's the last time it was coated?"

"No idea."

He scribbled. She breathed deeply. He was calculating how much her parents' life had been worth, not just those walls, that plaster. Before her mother's passing, she would never have shouldered such a feeling—hadn't she looked down on the home several times before, with each year since her move from the city adding a fresh layer of contempt for the squalor in which it was set? Why was she tolerating this?

Maybe she should have taken Sherri's lone suggestion about the process: find someone who knows the neighborhood. She disregarded that idea as casually as if it were an unnecessary stop sign. This man knew how to close high end deals. But through his eyes, she saw something beyond the money the home would bring: the memories she'd buried were reminding her of the buoyant life that had once been lived protected by that roof. Had she ever been involved on the selling part of a housing transaction, she might have understood in ways that buyers of gorgeous homes with great rooms the size of a small house don't; that selling a home is not, in fact, as easy as dropping off one's dry cleaning.

"Let's head upstairs."

He led the way inside and they arrived at the base of the stairs before she had said okay. The steps creaked as they climbed. She used the handrail that he ignored.

Once she reached the second floor, he was already assessing the bathroom. "Is this the only one in the house?" He nudged the back of the medicine cabinet.

"Yes." Strange how, growing up, the idea that a family would need more than one had never occurred to her.

His eyes roamed the walls. Moving to the shower, he peeked inside, then angled the shower curtain. The sunlight exposed mildew and water stains. "I would change this before we show the house." He released it. "When's the last time you painted in here?" He touched the blue her mother had picked out. The blue had faded.

"Not sure." How often do people paint their bathroom?

"Could use a fresh coat." He scribbled. "How many rooms upstairs?"

"Three."

"Let's look."

They entered and measured each room. Here, they noted a hole in the wall bordered by a square of dust, and there, he tapped windows and grimaced at the single pane. On his way down the stairs, he chuckled a bit, and she wondered if he would give her a knowing smile meant to indicate they were both in on a joke to which he was soon to deliver the punch line. But he shook her hand and told her he would mail her a packet soon, one that would have the price break-down, categorized in three tiers, depending on how aggressive they wanted to be. As she watched him walk to his car through the front window, all she could picture were his soft, pity-providing green eyes. This made her want to shake. In part, she feared this feeling would return every time they passed one another in their neighborhood.

They received two quick offers, and, at closing, as soon as she had signed the paper work, she split the check with her sister—sent registered mail to her sister's home—and Carol had wiped that day with that realtor from her mind. If you'd asked her about it, she would have mentioned that the man had carried out his business professionally, orderly, and enabled her to turn the property in a perfectly respectable way. She had no idea that the people who eventually bought the home renovated it, replaced windows, installed central air, fresh drywall throughout, and painted every new wall in a neutral, non-threatening cream color. That couple lived in it for six and a half years. Then, when their first child reached school age, the crime reports became more troubling. The schools, they more carefully considered. They listed the house, and it sat for months—almost a year. The man who bought it did so as the income census track was switching from low-income to medium, and he paid twice what she had managed to get for it. Though if this fact was relayed to her, she'd shrug.

Like the pictures in the photo album in her lap, that memory of unloading her parents' house had been sealed behind a thin film that only now she wished she could take out and cradle. She zipped through the pages, most of which were empty, and then on the last page, one photo centered on black sticky paper. Even in a sea of photos it would have reached for her attention, and not just because the curved corners of the photo and the rough finish showed its age. She and Sherri (Sherri, in her usual giddiness as if she'd never had her picture snapped, and Carol, reserved, waiting for the moment to pass) standing in front of her parents' home. Right there, like a postcard sent from a place she'd always dreamed of visiting.

Geoffrey had handed it to her, years ago, a find on one of his attic hunts. He had presented it to her like a piece of evidence, an accusatory slant to his voice: "what's this?" She'd regarded it casually, though inside a dam was breaking, gushing resentment at being transported to a time, a place long since gone, an era sealed away with her mother's death. With her son's patient though searching eyes studying her, she carried the picture upstairs until she felt right discarding it later atop the day's food leftovers. She'd reconsidered this decision; though, when the trash had been collected the next day, she accepted that the picture was gone, and, well, that was that. Yet there it was. *Geoffrey.*

By the time she'd met Mason while at Penn, she'd believed in her need to escape so intensely that every reason she'd imbedded in her head—dangerous neighborhood, poor conditions, no future—had taken root so well that she'd had no use for any truth she'd witnessed to the contrary. Mason's subtle flinch when she offered her address was further confirmation that her past was like a shoddy wardrobe in dire need of being donated. And now, as she absorbed photographic details, she felt like she was re-reading a novel, one she hadn't understood the first time through (the responsibility for which, obviously, had been the author's), yet years later, appeared more and more brilliant with each page turned. Uncovering so many things she realized she had allowed herself to miss, she felt guilt seep into her.

She plucked the picture from its page. Noting its small stains, she imagined Geoffrey doing his best to clean it. What had she run from? And whose fault had it been that she had been so averse to the memories the picture had raised? Hers? Mason's? Even if the idea had never been planted by her husband, surely he'd done nothing to discourage it. Could she even fault him if he had? Wasn't she the one who had adamantly insisted her mother come to *them* once Geoffrey had been born?

How much pain this must have caused her mother. She pictured her, standing tall, walking to church on those cold mornings, that faux fur coat Carol's father had bought for her—a snow leopard coat, wasn't it?—hugging her perfectly at the shoulders (the collar pulled up to guard her neck and jaw). It even reached below her knees (though on a taller woman it might have stopped at the thighs). Her face illuminated when she put it on, setting the big round, lion-head embossed buttons through the holes. Heads turned when she passed, and it was the softest thing to fall into, when Carol would hug her mother harder on those days. It never occurred to Carol it wasn't real, not then, not through her young adult years, not even when her mother had willed it to her and she pulled it to her when she'd brought it home and waited to hang it in the guest room closet. Mason doubted any dry cleaner could address its smell—and he stopped short of suggesting they try to take it to their man. Carol had thought her mother was playing one last joke on her—did the woman think she would ever wear that thing? Maybe that's why they'd donated it. Wait, donated? Had they?

She set the pictures on the carpet and rushed to the first floor guest room. Out of breath, she imagined that coat hanging in its clear garment bag. When she slid the door open, where it should have been instead rocked an empty wood hanger. She steadied the hanger and drew her fingers away slowly, as if she were stroking the coat one last time, feeling every fiber, remembering her mother's warm embrace, straining her nostrils to smell the jasmine and hints of cedar in her mother's *Charlie* perfume one last time. *Gone.*

Staring at that hanger, her mind wandered to the lawsuit Mason hinted at. What would Geoffrey have wanted? No, what would Geoffrey *want*?

The doorbell rang. She heard their little voices through the bedroom window, through which she could see the front door. Apparently nervous, they were unable to stand still on her porch: those neighbor children. Could she handle condolences from children? Though why their vapid parents would have ushered them over is beyond her. If she ignored them they would ring the bell repeatedly, for she just realized that she had left the car in the driveway rather than pulling into the garage. Mustering her energy, she opened the front door. Their smiles and giddiness evaporated. The taller one, James (she thought), nudged the squat one—Tucker, wasn't it?

"Um, Mrs. Stevenson, we were wondering if you had our basketball. It might have gone in your yard." They shifted their insignificant weight between their skinny legs.

She took a deep breath, feeling anew the irritation at having to correct these children's parents' assumption that she'd taken her husband's last name. How many times had she casually mentioned their mistake? Then she returned to their question: A basketball? Instantly, she remembered. The right thing was to descend the basement stairs, locate the bin in which she had placed that ball, and then return it. Their innocent faces appeared momentarily patient, and in their soft, naïve skin, she imagined Geoffrey eyeing her, he watching her for recognition of his statement of his graduate intention to study urban planning at Penn and how he planned to take up residence in that neighborhood. She'd held her tongue then—or perhaps hadn't protested nearly as emphatically as her instincts were commanding her to. Slightly stunned, she slowly acknowledged to herself that she bristled at the notion that, for the first time, he was not asking, he was asserting. Maybe this had been what had anesthetized her tongue. What she would not give to return to that moment and force the words from her mouth. They were still staring at her, and with each second their posture eased. She dusted some lint off the front of her blouse. "No, young men, I don't believe I've seen a basketball, but if we find one, I'll let your parents know."

They eyed her the way children do when they know an adult is lying to them but they lack the ability to challenge. The older one scrutinized her face, which she'd kept stone stiff.

"Well, thanks, Mrs. Stevenson."

And with that, her front steps were empty. True, they were unlikely to learn any lesson without their ball to test it, but even if they bought a new ball, she felt sure they would be a little more careful, or perhaps simply stop playing in the backyard altogether. She wasn't sure which outcome she wanted more.

7

At a body shop on the west side of Broad Street, among the smell of rubber and motor oil, Michael stared at his mangled BMW. He'd taken the week off work but he'd needed a few days before he allowed himself to face the car. Every moment since Monday he'd successfully suppressed throttled back to him when he touched the shattered windshield. Sure, the windshield would be replaced, the fender un-dinged, the body repainted, the accident expunged. That is, if the insurance company didn't decide it'd be cost prohibitive to do so. He fingered a ding in the fender's paint. Did he want this car back? Dad hadn't asked about the car's condition when he'd called to tell them that he'd hit someone. Part of him embraced the lack of concern for the car, but then he remembered how his father had been just as uncurious when he found out Aiden and Michael were living together.

The mechanic walked up, wiping a wrench with a pristine white towel. His grey overalls looked like they hadn't seen a day's work. *Never trust a well-dressed, clean mechanic, son.* Maybe the car was in the right place. "Still waiting on the insurance company, Mr. Davis. Soon as I get a response on the estimate, I can start the job." Even his teeth were immaculate. Feeling self-conscious, Michael tongued his front teeth. Had he brushed before leaving the house?

"Yeah, the insurance company said that they were processing the estimate. I'm gonna grab some stuff out of the car."

"Door's unlocked." He lingered a moment. "Sweet ride, by the way. You restore it?"

Michael eyed the large black leather steering wheel, the one Dad had replaced, the leather seats stitched with dirtied white thread. Between the front seats, the accordion-protected gear shift, the one Dad had tracked down at a junk yard, where he talked the guy into letting him have it for free. In the center of the leather covered dashboard, the clock that had stopped working years ago. "Nope."

The guy left him alone with his car. With Dad's 1970 BMW 2002.

His father had found the car listed in the paper. *Great car. Perfect candidate for a restoration project.* For two months he'd kept the clipped ad in his wallet, along with his family pictures.

"You're going to buy *what* and do *what* with it?" Mom had challenged. She was probably thinking about the beer home brewing equipment, next to the stained glass stock and accompanying tools in the basement. Dad had it towed into the just-cleared garage, which Mom had been on him to clean since they moved into the house six months before. When she got a handle on what this new little hobby would entail—the time and the money—she'd wished he'd kept the crap in the garage.

"Honey, when you grow up, make sure your dreams are within reach," Mom said, patting him on the shoulder. Perched at the window, he watched the tow truck lower the car. Rust splotched the dull red paint. The wheels were missing their hubcaps. The front fender looked as if it had fielded a series of hard-hit golf balls. The hood was a deeper shade of red than the rest of the car. One of the tail-lights was cracked, right next to the dirty silver 2002 tii lettering. As Dad later explained, it might've been an early model, a few years before BMW became *BMW*, but a name was a name, and he liked prestige at the best available price. Plus, that model had saved BMW from bankruptcy. Dad had devoted hours to bringing the car back to life and, as long as he'd owned it, the car shone, in part because he washed it weekly and waxed it monthly. Michael had never seen a person so invested in a car before, and he hoped that one day he would be able to care for something that way.

The day Dad had handed over the keys, Michael felt numb and wholly unworthy. "That car's given me all the joy it can, son. She'll take good care of you." Dad acted like he was offering a dog he could no longer care for. Sitting in that driver's seat for the first time as the owner, Michael said, '"I can't believe it, I can't fucking believe it," tapping the steering wheel, "it's really, finally mine." He wanted to tighten his grip and scream, but Dad was still in ear shot. He couldn't wait to drive it.

Now he couldn't imagine getting behind that wheel ever again. The dried blood in the cracked windshield made the whole thing resemble a political district map. If he got the car back, would he see that man's blood there every time he turned the ignition? He could not imagine what his father would feel seeing the state of this car. He never should have accepted those keys.

From the small glove box, he retrieved his driver's manual, his registration, his insurance card. Something was missing, but what? Not there in the back seat, under the cracked leather visor, beneath the grimy front seat or tucked in the trunk; not even stashed near the spare tire. In his backpack, which he hadn't realized was in there, he dumped the registration and insurance card, not really sure what use he would have for either. He zipped up before leaving the lot.

On the crowded bus home, he avoided any and all eye contact. "Yo, Nathan, next stop man," a man across the aisle from him barked. The man was shoveling a hoagie into his mouth. Maybe getting rid of his car would be a bad idea. He turned to the window. He hadn't realized how many cool houses there were. This is what he missed while looking straight ahead. Maybe he *should* ditch the car, take a break from driving, walk more, and explore the city.

The bus passed the park on his block. He yanked the cord, made sure the front 'stop requested' sign was lit, and stood. He had enjoyed how convenient the bus actually was. Two friends had suggested he ride a bike while his car got fixed. He'd almost hung up on each of them, wishing they hadn't even called in the first place.

Trotting home, he checked both ways as he crossed the street. He liked how empty the streets felt during the day. Then he turned onto his block and noticed a person knocking on his front door. He blinked a few times before he recognized the UPS uniform. He set a basket on the front step and had taken out a booklet and a pen.

"That's my house."

The delivery guy looked at him and smiled.

"You Michael?"

Looking around, as if worried that someone would hear his name and put two and two together, he choked, "yes."

"Cool." He handed him the basket. The cellophane crinkled. *What the hell*? Michael signed the electronic clipboard. "Have a good day."

He took the basket inside. Setting it on the dining room table, he removed the small white card. "Mike, keep your head up. Walter." He tore the cellophane. Set atop green plastic grass, a cheese and sausage assortment. Strange, but a nice gesture. Michael put the basket in the kitchen and plopped on a dining room table chair. He rested his chin on the table. That poor guy. He still wished he'd been able to find any information about his status at the hospital. Going to visit him still seemed like the humane thing to do, even if it might be a horrible idea. He stared at the ceiling and his eyes noticed a cobweb in the corner. He couldn't bring himself to wet a paper towel and wipe it away. Man, he really should leave this house, perhaps take Ron up on his invite to have a drink, but did he really want to field questions about how he was doing? And what if instead he was listening to casual conversation about a boring work week? A conversation that would make him want to scream from the top of his lungs how that bullshit didn't matter, none of it mattered when you put another human being in the hospital. He tapped his forehead on the edge of the table, held it there, then stood.

He walked to the dining room window and to the pot of dirt. He turned the blinds to guide more light to the surface then leaned down, scrutinized soil. *Still no sprout.* With his finger he nudged a few different spots. Should he water it? At what point did soil become too dry?

• • •

The next afternoon, a knock at the door seemed to shake the house. Should he answer it? Milton's head peered through the blinds and Michael opened the door. A six pack of Lager in hand, he said, "Let's go man, up on the deck." He was half up the stairs before Michael had a chance to decline. When Michael'd moved in, Milton handed him a frozen turkey. Looking at it, he said, "Thanks?" Soon, he would appreciate how his neighbor took it upon himself to organize the block clean-up on Saturdays and sprinkled salt over fresh blankets of snow when Michael slept in late. He had also offered on more than one occasion: "If you ever go out of town, let me know. I'll keep an eye on your place for you." One got the impression that nothing happened in the neighborhood without him knowing, and Michael felt lucky to have bought next to the man, but, sadly, he'd never invited him over, not to say "Hi," not to share a beer.

"I always forget you have this up here." Milton sat in one of the two lounge chairs on the deck. He'd helped the construction guys daisy-chain the lumber up the scaffolding. Michael's deck had been the first one constructed on the block. He felt ashamed now that it had never occurred to him to invite him to see the finished product. Then he pictured that neighbor he'd once had, the one who drove the loud Chevy—Mr. Wilson? Mr. Williams? His name had been repeated so infrequently he couldn't recall. He'd wave occasionally and he and Dad would occasionally chat when they happened to be bringing in the garbage cans at the same time, but he'd never been invited over, as if that just wasn't something you did. He opened the beer Milton handed him. Settling into the other lounger, he noticed how the tree across the street had seemly overnight grown into his view of the PECO building. He also noticed the construction on a roof deck at the end of their block.

"You really made this house a great home for yourself, Michael. You should be proud."

He wondered if it would ever feel like home again or, come to think of it, if it ever had. Milton reclined like he was tanning.

Without opening his eyes or turning his head, he asked, "So what happened to your fella?"

Instead of chuckling at the word "fella," Michael's smile evaporated. Of course, this was also a weird question. Had he been in a different mindset, he might have dodged it. But his defenses were rather weak of late. "He's gone. A few weeks ago." Michael sipped his beer but only tasted the warmth as he swallowed it. "A few months ago, actually."

"I'd say sorry about that, but I ain't gonna lie, he seemed like an asshole. You could tell by the way he parallel parked. Man had no respect for anyone else's bumper."

The thought of all the times he'd told Aiden to be more careful with the car crossed his mind. This brought a half-hearted smile. "Yeah." Michael wiped condensation from his bottle.

"You're not thinking about getting out, are you?"

Michael almost choked on a swig of beer. "What do you mean?" He wiped his face with his sleeve.

"Come on, Mike, you know what I'm asking. You don't think I didn't hear—that everyone hasn't heard about the accident? I'm sure you're spooked, thinking that your neighbors looking at you like you did it on purpose. But don't let that shit get to you. It'll blow over. After all, it was an accident." As he sipped, his eyes danced along the skyline. "Besides, when I get a good neighbor, I want to keep him. You leave, things will be unsettled for a while and I don't want that for this block. You know what I mean?"

Great, more pressure. Michael wished the beer was colder. "Should I go to the hospital, see how he's doing?"

Milton turned and studied his face. "Don't stir the pot," Milton said.

Michael nodded. *Stir the pot.* Was that what he'd done by not hitting that brake fast enough? God, how old could that guy have been? College aged? And that little girl. He pictured those little fingers that waved to him as she had passed right before. He'd waited for her to reach the corner. He had waited. Aiden would have rolled his eyes that Michael had waited so long. She'd had to have seen it too. All that blood.

That bike had just appeared.

The blood shot across the shattered windshield.

Or did they happen at the same time?

Was his car moving?

That kid was on the windshield one moment and then he was gone.

Could he even tell it was a guy?

Someone screamed.

How long did he stay in that driver's seat before creeping out?

Outside, glass crunched under his feet. Blood leaked off the hood. His heartbeat in his ears. His fingers were numb. The ambulance arrived; cops surrounded him, asked questions, wrote down information. *Am I in trouble?* A crowd had gathered, shaking their heads in his direction. Anger in their eyes. The ambulance pulled away, cop cars left. Two cops—one woman, one man—stayed with him, the questions kept coming. Pictures being taken. Was that a helicopter overhead?

"Do you want us to escort you home?" The officer was saying. Michael was staring at the blood in the street. He shook his head. She removed her hand.

What was he supposed to do with his car now that they had taken their pictures? The bloody windshield. *This is bad, very bad.* The crowd thinned, people were cussing as they left. Cops pulled away. Twice he dialed his insurance company before his fingers stopped shaking.

"Would you like us to recommend a body shop?" The woman on the other end of the phone asked. She was smacking gum. Michael was in a bad movie, he had to be.

"Yes," he said. "I guess." How did he get home that day?

Home. He looked at the pressure-treated wood of his roof deck, the wood that needed staining before it rotted. He had waited the three months for the wood to dry out and then had forgotten about it. Had he waited too long? He recalled stepping onto those wood planks for the first time, by himself, surveying his view, the trees sprouting—the ones that would grow to obscure his view—and feeling, for the first time: this really is my home. I am safe. He hoped Aiden would settle in too.

Where was that safety now?

"Still with me?" Milton's voice bounced with the energy of someone trying really hard to steady the ship.

"Yeah."

"You have a good chance here, to start fresh. Take it. You need friends around you. Get some of your people to move into the neighborhood. That will anchor you."

Michael felt like he'd just been hit on by a co-worker. He gave Milton a perplexed look.

"You know anyone looking to rent?"

Michael played with this idea. Friends in the area. Could he make that pitch? Would he be like some sleazy salesman trying to pass a lemon off? Wait. Is that what his neighborhood was to him now? In the past few days, how many times had he felt like bolting?

"No, all my friends are good for now." He smirked a bit. "Besides, I think they'd prefer Old City to our neighborhood." *Our neighborhood.* That phrase comforted. Like saying "I love you" cemented the feeling for another person. *Another person.* Sure, a few friends had called, but who had bothered to stop by? Why did the first have to be a relative stranger? Isn't this what he wanted out of the place where he settled: a sense of community? But had he earned this yet? He couldn't shake the feeling that Milton was after something. Why was he so distrusting?

"Here." Milton put a beer in his hand and stood. "Be right back." He trotted down the steps, heading to the bathroom. Moments later, he was back and settled. "You sure have a nice view from up here."

"Yep, I guess I do." Michael kept looking forward. If only he could appreciate the view of the downtown buildings, the trees swaying in the breeze rather than Aiden, the car, that kid, the house. He could see Milton studying him and, noting the pity in his eyes, he understood how unstable he looked. And maybe something else was there too, a slight trepidation.

Of course, Michael couldn't know that Milton had almost mentioned Rose's interest and that he was hesitating because, one, he understood how important it was to know who was talking about you and, two, that knowledge had a way of helping people make bad decisions.

8

The day after the accident, Keisha was having trouble finishing her math homework. Sitting in her room, she couldn't stop thinking about the accident she'd seen and how she hadn't told anyone the full story, in part because no one would have believed her, especially Mom, and all because she'd fudged that one tattle on Natalie, who deserved what she got, because she always got the new clothes and Keisha was tired of only getting hand-me-downs. She'd said she was sorry about that one time; she really wasn't. Mom had even come to get her that day in that crowd, and while being dragged away, Keisha had tried to tell her, but Mom wasn't having any of it. Up in her room, Keisha's math text book sat closed next to her leg. Using her finger, she traced the green flowers stitched on her comforter. She had been swinging her teddy bear around, but that made her a little dizzy. Besides, the stuffing was coming out of a tear in its ear. Mom could fix it, but since she was probably downstairs hunched over that pile of papers on the kitchen table, she left her alone. Those big veins in her neck scared her. Would her veins get all big like that one day?

She stopped tracing, slouched her shoulders, took a great big breath, and then puffed her cheeks as she exhaled. She wanted to be a hot air balloon and float away. She pictured her mean teacher standing over her desk, folding her arms while Keisha asked her a math question. Why couldn't those stupid word problems be easy like her science homework, all that plant stuff that she understood because she could picture it? She nibbled at her pencil's eraser and then smacked that funny, dry taste away.

The front door slammed and she shoved her book under her pillow. Maybe he wouldn't ask about her math if he didn't see the book. She looked at her bear, who smiled back. Downstairs, Mom and Dad were talking but she couldn't hear about what. Were they finally going to talk about all those people who were at the house last weekend?

Last Saturday, a white man in a suit showed up with a stack of papers, a picture of their house on them. He made the stack neat on their kitchen counter, next to a bunch of his business cards. When the doorbell rang again, her parents had tried to scoot her out the front door as fast as they could. Two people holding hands moved into her front room while her mother fussed her into her jacket. "Hi," Keisha said. The black woman looked at her and smiled with her big white teeth. The white man had a measuring tape. He started taking pictures of her walls, the floor, the ceiling. Walking towards the park, from the front window, she saw the flash going off.

At the park, Mom folded her arms on the bench while Dad sat forward, his hands clasped between his knees—just like when he's watching basketball (he was always watching basketball). Keisha ran to a part of the park, where someone had ripped out a plant and left it by the hole in the ground. She carried it to her parents.

Keisha eyed every part of it like she had just discovered a treasure map. "Look, Mom. I've been reading about plants in school. I learned about all the parts." Without looking to see if they were paying attention, she pointed to the cluster of brown strands hanging from the plant's end: "These are the roots and they are really important for any plant because they are what dig into the ground and allow the plant to grow big and strong. Also, the roots are what take all the water and the food from the ground and bring it back to the plant, then all the necessary stuff gets carried all through the leaves." Mom and Dad stared at the house. Natalie was sitting on the ground, picking at rocks, shaking her head when Keisha looked at her.

Finally, she asked, "Daddy, what were those people doing in our house?" Her parents looked at each other like when Uncle Steve moved out of Aunt Tiffany's house. Natalie smiled like she knew a secret.

"Don't worry about it, honey," he said.

"Honey, go put that back where you found it. Don't get all dirty before dinner."

"Yeah, stupid."

Keisha stuck her tongue out at her sister, who cocked a fist in her direction. Keisha dashed away.

Now, thinking of that stupid smirk, she crept across the carpet to the stair's edge. The closer she got, the better she could hear. She kept her hand over her mouth, for if her parents caught her listening, she wouldn't be able to watch TV for a week.

"We're out. We got a 45-day escrow on this place and a 30-day one on the house we liked in West Philly."

"How are we supposed to get everything wrapped up that quickly?" Her mom's voice had a little edge to it.

"We can get this done. Besides, we knew it was going to be like this."

"Uh-huh."

"I can't wait to see what we can get done with that new house." Dad's voice picked up a bit, like when he was talking about the family driving somewhere long. "Now we just have to make sure…" Dad stopped. Worried she'd made a noise, she backed into her room and eased her door shut.

She yanked her teddy bear towards her. With the bear pulled to her chest, Keisha paced like her mother did when she read mail. Why do we have to move? She squeezed her bear. How was she supposed to get her stupid math homework done now? She crawled into a corner.

Later, the scribbled dogs and houses had taken over most of the white space in her workbook. Then Dad's boots thudded against the stairs' carpet. The thuds got closer. He knocked. Without her saying anything, he opened the door and poked his head inside. He was going to be mad.

"You getting that homework done, baby girl?" he asked.

"Trying to." She wanted to cry. His voice was too soft, like that time he told her she had a cavity that needed to get filled.

"What are you working on there?" He stepped into the room.

"Math stuff." She picked at the page's bent corner.

"You go over this in class today, with your teacher?" He sat on the bed.

"Kinda. She doesn't explain stuff. She talks so fast, writes stuff on the board, then gives us busy work. She doesn't let us ask too many questions." She wanted to tell Dad how her teacher smelled funny.

"Well, let's see what you got there." He grabbed her workbook and eyed it real close.

"They're these word problems, Dad. I just don't get what they're asking."

"Let me see: 'Jackie owns a farm and she is trying to sell some of her crops. How much money does she make for her 13 crates of carrots at 3 dollars a crate?'" Dad looked at her.

"I don't know. Do you times the 13 and the 3? Is that right? And why does she have to sell her food? Doesn't her family need it?"

He smiled like Mom had asked what happened to all the ice cream. "Yes, honey. See, you got it licked. Easy." He tugged on her ear. "As far as saving food for her family, that question has nothing to do with this here word problem. Don't overthink it."

"Yeah, Dad, but I don't know why they can't just ask you how to times 13 and 3. I can picture that in my head. What about this one?" She pointed to the one about horses and what they eat and bales of hay and different days to feed them. Where should she start with that one?

He mouthed the words to the problem. "Well, honey, you see you gotta divide. You just…" He stopped and she looked out the window, wishing she understood how people seem to get this whole dividing-things-up stuff. "If it's bothering you this much, get through what you can. When you get a chance, you ask your teacher to help you. And if she doesn't listen to you the first time, ask again. If that doesn't help, well, you let me know and I will call the school. Okay?" He patted her on the head.

"Okay."

He leaned forward and rubbed his knees like he did when the basketball score was close. He cleared his throat and then touched her shoulder. His hand felt heavy. "Don't worry," he said.

She looked at the flowers on her comforter.

"Baby, were you listening to your mother and me talk a little while ago?"

She nodded.

"So you heard what we were saying about selling this house?"

She felt tears coming.

"Keisha, I know it doesn't mean much to you now, but we are going to make good money on this here house and then buy something better in a new neighborhood." His voice got low again. He was looking at her. Her eyes itched but she didn't want to cry. She wanted to be a big girl, just like stupid Natalie, who she was sure knew they were moving. She clenched her fist. "It's going to be all right, baby, I promise." He moved his hand from her shoulder. "By the way, your mother told me that you were by that accident on Monday. That so?"

"Yes, sir."

"She also said that you say you saw it, that the man on the bike caused it. That so?"

"Yes." She pulled her teddy bear close.

"You want to talk about that?" He moved close to her.

She had been coming home from school, and when she reached that corner, she stepped off the curb. Her shoe hit the concrete and the car screeched. Her heart skipped a beat and she jumped back. She could smell the burned rubber. The driver, his window down, mouthed sorry to her and motioned for her to cross. She waited to see if he was serious, and when he nodded, she crossed. The engine hummed as she passed. The man even waved to her.

Then it happened.

When she turned to thank the driver for being nice, his car went. That man on the bicycle whooshed right into the car. The driver yelled and there was a loud crash. Keisha screamed.

She covered her eyes. A man cried out. Her heart was jumping in her chest. Through her fingers, she could see all the blood on the ground. She turned and shut her eyes so tight they hurt. Then everything got real quiet, except for the humming of the engine. Then she felt people come around her and she opened her eyes. The bicycle wheel was going round and round on the ground as people moved in front of her. She heard sirens, then people shoved her even though she wasn't in anyone's way.

"You see that shit?" one man said to another one.

"Motherfucker probably did it on purpose. That white fuck," another said.

She stepped back. When her dad yelled at people like that when they were stuck in traffic, she crouched down as low as her seat belt would let her in the backseat.

The sirens got louder. When the police showed up, and the ambulance got there, the people moved back a bit. She got pressed against a wall. Then Mom was there, and, before she knew what was happening, Mom was dragging her home. The veins in Mom's neck got big so she shut up.

There in her room, she looked at Dad: "How come I couldn't tell no one about what I saw?" She closed the rip in her teddy bear's ear with her fingers. She pressed hard and then took her fingers away but it wouldn't stay closed.

"Sometimes you just have to let adults figure things out. Some things you have to avoid getting mixed up in. There were plenty of adults there, sweetheart." His voice got real soft and he put his arm around her. She leaned into his chest and smelled. He was wearing the cologne that smelled like the woods, the one that they had bought him for Christmas, the one she picked out, the one Natalie hated. Keisha relaxed.

She wanted to tell Dad that she was the only one there to see it, but she didn't want him to think that she was lying. He might have stopped rubbing her back.

She remembered how the people in that crowd that day looked like they wanted to fight, with their fists clinched, shaking their heads. She could still hear their curse words jumping out of their mouths. She flinched.

"Daddy, why would people think that white man driving would have tried to hurt that black man on the bike?"

He sighed real hard, like a lot of air rushing out of a bike tire. "Well, some people like to believe the worst about people."

She sat back and pulled her teddy bear to her chest.

"Try this. Is there anyone you think that doesn't like you?"

"My teacher, Mrs. Martin." She opened and closed the rip of her teddy bear's ear.

"Why do you think she doesn't like you, sweetheart?"

"She always looks angry when I answer a question wrong, makes me feel stupid." Keisha really meant that her teacher made her feel retarded. But her father told her not to use that word.

"Well, maybe she thinks you can do better, that's all. She probably likes you just fine." He moved a braid away from her face. "She's doing her job, and every student of hers might need different attention. Maybe she is trying to find the best way to encourage you." He lifted her chin. "Have you told her how you feel?"

"No." She met his eyes. She didn't understand what that had to do with what those people thought about the man driving. "Could there be another reason, Daddy?"

He eyed her the way he looked at funny-looking food Mom made from a new recipe. "Some people want a reason to hate white people, baby. When you get older, you'll understand a bit better. But for now, you should know that that was an accident, that that man driving probably didn't mean to do what he did. Okay?" He hugged her tight, kissed her forehead, and then stood up. Now she had something else that didn't make sense. She bet Mrs. Martin still hated her.

That night, she dreamed about carrots and Jackie's farm. She could see her having to gather her vegetables to try and sell everything, like at a sidewalk sale. She imagined that Jackie was sad when she put all of her carrots in her wood crates. Keisha imagined that Jackie had two daughters who watched her load crates onto a truck. A dog barked. As she worked, Jackie stepped in the mud over and over and all Keisha could do was watch. Jackie was white.

• • •

The next day, Keisha crossed into the schoolyard and kids were gathered around a boy who was always getting into trouble for ditching and spray painting graffiti on the bathroom stalls. He was jerking his hands around, showing everyone how stupid he was. Kids watched him like he was popcorn in the microwave, waiting for the last kernel to pop. Behind the dirty chain link fence, she stopped.

"I'm telling you, I was there. That car plowed right on through that guy on the bike, sent him flying and shit." She rolled her eyes. Why did people love giving him cookies and chips out of their lunch when he sat by them in the cafeteria? Her neck got hot. The bell was gonna ring soon.

In the classroom, she ran to her desk so she could spread out her homework before class started. She unzipped her backpack and scooped her books out. Sticky notes, with all of her questions scribbled on them, stuck out. She needed to understand that stuff if she was going to change schools. She didn't want to look like a fool to her new classmates for not knowing stuff. When the bell rang, and nobody was at Mrs. Martin's desk, people exchanged looks. Danielle, who's annoying and sits up close to the white board, giggled.

Ricky leaned towards Chris and whispered. Someone in the back of the room shouted. Timmy and Colin ran around their seats. Last Halloween, they walked around taking people's candy and then playing catch with it across the room. Of course Mrs. Martin waited before she yelled at them. Concentrating on her word problem answers, Keisha hummed. She grabbed her pencil when she realized that she'd forgotten to carry a one. Any minute, Mrs. Martin was going to walk in and, if Keisha kept her head down and kept working, she wouldn't get in trouble.

The door jerked open, and most of the kids darted to their seats. Timmy and Colin stopped in the middle row. Ms. Erin, wearing one of those nice, professional-looking business suits, walked in!!!! Was she taking Mrs. Martin's place? In second grade, if Keisha raised her hand, Ms. Erin came by her desk and stayed with her until she figured something out. It sucked that she had quit at the end of the year. Timmy and Colin looked at Ms. Erin and then walked to their desks. Standing at Mrs. Martin's desk, Ms. Erin clasped her hands together. Keisha beamed extra big, hoping she would notice her.

"Hello students." She looked at everyone. She kept her eyes on people until they looked back. "My name is Ms. Erin, and I am filling in for Mrs. Martin today." Slowly, everyone started looking at her in the front of the room.

"Okay, young ladies and gentlemen, how is everyone this morning?" No one said anything. She cleared her throat. "Let's try this again. *Class*, how is everyone this morning?"

Everyone said, "Fine, Ms. Erin."

"Good, now, young ladies and gentlemen, according to Mrs. Martin, you have been learning about plants." She scanned the room and a few people nodded. "Okay, then, take out your science workbooks and turn to page 23. There you will see the 'Plant Parts activity sheet.'" Keisha pulled out her book and found the page, the one with a drawing of a plant with lines coming off it. This must have been why she had to read all of that easy stuff last week, about the plant parts and what they did. As people looked at the sheet, they scratched their heads. Like she was counting heads on a school bus, Ms. Erin bobbed her head. "Young man in the brown sweater, are you with us?"

As usual, Charles was scrunching up his face. One time, when he got called up to do a presentation and he looked like this, he peed himself. Ms. Erin walked towards him. She kneeled at his desk and flipped the pages for him. "This one, honey." She stood up and patted him on the shoulder. Mrs. Martin would have yelled at him from the front and shook her head all nasty when someone else helped him find the right page. "Now class, last week, you read about what the parts of the plant are and what they do. So today, by yourself, I want you to fill out this sheet, putting the correct part next to the correct line. In case you forget what the parts are, look at the bottom of the sheet." She raised her book so everyone could see what she was pointing to. No one was ever this quiet for Mrs. Martin. "Once everyone is done we will review the answers." She grabbed her pencil. Why couldn't all of their lessons be this easy?

Ms. Erin walked around, peeking over everyone's shoulders. When she returned to the front, she stood by the whiteboard and held her hands together. She looked at Keisha and smiled. Why didn't Mrs. Martin smile like that once in a while? Ms. Erin came towards her.

Kneeling beside Keisha's desk, she took her paper in her hands. After studying it, she set it down. She knew she got all the right answers. Ms. Erin looked her in the eye. "Good job, Keisha. How are you doing?" Keisha wanted teeth as bright as Ms. Erin's.

"I'm good, Ms. Erin." Keisha looked at her desk. "Everyone wishes you were still teaching here. Are you coming back?" Keisha wanted her to say yes, but then she remembered that she was moving. She'd be jealous if those stupid boys in her class got to have her as a teacher again and she couldn't.

Ms. Erin looked kinda worried for a second, like she had left something important at home. "No, dear, I am just here to fill in a bit." She tapped her nails on the desk once she stood. "Class, is everyone finished?" Silence. "Okay, let's try that a different way. Who is not done?" No one raised a hand. "Okay, would anyone like to volunteer the answer to the first line?" She walked to the front of the room.

Rodney and Keith volunteered for the easy ones: "leaves" and "flower." Sara acted like she had ants in her stockings for the "fruit." Zachary and Tasha said the "stem" and the "seed" and then Keisha raised her hand for the "roots." She had to be careful how many times she raised her hand. When she did something right, people shook their heads, like she got lucky. People were always thinking she was getting lucky. One time a bunch of the kids were playing HORSE during recess and Keisha swung the ball towards the basket and it went in. She won. She was still the last to get picked for teams.

"Okay, now let's move on to the second part of the activity. Let's get you all in groups,"

She was pretty sure Ms. Erin winked at her as people moved into the groups she assigned. She couldn't wait until math.

• • •

The bell rang and people pushed and shoved out the door. Keisha gathered her stuff and Tasha stayed behind—they walked part of the way home together. She waved for her to go, then Keisha walked to the front, where Ms. Erin was putting her notebook into her bag.

"Goodbye, Ms. Erin." Keisha picked a chip in Mrs. Martin's wood desk.

"Goodbye, Keisha." Ms. Erin's eyes scanned her, like people did when they thought she was making something up. She wanted her teddy bear. "Are you okay, Keisha?"

Keisha moved her hand when Ms. Erin looked at it. "Yes, I just like having you as my teacher, that's all."

"Okay, well, I enjoy having you in my class." Her eyes didn't leave Keisha. "You sure you're okay though?" Ms. Erin's mouth got all serious. "I heard from another teacher that you witnessed that bike accident in the neighborhood on Monday, the one everyone is kinda upset about. You okay with that?"

She looked at a bird that had just landed on to a tree branch. It chirped at her. "Yeah, I guess. Nobody talks to me about it though. People think I made it up."

"Well, honey, can you talk to your folks about it?" She put a hand on her shoulder.

"No, not really. They just tell me it's none of my business, just let things be. Besides, we're moving soon anyway." Two more birds landed on the branch. They didn't chirp, they just looked at each other. The first one flew away. Keisha looked at the clock. "I gotta get home, Ms. Erin. Bye." Keisha wanted to cry. She bet she wouldn't understand math anymore without Ms. Erin either.

• • •

Tasha was waiting by the gate when she walked up. "Why were you talking to Ms. Erin?"

"I wanted to say goodbye." Keisha picked rust off the links.

"Goodbye?" Tasha walked. Keisha lagged behind.

"She's my favorite teacher." Keisha felt her eyes tearing. "I hate Mrs. Martin."

"We might have her as a substitute again. Why you acting so weird?"

"I'm not," Keisha said.

"If you say so. You coming over later to hopscotch?" They spent Wednesdays at Tasha's house because her parents didn't mind the chalk on the sidewalk. On Fridays, they watched cartoons at Keisha's.

"No, I have to get home today." She wanted so bad to tell Tasha that she was leaving her stomach ached. But Dad said to keep it a secret.

After Tasha turned towards her street, Keisha felt lightheaded, like she hadn't eaten all day. Soon, she reached the accident corner. The blood in the middle of the street was gone. Had the rain washed it away? There was a dark spot though. Her stomach knotted. There were no candles or stuffed animals near the corner. That was good. Then she remembered that scream. She blinked really hard. She shook her head until that sound vanished.

She looked down the street again and a piece of newspaper drifted right into a parked car and spread out on the wheel. She should have taken Montrose St. She looked at the dirty ground in front of her. She looked down the street. No cars. She stared real hard to make sure she didn't see one far away, then she felt a hand on her shoulder.

"Baby, what are you waiting on?" Keisha turned. Ms. Rose was smoking one of her nasty cigarettes. Keisha always held her nose when she walked by the Laundromat and Ms. Rose was on her break. Keisha and Tasha got soda from the vending machine in there when they played on the jungle gym across the street during the summer. Sometimes she stopped and listened to what Ms. Rose said to people there because they were always stopping to ask Ms. Rose something. She felt grown up listening to those conversations, like she could be trusted with stuff.

"Just making sure a car isn't coming, Ms. Rose."

Ms. Rose looked down the street. "Can't you see ain't nothing coming this way?"

"Yes, Ms. Rose. But I'm just being careful because of the accident I saw on Monday."

Her eyes got real small. "What do you know about that accident, baby?"

"I saw it, Ms. Rose. I saw that bike go right into that car."

Ms. Rose's look turned all serious. "You really saw it go down, baby?"

"Yes, Ms. Rose. That man on the bike didn't stop."

"Hmm." She looked down the street and then at Keisha. "Why weren't you in school?"

"We had a half day, Ms. Rose."

She puffed her cigarette. "You tell your momma you saw it?"

"Yes, Ms. Rose, but she said not to get all mixed up in other people's business."

She looked like she was concentrating. "Hmm, is your mother going to be home later?"

"She should be."

Ms. Rose looked like she was thinking real hard. "Well, you tell her I'm coming by to talk with her about something, okay?" She nodded. Ms. Rose puffed her cigarette. "Come here, baby, give me your hand." They crossed.

At the corner, Ms. Rose walked straight. "You get your homework done now, get them grades up, you hear?" she said.

"Yes, Ms. Rose." She passed a house and Keisha couldn't see her no more. She wanted to ask Ms. Rose what she thought she should do about telling people about the accident, because she seemed to know just about everything. She kept walking.

She checked for cars at every intersection she reached, and in the middle of the streets, she kept her head down and listened to the wind and watched the dirt swirl with the breeze. A few blocks from her house, she crossed to the opposite side so she could walk in the sunlight poking through the clouds. Plus, the sidewalk had better cracks on that side. When the new houses on the other side of the street got finished, the sidewalks were all smooth and new. The cracks made walking fun.

Oh! A car door slammed and then a cab sped past her. She had ducked because she thought it was a gunshot, or at least what she had always imagined one sounding like. As she turned, the Hello Kitty charm on her backpack jangled. A man walked towards her and she sucked in her breath. *The driver.* Two plastic grocery bags swung in his hand while he clutched one paper bag close to his chest. At the top of the bag, apples bounced. He was practically running as he crossed the street. They were a few cars' distance from one another by the time he stepped up his steps. His grocery bags swished back and forth as he searched his pockets. The way he was balancing those bags, he looked like a clown who was about to drop everything. He stopped for a moment and turned in her direction, like a squirrel she'd surprised. He yanked keys from his pocket. The bags lifted with his hand, which was getting red where the bag handles pulled on his wrist. He must have forgotten which key worked because he kept changing keys.

"Fuck!"

When Dad said that word, he threw his tools. This happened when the car out front still didn't work. She couldn't move. She could see the veins in the man's neck. He dropped everything on the ground next to his front steps and an apple tumbled towards the street. She watched it roll, and then ran for it. Before it found the gutter, she picked it up and dusted off the dirt. "No, don't worry..." He sounded like Dad telling her not to pick up any trash in the street, even though she wanted to throw it away.

Trotting to the man, she held the apple out. He took it from her real slow, like maybe he thought she was fooling and would snatch it away from him. He looked sad, even behind his sunglasses. His skin was real pale. "Don't worry," she said, "I caught it before it hit the street, so you still should be able to eat it. As long as you wash it first."

"Ah… I… thanks." His voice got real quiet. "You didn't have to do that, but thank you." His voice cracked, like he was about to cry. His lips parted like he was going to say something. Did he recognize her? He closed his lips tight, dropped the apple in the bag, then turned, pushed his door open, gathered his groceries, and shut and locked the door. She wanted to knock on his door, tell him that she knew he didn't mean to hit that man on the bike. But he would probably just wait for her to stop talking, nod to her, and then tell her to go play.

So she started walking home. Should she tell Mom or Dad that she saw him, that she helped him save his groceries? They would probably tell her that she shouldn't talk to strangers, especially him. But wouldn't everyone be strange in their new neighborhood? She wouldn't tell Natalie either, because she didn't deserve to know. Now, when she saw her sister smirk, she would know that feeling.

9

Rose rang the doorbell, waited about the time it took to light a cigarette, and then knocked twice. She didn't want to look like one of her customers who constantly checked the clothes in the dryer before the buzzer sounded. The door opened. "Hey Donna, how you been?"

"Ms. Rose." She didn't budge in her doorway. "Keisha said you were coming by."

"May I?"

Donna held her gaze for a few moments then her eyes softened and ushered Rose inside. The door closed. The women hugged in the way you do when you think the other person is fragile. Rose's eyes darted to Keisha, who was at the top of the stairs, but they didn't stay on her long. "You got any coffee on? I thought we could talk a bit, if you don't mind."

Donna considered her. "No, but I can get some going. Come into the kitchen." Rose stepped around some boxes on their way to the kitchen.

"How you been, Ms. Rose?"

"Getting by, getting by." She sat at the kitchen table. Donna moved a paper stack on the table out of the way. "Heard you were moving, looks like that's true," Rose said. She felt a little sad that a nice family like this was moving on. She wished she'd been by more often to visit.

Donna filled the coffee maker with water and switched it on. "Sugar?"

"No, just black."

Donna leaned against the counter. "What's on your mind, Ms. Rose?" She sounded tired.

Rose turned her head just enough to catch little Keisha crouching by the top of those stairs. Was she inviting trouble into this little child's world? "I, uh..." She swallowed hard and coughed. "I know you got a lot on your plate, with moving and all, but I wanted to talk to you about something." Rose cleared some phlegm from her throat. "About the accident."

Leaning against the counter, she crossed her arms. "I was hoping that wasn't what you were here for."

"I saw Keisha this afternoon, and she told me she witnessed it. She tell you that?" Keisha flinched, so Rose averted her glance. In that moment, she had half a mind to excuse herself, stand, and walk right out that door without looking back.

The coffee maker spurted drops into the pot, which needed a good scrubbing. "When I grabbed her from that crowd, I didn't want to hear it." Donna cleared her throat. "Even if she did see it, we don't need to get mixed up in that business." Stress washed across Donna's face. Rose understood the reluctance. How do you place your child in harm's way, even with the best intentions? "Mmm, I hear you, baby; but listen, that man who was driving, he's a customer at the store. I've talked to him a bit. He's a good man, lives in this neighborhood. If he didn't do it, someone needs to speak up."

"Rose, I'm not risking my daughter—or this family— to help a strange white man."

Rose couldn't say she'd do a thing differently, were the roles reversed. But she reached for middle ground. "Now listen, I respect what you're saying. I'm not talking about getting her out there; no, I'm saying, if we can talk to her, find out if it's true, then we can spread the word, organize folks, cool people down. This nonsense people are talking scares me."

"She's *a child*, Rose."

The request was slipping away. Did they still go to church, Rose wondered. "All shapes and sizes."

"I thought you'd left the flock." She put a little too much bite on that last word for Rose's liking. The coffee pot coughed up a gasp of steam and Donna poured the coffee.

Rose watched the steam rise from the cups. "Now, just so you know what I was thinking, before you decide. I was thinking, get some flyers printed, and organize a gathering— maybe at that bar that took Reggie's Place's spot. With folks from the neighborhood—old and new—we can squash this before it turns nasty."

Out of the corner of her eye, she noticed Keisha creeping down the stairs like a cat afraid it would wake the dog. She could see Donna searching for a way to tell her no. But maybe if the little girl wanted to help.

"Rose, your heart's in the right place, but we can't." Donna's voice tensed, and her face shrunk with the burden she was dodging. She brought the cups to the table.

"Momma, I can help pass out those flyers." They stared at Keisha, who looked so confident standing in the entrance to the kitchen. Their mouths parted. Those dark eyes were eager to court the world, make a difference, even if she didn't know what road lay ahead. But Rose did. Could she really ask this of a child?

"Keisha, the adults are talking. You go on back upstairs until dinner's ready." Keisha hesitated before scampering away. As Rose watched her clamber up the stairs, her heart crumbled. How hard should she push this?

"I respect what you're doing, Rose; I do. But this isn't our fight. And soon, this won't be our neighborhood."

Rose's mind lingered on this last bit of information. "I might be leaving too, Donna. Maybe taking up a cousin's offer to live in DC, enjoy a change. But if I leave—which I think I might—I want to leave this neighborhood, this place that gave so much to me, my family... my Charlie." Her voice thinned. She felt a surge of sadness and fought all that it threatened to bring to her mouth. She pulled her coffee close and watched the surface ripple. A soft undulation. "I can't explain why this is important to me, Donna, it just feels like the right thing to do, the thing that Charlie would have championed." Donna's face softened. Rose brought the coffee to her lips and gave it a good, long blow. "Besides, and I know I have no right to ask this, but if you are able to help—if Keisha can—not like you folks will be around for the fallout. She'll be out of harm's reach if you're moving." She closed her eyes as she took a long sip of the hot coffee, which had a right amount of bitterness as she swallowed.

Donna exhaled long. "I can't say Tony will allow it, but I will ask. But what is it you want from us?"

"Come to the meeting, that's all I ask. If you don't like what you hear, stay quiet. If you feel right about it, speak up." Donna gave a long sigh. "But first we have to figure out where to hold it." Rose set her coffee on the table and tried to dampen a smile, which really masked her fear. Now she was committed and she prayed—if she still could—that all she was asking of these people really was all that would be asked of them.

• • •

Later that day, at the bar's corner, she waited for the owners to raise the security shutter. For whatever reason, Rose was surprised when a young man all clad in black came out the door bouncing a set of keys. Seeing her, he slowed.

"Hello baby, how are you?"

He paused the way people do when they distrust a person's cheeriness, sensing some request for money right behind the greeting. "Hi." He stepped between Rose and the security shutter.

"One of the owners in?"

He crouched and fiddled with the lock. "Erin's in the office."

Although they'd never met, Rose remembered the woman, with her tidy blonde hair and slender glasses. "You think she'd mind if I talked to her for a moment?"

He freed the lock and raised the shutter. "I'll ask."

Rose hadn't bothered keeping track of the minutes until Erin stepped out the side door with all of the perkiness of someone fresh from an afternoon nap. The closer she got, the more Rose saw that the bounce in her step was hiding the stress in her face, the kind people wear when sleep eludes them night in and night out. In the days to come, Erin would wrestle with her anxiety about the direction in which her life was headed. She would finally ask her partner and boyfriend Tim for his blessing to step out of the restaurant and back into the classroom, all while he had designs to expand their business into another part of the city. And when they'd reached consensus on the best way to handle the expansion and her return to her career, she'd stop at the drug store on a hunch and come home to take the pregnancy test she'd bought. And when it came up positive, her anxiety over the future would climb. But that would all be a few weeks away by the time she stopped a comfortable distance from Rose and offered a polite "Hello." She crossed her arms but quickly moved them to her side.

"Erin? My name is Ms. Rose. I've lived in the neighborhood for quite some time."

"Nice to meet you, Ms. Rose. What can I do for you?"

"If you wouldn't mind, Erin, might we step inside?"

• • •

When this white couple had gathered the neighborhood to come hear what their plans were for Reggie's Place, Rose knew the change was taking root—they had all seen it, everywhere lately, burrowing, in fact, deep into the soil under their cracked sidewalks and thrusting everything up like a stubborn tree root mangling concrete, with nowhere else to go. Their community was sliding away and, although they weren't happy about it, this place had offered to include them. They might as well listen. So nine months ago, the neighbors sat crammed together on folding chairs on the restored hardwood floor, surrounded by grey walls that still needed paint. Along with friends, Rose waited for them folks to announce what they had in mind.

"Hello, everyone. I'm Tim, this is Erin. As you all know, we bought this place." *He should've worn a suit for a night like this. Did he really think a pair of wrinkly shorts and a t-shirt would make them feel comfortable with him?* He continued: "We wanted you to know that this place is yours too. We look forward to being good neighbors."

Erin's eyes had passed over all of them while he spoke, like she was surveying them. Her eyes were not lit up like his were. Rose eyed the wood bar, which had been shined nice and bright like a church pew, like a dirty coin that had been polished. *A bar should never shine like that, especially* that *bar. Why are white folks are always so happy about their drinking?* Still, they seemed young, spirited. The girl's blonde hair was tied back. Those glasses that looked like two rectangles were perched on her button of a nose, making her look like some librarian. Rose didn't think much of his short, stocky frame, but the closer she looked, seeing enough grey hairs in the growth of his beard, she knew he must've seen a little of life. They were bringing the change only young people attempt. Young folks, they made things happen because they grabbed for the future. Not like older folks, who knew how things slipped through your fingers when you held them too tight. But kids, especially ones like those two, did it because they were young enough to bounce back with their lives if it didn't work. The people listening to them speak were waiting to hear how expensive it was going to be to be part of the new neighborhood. But as Rose listened that day, the details flowing, the smiles passed, the constant moving about the room and getting closer and closer to people, these people showed how to calm grumblings.

This was why, sitting in Donna's kitchen she had thought of that couple first for this mess. As she gathered her thoughts on the trek over, she was hoping she would not have to remind them that they owed the neighborhood just a little. She also tried to forget that she couldn't think of another option. She'd seen what a large room brings out in people.

Erin held the door for Rose, who stepped first into the quiet bar. The man who'd opened the gate was setting things up. She watched his hand wipe the wood bar. Ella Fitzgerald played through the speakers, at a level that made conversation tolerable.

"So, Ms. Rose, what can I do for you?"

"First, let me say I am sorry to barge in here like this. I hope I didn't disturb you all while you were getting ready."

"No, you're fine."

"Okay, well, I..." Rose's eyes settled on the softness of Erin's skin. No cumulative effect of experience had found its way to her face—her tired eyes notwithstanding. Was Rose about to unfairly burden this young woman? But then Erin was a neighbor, and as such, Rose felt entitled to lean on her as if she were family. In the end, this was her fight too, wasn't it? She looked to be the age Charlie would have been, give or take a few years. "I'm sure you heard about the accident that happened with those two young men on Monday?"

Erin's smile dropped for a moment before she lifted it. She cleared her throat and nodded.

"Well, I'm sure you also heard about the conflicting opinions running around this neighborhood. I want to gather clear-thinking folks to begin calming things. The last thing this neighborhood needs is for foolishness to start." She realized it would probably be a bad idea to reference that 1997 Grays Ferry riot.

"Okay?"

Rose stirred, and then she remembered that she left out the important part. "I wanted to gather folks here, in your business. It would be good to see that you folks care and that something they remembered—the bar that had been here before you all did what you did with it—had been changed for the better."

"Hmm. Ah, let me...ah...give me a second." She turned and called over her shoulder, "Tim" towards the kitchen, where a lot of pots and pans were knocking around. "Can you come out here?"

• • •

Over the following hour, after Tim had appeared, toweling off his hands, the three of them discussed Rose's proposition. His immediate acceptance of the plan made Rose flinch, like he'd sensed an opportunity. But she accepted the drink he offered and sipped it while they hashed out details. How many people? Oh, probably not more than 30 (though she hoped for at least 50). Food? No, that wouldn't be necessary. Should we be here? Oh, most definitely. And no, they wouldn't need a staff. They were closed on Monday nights, would that work? I don't see why not. And on, and on. Questions got answered, more surfaced; Erin's delicate disposition wilted. This confirmed, though, that the woman had some sense about her. For what sensible person wouldn't see the approaching storm and pray that lightning didn't strike? Tim looked all too eager to hold the umbrella.

They sealed the agreement with firm handshakes, and as she left, she realized she'd set things in motion that would now not be undone. Was she right to place these people at its center? Would people think they were trying to manipulate the community? Would they be the poster children for the gentrification, and as such, targets for unrest? And what if something happened to Keisha and her family because of her involvement? She might have that light in her eyes crushed before it even had a chance to turn into a fire.

As she walked home, she heard Edgar's voice: "The success or failure of this little gathering of yours," he would say, "will fall to you. If the neighborhood should devolve into violence, some people will hold you responsible. And then what?" But she'd kept this at bay not even allowing for the thought to form. But, for once, she would act and not stop because of what might happen if she kept going, because what might happen was what needed to happen.

She turned down a street she hadn't visited in a while—one of those narrow streets that allow for one lane of traffic and parking. People avoid these when they're in a hurry because they're too tight to take quickly in your car. Plus, the wonderful, arcing trees were thinking about blooming. The sun fought to shine between their thick limbs. She happened upon a vacant lot where she was sure a house had once stood. On the feeble wood fence that guarded the property hung a permit, dated for last fall. Through the fence she could see the layout of what would become the foundation. The concrete looked naked and hungry—if such a thing could be said for a gray slab.

Of course, she was too tired to allow her mind to dream all kinds of nonsense. The funding had probably fallen through and the workers turned to another project, the investors resigned to write off what had been started, leaving this scar on the street for the residents to endure. The paper was full of stories like this.

Abandoned. She thought of Keisha and her stomach soured. Would she be able to see this through long enough—past any meeting—to ensure she was protected? She thought of leaving for DC. She'd better get home. Her nephew and his friends would be there soon, and the thought of cooking for young men again warmed her enough to move her legs.

At her house, the stubborn key fought the old lock; it might have been the light bulb that had been taken from her front door light; it might have been the cheese steak menus shoved through her mail slot; or it could have been the dead silence that greeted her when she crossed her threshold, shut the door, and waited. She knew she only had to take the chicken out of the fridge, clean it for cooking, and get out the spinach and potatoes. Yet her feet remained anchored.

She used to love the early evenings, for this was when Charlie would come in from playing. While she would be putting the finishing touches on their meal, Edgar would be tinkering in the basement. After she'd set the table, she would call her men to their places and present the hot plates. Together, they would enjoy what they'd been fortunate enough to enjoy: the food, the company. Amen. She smiled as they ate: she'd done her duty. Then Charlie left.

She'd waited for those letters, sparse in their words, heavy in their fear for what might await him in that desert half way across the world. She learned that the barking of the neighbor's dogs meant the mail was close. Why had she held her tongue? Why had she waited for Edgar to tell him no? Once Charlie had left, Edgar said he'd been waiting for her to step in. Then that officer arrived at their door and soon she was merely lingering in the world, orbiting her husband and eventually guiding him through his cancer in that home in which she now stood.

For the first time in years, she felt strong.

She thought of little Keisha, and that nice white couple. She climbed her stairs and turned on the bedside lamp. At her dresser, she opened the cedar jewelry box Edgar had given her for Christmas all those years ago. The thin gold chain she plucked dragged against the box's faded red felt lining. She draped the chain against her hand in the dim room light and tilted the dull gold cross in her palm. She hadn't held that since the day she'd buried her Charlie. She clutched the chain and the cross, rubbed the edges against her rough skin. Then she released her fingers, spanned them wide, and then drew them in a ball again. Each time she did this, the stabbing from the cross dulled, as if it had settled into her skin. Or maybe she'd just adjusted to the pressure. But whatever it was, she couldn't figure out why she kept repeating this, nor did she question it.

• • •

Later, after the dishes had been cleared and the smell of a well-cooked meal still lingered, the voices of the three young men in her dining room swelling like a baking pie, she felt soothed. She didn't realize how much life had been gone from the house until it had returned. This house, this block deserved that life, that laughter, that energy.

She returned to her seat at the table and her nephew refilled her wine glass. "So, Aunt Rose, we think—that is, if the offer still stands—that we'd like to take you up on your generous offer of the house. It'd be great to have all this room, and the location is perfect. There's so much happening in this neighborhood."

She smiled and raised her glass. "Make it your home, boys, that's all I ask." They clinked glasses. She realized she worked best when her hand had been forced, even by her own design. But she had far too much to handle here before she stepped one foot in D.C.

10

For five hours and 23 minutes, Michael's legs had ignored the tingling sensation, but now, nestled there in the cracked-leather cushioned office chair, they were going numb. If only his brain would follow suit. eBay was providing endless amount of short-term accomplishments. The vintage four-ounce glass baby bottle had ended without a bidder. The *Vintage Matchbox Lesney Lincoln Continental #31, 1964* sold for $10.45. For a while, it looked like it might move for $9.45. The *Estate Vintage Chinese Crackle Glazed Green Ginger Jar in Mint Condition* was really tempting, but there were people all over that auction, and as the seconds ticked, bids exploded on the screen, sending the price higher than Michael could have predicted. He thought he'd seen enough of these vases to predict what it might go for, but this one—with its 17 bidders—surprised him. He'd almost gotten swept into the bidding just for the thrill of conquering something. But he chickened out. Or did he wise up? The ten-speeds he monitored got boring quick—as if he wanted a new one, or would spend more than $100 for one, but maybe that was the going price these days? Actually, it was the pictures he couldn't handle. If the bike looked in the least bit damaged, he moved on. He watched vintage Sega and Nintendo systems, typewriters, Persian rugs that were bigger than any room he owned, VCRs (he wondered what he could get for his), hedge-clippers his mother might like, literary anthologies and math textbooks he remembered from college, and 1000-thread count sheets (new), metallic placemats (also new), and a fire pit that was too big (and perhaps too dangerous) for his wood-fenced, shoebox of a back-yard. He couldn't remember how he happened upon the *Vintage Rawlings PRO H Gold Glove Series Baseball/Softball Glove*, which hadn't even been viewed by anyone besides Michael, and this alone compelled him to at least consider meeting the opening bid of $39.99. But really, what would he do with a baseball glove? Luckily, just like all the other auctions he'd monitored in that time, it ticked down and then was gone, disappearing into a void from which it would likely never return. A dark, bottomless, void… He put his head on his desk and considered banging it, repeatedly, on the surface, but, just his luck, he'd split the pressboard, and then he'd be down one more thing in life. *Great.*

Then of course was Elizabeth's email just waiting to be read yet again.

There, minimized in the monitor's screen, it sat. Aiden, you cunt; how could you have moved into his house? And why did Google Earth have to have a current picture of that red front door with that pathetic Pottery Barn wreath hanging from the pretentious brass knocker? Why did it look the same in person, 455 steps from Michael's front door?

Just when he was forgetting those puffy, slightly chapped lips; those lips which, on their first date, he'd wanted to reach across the table and coat with Chapstick: see, he needs me, Michael thought. When he opened the mail, he pictured those chapped lips mouthing the words of their bills, the junk mail, the endless slew of fast food and restaurant menus shoved in their mail slot.

He's moving in with him, at his house, which is a couple blocks from you (as you know). I didn't want you to have to find out by running into him/them. Hope you are hanging in there. Call me and I will bring over a bottle of wine.

For how long had Michael been pinching the shit out of his arm? He looked down. A small hickey, like the kind Aiden loved to give. He brushed the puffy purplish oval. Were they a regular fixture at the dog park now, going as often or even more than they used to—the one thing Aiden enjoyed doing in this neighborhood? They lacked both the time and space to buy their own—soon, soon, they'd discussed, and Michael had factored that into his home-buying mania. Watching him with those French bulldogs, he couldn't wait to provide the home for them and their new puppy, the one he pictured slobbering Aiden's face as if it were an ice cream cone. He'd name it Griffin. Now he wished he'd bought the dog before the house.

God, had he really bought another pack of cigarettes? After lighting a cigarette, he eyed the two Red Bull cans, their tops mountained with ash. He sneered and walked to the open kitchen window. A bunch of jubilant voices penetrated the screen. As soothing as sirens behind you while driving home from a bar. Can't these people find something better to do on a Friday afternoon? And why did the sun have to be shining so brightly? He should have been on his second latte, enjoying the panoramic view of downtown from his office, savoring each sip before he returned to his inbox. A mosquito landed on the other side of the screen. He assaulted it with smoke. It tensed and then drifted away.

He stormed to the upstairs bedroom, where the voices lightened to a dull white noise, and he stubbed his cigarette in an empty tea-light tin. He flopped on the bed.

455 steps, 48 houses.

If he took bigger strides, he could make it in 438 steps.

The voices outside swelled.

Bolting out of bed, he went to the open window. What the fuck were all those people doing out there on a weekday? Didn't they have jobs? Wait a minute. He scanned the flyer on the table, the one whose orange paper stood out amidst the junk mail. Had he meant to save it? *Dedication for the new park, Saturday.* Saturday?

He trotted downstairs and, at the computer, he pulled up the browser's homepage. Saturday. The security gate creaked. A knock. If he went to the door and peered through the peep hole, they might hear the groan in the hard wood floor. Then they'd keep knocking. What if they wanted him outside? Didn't they know?

The other day, a neighbor woman stopped by, said she saw he was new to the neighborhood (after this long, really?). Door-to-door Mormons would be jealous of her cheeriness. She mentioned a park dedication. "I'm just passing through," he'd wanted to say, as he waited for her mouth to stop moving. She had one of those you-just-need-one-great-big-hug looks and was leaning forward. He took her flyer so she wouldn't move closer. Just how many of these did they have to waste?

Another knock, a long pause, and then the gate groaned and settled into the latch. He sighed. Where were his cigarettes? She'd be back, wouldn't she? People with that sunny-ness always persisted. His skin itched. Maybe it'd do him good to check this gathering out, convince him that he was being paranoid, that not everyone knew, was out to get him. As long as no one tried to start a conversation. Then he imagined Aiden: "Why the hell would we socialize with *those* people?" Grabbing his cigarettes, he headed towards the door.

Though the sun was radiant in the clear sky, Michael rubbed the goose bumps off his arms. Dozens of people gathered under the blue tent in the intersection. Not the best place for a party, Michael thought. Their jovial energy pulsed towards him, and he twitched. It'd been a whole day since he'd left the house, to get groceries. A couple kids flew by on their skate boards, their screams lingering even after they disappeared into the crowd. The PA system blared George Clinton. He willed himself forward and walked towards one of the large speakers supported by what looked like a large black tripod. A few people nodded hello; one guy raised a beer. Had they waved to one another every so often when they happened to be coming home at the same time? *Was that beard new?* Did that guy know who he was waving to? His throat dried. *Did the music just get louder?* He crossed to the opposite corner.

Skidding to a stop, the skateboarding kids hopped off their boards. Juice boxes in hand, they hugged people who were likely their parents and Michael's eyes misted watching them dangle their hands around their parents. The adults patted their kids' heads, continuing their conversations with the people next to them. They were smiling, beaming. Behind them, the wide-open barren park teased. Counting the couples, his eyes tightened.

That cheery woman, with her toothy smile holding her face hostage, bounded towards him. The woman for whom every morning was a blessing, every rain drop a convenient car wash, every wind gust God's free leaf blower cleaning the street's gutters. *455 steps, 48 houses.* He crouched and untied and then retied his shoe. And then repeated.

Someone tapped his shoulder. He braced for that woman but eased when he saw Milton. There was something supervisory in his gaze.

"How's it going, man?"

Michael tensed. His fucking department manager used that when he was about to unload another project on his desk. He stood. "Ah, fine?" he said. Over Milton's shoulder, he spied the cheery woman, who'd stopped to bother someone else.

"You ever need anything, remember what I told you the other night, you've got a friend a few doors down." There was a subtext to his offer, that Michael had something to worry about. And he wasn't stupid; he felt the air's weight. He'd read the paper, he knew the neighborhood was a racial powder keg waiting for someone with a willing match. A small spark can make a very big fire. "I have some people I need to touch base with but I wanted to chat a bit more. You hanging for a bit?"

He nodded because that seemed like the best way to suspend the conversation, and Milton strutted towards the crowd, nodding at people as they passed him. When he reached the cheery woman, they hugged, complete with the double back slap, like someone had died.

More people entered the street. Michael noticed a couple, the only other white people. Pushing a stroller, the couple exchanged handshakes with neighbors. Their kid, hidden by the stroller's canopy, held its arms out, opening and closing its fingers like crab claws. The smell of BBQ wisped by. He turned to the park and its "grass." Scattered sprouts stood a bit taller than others amidst all the dirt that hadn't yet let anything else poke through. He thought of his pathetic little planted seed who'd—predictably—refused to grow. Maybe it was just his curse. Just about to race across the growing mass of people, he heard a cough.

The face that said, "Hello, young man," slowly registered. Like trying to clutch water, he struggled to remember the name. Tired but feisty eyes. Those graying dreads that—oddly—reminded him of stratified Earth that had seen its share of upheavals over the decades.

Something in her face relaxed, like she'd wondered whether she should have said hello in the first place but was glad she had. "Do I look familiar?"

First Milton and now this stranger. Where was all this warmth coming from? Then it clicked: that nice woman from the Laundromat. He could feel those pats on the shoulder, those silent nods in his direction when he'd entered the store. Those casual inspections of his clothes as he loaded them, those moments when he looked for her approval as he mixed clothes with bed sheets, that subtle frown when he over-stuffed, and an easy smile when he pulled clothes out and used an additional machine. "Hi, Ms. Rose."

"That's right. You remember." She was clutching an awful lot of papers in one hand, which she'd just rolled as he looked down. Flyers, they'd looked like.

She took a deep, slow breath and her free hand was fidgeting. She had to be a smoker, and Michael almost offered her one of his but found his hand was not cooperating. Something like tranquility crossed her face. "I haven't seen you in the store in a few weeks, baby." Again, with the subtext. Why didn't they just come out and say what they were thinking?

"Been a rough couple weeks. You know." It was strange engaging in small talk with this woman he hardly knew. But he sensed a genuine concern for his well-being, and how he could read that in her face he couldn't tell. This realization made him sweat. In that moment, she knew, too, and she was reaching out to him. Was he supposed to take that invisible hand? He thought of Aiden, someone who had supposedly loved him, knew him better than anyone, and not even a phone call, a text; nothing. *This is what you could expect from those close to you.* If you couldn't count on your friends, should you trust a relative stranger?

As his mind raced, she nodded and her eyes probed his face. He had a strange sensation as if she was peeling back layers of him that he was unaware of. Her eyes grew distant, as if her mind had moved her somewhere painful and joyful at once, and then she smiled. "Well," she unrolled her fist of papers and bent the corners back. "I want you to have one of these." She handed him a paper and waited a moment. Was she deciding to hug him? "I may not know you, young man, but I know when a man gets into something that wasn't his fault, when he needs someone looking out for him. You remember that and you consider what's on that flyer. You take care, baby." She gave his forearm a good squeeze. Smiling, she drifted away, merging into a cluster of people, who nodded. To each person, she handed a paper. She mouthed a few things but seemed to make sure she didn't look in his direction. Eventually, she landed next to Milton, who hugged her. They chatted, and then he took one of her papers. He studied it and then seemed to be searching for Michael in the crowd, but she waved a finger in his face. She said something and then Milton nodded. She motioned with her hands in a few different directions. Michael's throat dried and he felt light headed. He folded the paper, jammed it into his back pocket, and headed home, counting the cracks in the sidewalk with each step.

• • •

Out of the corner of her eye, Rose watched Michael keep his head down. *Look up, young man, keep that head up. Nobody will help someone who won't first help himself.* "So, can I count on you, Milton?" She asked to be polite, though she hoped her eyes did the begging she meant.

"This man needs help, but I don't know what this will do. How many folks you hoping to corral for this?"

The hint of amusement tinged with skepticism in his voice stung. "At least 25 or so. Any less might be pointless." She pictured every face she'd handed a flyer to. She was far from finding the right people to attend (though she'd given them flyers and a smile anyway).

He scanned the crowd. "This the only place you're canvassing?"

"So far. I was hoping to walk around a bit and stuff flyers in doors of the folks in the neighborhood I've known for a while."

"Who'd you have in mind?"

"Estelle and her husband Larry, over on League Street."

"The Stewarts?"

"That's them." Rose hadn't seen them in so long she'd forgotten their last names.

"They don't live there anymore. Last I heard, they moved to an assisted living facility. A young couple moved into their place last year, fixed it up real nice."

"You know the new couple?"

"Well enough to wave, not enough to bring them into something like this."

"Oh. Hmm, I was thinking of Terry and Tina too, over on Christian and 25th."

"They're gone too. They'd been renting and their landlord didn't renew their lease; had the house fixed up and sold it. Those guys did good work on the house."

Where had she been? "Oh, ahh... I'm almost afraid to ask about Jill and her two young boys." She couldn't remember the last time they'd come into the Laundromat.

"I don't know her, but you might want to check. Seems every day someone moving on—or getting moved—around here lately."

Rose studied the crowd, which had swelled in the time they'd been talking. She was all for new blood but was this more of a transfusion? Was there enough of the old blood to pitch in? Could she manage the new blood? Did she have any time to understand where they were coming from? Would any of them care about this neighborhood enough to help this young man?

"Well, I got my work cut out for me then, baby. Thanks for giving me your insight, Milton." She smiled, feeling a little sad with just how taxing this job was going to be. Then she saw Willis. Before she could move, he had joined her and Milton. He snatched one of her flyers.

"This all your doing, Rose?" She nodded. "Why not put something together for all the folks who don't want to be forced out, huh? Why side with one of these new people coming in, making it difficult for us, the people who have been here for decades, to hold onto our homes, walking around making us feel uncomfortable for sharing the same air as them?"

"We all see things the way we choose to, Willis." She held his gaze without flinching, and as she guessed, he couldn't handle that. He smirked, said hello to Milton, and left, thankfully, taking the dark cloud with him. She knew if she was going to make this happen, she had to get to as many people as Willis was about to, and before he managed to open his mouth.

Donna and Keisha approached. Keisha was grinning. "Hi Mr. Milton. Ms. Rose, can I pass out flyers now?" She held out her little hopeful hand and Rose wondered if those little hands could manage those pieces of paper.

"Milton; Ms. Rose, everything all right?" Donna asked.

There was an understandable edge to her voice and Rose instantly adjusted her composure. "Yes, Donna, everything is fine." She handed Keisha a small stack and Keisha counted every one, mouthing the numbers, smiling like she was counting her piggy bank.

11

From the cats at work, from the neighbor two doors down, the woman who always asked for help replacing the bricks around the tree on the sidewalk—the ones constantly knocked down by people new to the neighborhood who couldn't park their cars—even his mother had an opinion about that accident. But Nathan had better things to get worked up about, such as the school kids cackling as they walked down the street, which made him detest the spreading water damage in the ceiling's sheet rock even more. They cursed and he shook his head, picturing the empty bags of chips that would be left in their wake. Was he ever so disrespectful? His eyes roamed that stained ceiling—the stains had probably been there longer than he'd realized. Could he handle one more thing? He walked upstairs.

He collected Darian and moved to the master bedroom, where he set him on the bed. Behind the little man's head, marching through the bedroom window, a thin line of ants crossed the molding, down the wall, and neared a spider web, one that Nathan swore wasn't there yesterday. Giggling on the bed, Darian rejected the little hoodie sleeve, which dangled off his body's right side. Nathan stood, stretched, and exhaled as hard as he could. Man, where was his break in life? After four years, this was supposed to have gotten easier.

He'd been reading the pamphlets he'd sent away for, and the idea that his son'd be better off with "proper institutional care" was making a stellar sales pitch. But Nathan was giving a life with his boy a chance, so they were going to catch a pick-up football game. This is what fathers and sons do, right, they watch football games? Darian swayed while he failed to grip his hood's drawstring. Nathan imagined his son's empty bed.

Crouching by Darian, Nathan coaxed the pudgy right arm into the sleeve. Darian's head bobbed to a song only he could hear. His saucer-shaped eyes searched every wall. Nathan steadied him by the shoulder. He closed his eyes and breathed. Third time's the charm, he thought. How had Erica managed this? "Come on, little man, we got this." Guiding the sleeve over Darian's balled fingers, he moved the fabric over his son's caramel skin—a touch lighter than his own, the color the boy'd taken from Erica—but the hand dropped. His boy's big round eyes fell on Nathan. Darian's mouth, the one that never seemed to close, quivered. Then he giggled. Why did his son have to have Down syndrome?

The ant line swelled. Darian flailed his hands, almost knocking Nathan in the nose. He grabbed one of his boy's wrists. "No, we don't do that." Darian giggled more.

"No," Darian repeated, a little garbled.

Nathan eased his grip and then let go. He stared at that ant line, so brazenly entering his home, and then he thrust the brittle-framed window closed. He checked his watch. The guys would've formed teams already, maybe started playing. Even though he wasn't playing, he wanted to be on time. Or maybe he wanted to see how quickly he could get his boy ready.

"All right, then, plan B." He flipped Darian and forced the arm in. Darian seemed to do better when you weren't right in front of him. He hated catering to this, but time mattered. He turned him back around and pulled the hood over his eyes.

Finally. "Boo!" he said. Darian giggled.

"Come on, boy, we got a game to catch." He jostled his son's head, and his eyes bobbed, like he didn't recognize his father. Feeling his eyes moisten, he carried his boy down the creaking stairs.

• • •

Nathan strolled onto the public rec field on Washington Ave. They shouldn't have taken 20 minutes to walk six blocks, but Darian walked every way but forward. Nathan approached the bleachers. An older black woman was leaning back, smoking, and casually watching the game. Nathan sat on the second tier.

She looked at Nathan and Darian, then at her cigarette. "Oh, sorry, baby." She stubbed out her cigarette and then walked it to the trash. She settled again on the third tier.

Nathan glanced at the basketball courts, with their Sprite-sponsored backboards and net-less rims a few yards away. Behind him, the breeze rattled the dirty chain link fence. On the chewed-up field, the guys, wearing t-shirts and sweats, chatted, pointing to one another. When one team tossed the ball to the other, the sides set. He felt a little strange when some of his friends nodded at him. Of those, Tony eyed him a bit too long. None of them was used to seeing a brother show up with a little kid and no woman by his side. Nathan adjusted his little man's hoodie and pretended not to care about their judgment—he'd made his own life choices, and the past four years had not let him forget.

He'd been able to buy his house when he was 23. It needed a ton of work, which was how he could afford it. When Erica saw he had his business handled, she was much more affectionate, more attentive. Picking her up for a date, he was invited in. "Here, let me rub your shoulders." At 24, they got stuck. Erica's eyes, however, danced as she stroked her belly.

If he had known then what he knew now, would he have changed anything?

Randy called a play. He glanced at his receivers, then at the defensive line. The ball snapped. He drifted back; the lines collided. One receiver cut in, the other ran deep. Randy pumped his arm twice, then drilled the ball downfield. Through coverage, Marcus snagged the pass and found the end zone. Next to Nathan, Darian bobbed. He steadied the wobbly child. Darian pointed towards the playground, where kids were screaming and chasing each other around the swing and slide set. He grunted and snorted, almost like a donkey.

"Relax, buddy," Nathan whispered in his ear while stroking his head. He leaned his head against his and felt his eyes get tight. Those damn perfectly pitched voices of theirs, rising and falling like the rhythm section in a band. On the field, the teams lined up.

"How old's your boy?" the woman asked.

"He's four." He adjusted little man's hoodie. On the field, Ray was standing too far back to return the kick.

"He like to come here to watch the games?"

"Mostly, he likes being out of the house." His palms sweated. This is what parents did, right, bring their kids to a public place and mingle with people? Why was he so nervous? At least he hoped it was nerves. He nudged the hood up.

"Well, sure is good to get out of the house. You live in the neighborhood?"

He felt like when one of the crazies began a conversation and all he could do was adjust his seatbelt. He turned to the woman and was disarmed by her warm smile. "I live on Catherine, by 23rd."

"That's a good block. You know the Matthews?"

Nathan ran through the short list of the names of his neighbors. The nonexistent list. "Matthews… No, don't think I do."

"Hmm, you sure? They've been there for a long time. They have the red house, three big plants out front, a wood bench."

Nathan was feeling like he hadn't done his homework. Maybe he needed to walk his block more. "Oh, yeah, I know the house you mean. I haven't seen them in a while."

James dropped, clutching his ankle as he curled on the grass.

The guys surrounded him. "We going to have to put you the fuck down, man?" One of them asked. A couple guys chuckled.

"Can you walk that shit off?" another asked.

"Man, help him up," Desean said.

Two guys helped the guy limp towards the fence, where he winced his way to the ground and eased off his shoe, his mouth all twisted.

"Nathan, man, can you still catch? You up for this?" Desean yelled.

His palms moistened. "Can't man." He indicated Darian.

"Ms. Rose, can you help us out here, watch his son?"

Nathan felt a hand on his shoulder. "Son, I can watch your boy. In fact, I'd enjoy that very much." Rose extended her hands.

He looked at Darian and then at Rose. "You sure? He can be a handful."

"I can do handfuls, baby; just give him here and go play your game."

Darian peered with his vacant stare. "You stay close to this lady, 'kay?" He giggled. Feeling a little uneasy, Nathan stood. Rose looked like she'd been transported to another world. He hadn't seen a woman smile like that since the day Darian was born. This unnerved him, like maybe he wouldn't get his boy back, but he leapt off the bleachers.

In the huddle, Desean introduced Nathan, and the lines set. As Nathan took the right end, he watched Rose. She pulled Darian's hoodie down and bounced him on her lap. They were looking at the playground and Rose was pointing to the kids in the sandbox. More kids ran into the playground.

"Hut, hut… hike." As everyone scrambled, the two lines collided. As

Nathan dashed downfield, Desean pump-faked to the other receiver, so Nathan cut in. Behind Desean, Nathan saw Darian wander towards the kids on the playground, with Rose following far behind. He almost ran for his son, but then he saw the football spiraling his way. He raised his hands as the ball bounced off his chest.

A couple teammates hung their heads as everyone returned to the line of scrimmage.

"What the fuck, man? You had that all the way," Desean said.

"Sorry man," Nathan said. "But I gotta catch my kid." Darian closed on the kids, who stopped what they were doing to watch him. Some curled their lips. Nathan clenched his fists as his heart raced. How could he have let his son down like that? In moments, he reached his son, picked him up.

Rose put a cautious hand on him. "He wanted to play with the other children."

"He's… I didn't want him to play, I just want him to stay put."

"Oh, I…" She searched his eyes. "I'm sorry, baby. I guess you never can keep them too close when they're that age." Her voice had saddened in a way that gave Nathan pause. He held Darian close, who squirmed. "Let me give you something." She handed him a flyer. "It's an important meeting about our community. I hope you can make it." Nathan folded the flyer without reading it and shoved it in his pocket. "You love this boy every day of his life, young man." Rose patted his shoulder and walked towards the bleachers. The game had resumed. Nathan thought about following her and apologizing, but for what, he wasn't sure.

Nathan stalked off, and as they left, Darian's little hand reached towards the playground.

They walked close to the buildings, and although the sun loomed over them, Nathan shivered in the shade. His blood churned against a heavy heart. He felt himself drop that ball, he saw Darian ambling towards those kids. That judgment in their little fucking eyes. How long before they would have laughed at his boy?

A Septa bus zoomed past, passengers jamming the aisle. The driver honked, though Nathan didn't catch who it was. *Probably Carl or Steve.* Running towards the corner, a few feet ahead, Darian crouched and glared at a penny.

"Take my hand, little man." His head tilted at the empty hand. Nathan took Darian's hand in his, and they crossed the street.

After a few blocks, they reached Nathan's old elementary school. Kids were playing basketball on the cracked blacktop. He stepped closer to the rusted chain link fence. One team launched into a fast break after rebounding, leading to a missed lay-up. Darian stared at clouds drifting by. How long could he fight back the tears?

He thought about that meeting they'd had with the local elementary school last year. He and Erica had had questions about the letter they'd received. Sure, they knew their son was different, needed special care, attention. Turns out, they were kidding themselves with false hope. "Mainstreaming at some point," the principal mentioned. Erica stared at the ground.

"But to be honest," with her pressed pants suit and pulled-back hair, "and off the record, this neighborhood lacks the funding for the services your son needs to succeed. He might be better served in a public home, as horrible as that might be to hear."

He thought about those pamphlets he'd been reading. How was he going to make this work? Where was this money going to come from?

As he watched the kids on the court in front of him, his heart was not so much sunk as it was hollow. Would Nathan ever see his son play a sport? He gripped his son's hand tighter.

"Come on, Darian, let's get home and get our food together."

Could he manage one more obstacle? Darian's hand felt so delicate. Had Nathan's mother ever thought of giving up?

• • •

With his little toes, six-year-old Nathan had nudged the tissues stuffed in his shoes. He was sitting on the edge of a folding chair in his living room, surrounded by people. When they weren't looking at each other or patting each other's backs, they were hugging, crying, eating; but none paid him much attention for more than a moment. Swinging his feet back and forth, he sat as far forward as he could without touching the carpet. Every few swipes, he was able to sway the carpet strands standing higher than the rest. First one way, then on the return kick, the carpet kept returning for more. From time to time, he'd feel a pat on his head. In the kitchen, people were gathered. Among them, Cheryl and Tony (who lived at the end of the block—they gave out the best Halloween candy) were sitting at the table. His mother, leaning against the kitchen sink, was sipping coffee, next to Leonard and Cynthia (who lived a block over, and who played cards with Mom and Dad on the weekends), and Cousin Dennis and his wife Roberta (who lived in Baltimore). Mom's work friends filled in the rest. They all seemed to know him, which made him feel strange. Dad's co-workers had already come and gone. These were the ones who had kept hugging him as they left the church that morning. They kept smiling and crying at the same time. Sitting in his seat, he wished people would stop whispering around him. He'd known that Dad had been killed in a convenience store robbery.

Smelling like cigarettes, his Uncle Charles and his Cousin Jack carried their beers through the front door. In the kitchen they grabbed two more. Mom smiled, her lips quivering, as she held her balled fist to her face. Uncle Charles whispered something to her and she nodded. Then he walked to Nathan and clutched his shoulder. "Come on, son, let's go downstairs." He edged off his chair. Holding the basement door, Uncle Charles said, "Lead the way, Nathan."

On their way down the stairs, they passed the gash in the dry wall, the one Dad made forcing his easy chair down the steps. With the chair wedged in the stairway, Mom had berated him. But he kept jamming it, using his shoulder, his legs, a crowbar to get his favorite chair downstairs so he could watch his games in peace. Somehow, he made it happen. Now that chair faced the TV. Uncle Charles and his Cousin Jack set up folding chairs on either side of it. Nathan's father's Eagles jersey hung from a hook on the wall.

"Turn the television on, son, the game's on. Your father would not want us to miss the season opener on account of him."

Nathan climbed into the stuffed chair and clutched the remote. The TV came on; the volume was real low. The ceiling creaked. People murmured but Nathan couldn't tell what they were saying. Uncle Charles grabbed the remote and raised the volume. Cousin Jack shook his head. "Your father liked to *feel* the game, son. When someone gets hit, you want to flinch." Nathan nodded. He felt kinda empty. Uncle Charles put his hand on Nathan's chin and turned his head. Looking eye-to-eye: "Your father loved you, Nathan, and that's all you need to know. Got that?" Nathan nodded. "And when you get old enough, you put on that jersey hanging over there, but not before. Got it?" Nathan nodded. "Now dry those eyes, son; the game's on. There'll be plenty of time for crying later." Uncle Charles passed the bottle opener to Cousin Jack.

Nathan had watched some games with his Dad, but only when Mom wasn't home. "When you get older, boy, I'll explain it all to you," he had said. He cheered when Dad cheered.

The teams on the field spread out to opposite sides. One of the players ran and kicked the ball. Another player caught the ball, ran a little, and then players flattened him.

"Nice." Cousin Jack nodded like that was supposed to have happened.

"They stopped the ball at the eleven-yard line, so now our team has the opposing team in a good position for this set of downs." Nathan nodded to Uncle Charles. "Don't worry, son, I got you. You'll get it." As he reclined in the chair, the cushions swallowed him.

The next season, Nathan's mother, with help from his uncle, moved the TV and stuffed chair into the front room. "Now, he starts cussing watching these games, the TV goes, got it," Mom said. Uncle nodded and so did Nathan. On Sundays, his Uncle took the couch. On the floor, his elbows propping up his head on the carpet, Nathan sprawled in front of the TV. Draped over the chair, his father's jersey. In the kitchen, his mother read.

"How do you think they'll do against the Falcons?" his Uncle would ask him. Or against the Cowboys? The Giants?

At half time, Mom took her book upstairs. "Don't sit so close to the screen, Son."

Week in and week out, Nathan studied how on the field, men were getting it done down by down. Regardless of the score, those men crouched at that line, whether offense or defense, and pushed until the last second. He yelled every time the Eagles scored, even if they were down by 21 with under two minutes left in the fourth quarter. "Never lose faith in your team, Nate, never give up."

When he was in junior high, his Uncle pushed to get him in the local league. "He needs this, to be a part of the game. He'll learn things no school will teach him."

Mom looked worried. "His grades slip, even a little, he's done. Got it?"

Uncle Charles took him to tryouts and bought him the equipment. When his work schedule allowed, his uncle made most of the games. Mom made the other ones, though she brought a book.

The walks home were reserved for man talks. "Your father would be proud of you, son. He'd also tell you to cut in the moment you feel someone trailing you." Nathan nodded. "How're you doing in school?" Nathan shrugged. "Don't forget your education, son." Nathan tossed the ball to himself. "Also, when you are dashing out, don't turn to look for the ball until you've hit your spot. This tells your defender when to look too." On Sundays, Nathan studied the games to see what his uncle meant. His muscles leaned and legs strengthened. He was passed to more often, benched less. Mom stopped bringing a book to the games.

In high school, he made the JV team his freshman year. Before the first game, his uncle died. Lung cancer. "Just like your father, he'd be proud of you, Son. Don't forget that," Mom said. When he crouched at the line of scrimmage, he heard his uncle's voice in his head; same for when he sprinted down the sideline, waited for a pass. Senior year, he started as a receiver on Varsity. At night, when he should've been stressing a mid-term or paper that he hadn't yet researched, he dreamed often of catching the winning touchdown pass. During classes, he listed his dream colleges. He was bound to get a scholarship somewhere, his coach told him. The scouts never showed. When the deadline passed, he felt the rage build, as if he'd been cheated. "You got two ways to handle this, Nate. You can complain or you can suck it up and move on. What's meant to be will be."

• • •

Nathan tossed in his bed. While he dreamed, his eyes fluttered. No heat escapes the bus's vent; the riders, sandwiched in the aisle, all the way to the rear door, groan with every bump the bus catches. Nathan slows to a stop. The brakes squeal, people shove their way forward. People jockey for position in the vacated space. He watches through his rearview mirror. Like he is in a carwash, rain dumps on his windshield. He is behind schedule. His riders are behind schedule. The heavy air is musty.

The left wiper drags along the windshield.

Now stopped, the bus is as close to the curb as the car parked in the bus area will allow. The doors open, he lowers the bus for this old lady, who screams at him about the rain. The bus drones, like a truck backing up, then it jolts. The old lady glares at him through the thick frames of her glasses as she shakes off her umbrella. He closes the door, he flips the hydraulic switch. Sputtering. Eyes fall on him. He toggles the switch. Cars honk, they speed past.

The wiper drags across the windshield.

He toggles the switch. The motor chugs. Nothing. The passengers surge forward. The old lady thumps him with her umbrella. Other people converge on him. They yell, point, bark, snarl. "Get this thing going." He jerks the switch faster and faster. Nothing. Where's the alert button to Dispatch? Where his monitor should be, to his left, wires dangle. The anger around him constricts.

The windshield wiper accelerates, looking like someone wagging their finger at him.

Bodies press against him. Hands reach for his face, and he screams.

He awoke in a damp bed, thirsty. Oh man, what he would've given for a decent night's sleep. According to the bedside clock, he had a good 20 minutes before closing his eyes and expecting them to stay shut. Throwing his feet over the side of the bed, he stood.

He tiptoed down the hall, the wood floor creaked. At the next room, Nathan stopped, eased the door open. Streaming in through the window, moonlight bathed the small bed in the corner. Darian's hand balled up next to his face. *So delicate.* How could something so miraculous have something so wrong with him? Darian's chest rose and fell. How was he going to help his boy? Nathan eased the door closed.

Towards the computer room, he walked. He sat; the chair's cracked pleather scratched his legs. He turned on the monitor and opened his web browser. He checked Facebook, and he scrolled through nonsense updates until a friend's post stopped him: Sick of this shit, man. *People running over black people with their cars and not a damn thing happening to him because he's white.* Shaun didn't live in this neighborhood, but it didn't take much for that negativity to spread, and before everyone knew it, shit would explode. And over nothing, unless you were the guy who got hit.

In the summer '97 the neighborhood had seen true racist violence. Man, that summer, Nathan lived a few blocks from that black family who got attacked right off Gray's Ferry. He wasn't there when it happened, but he knew people who'd seen those ten white folks gang up on those two black kids after that block party. They had followed them to their house, and on their stoop, they beat the crap out of them, even kicked that mother who had tried to step in. She got her windows broken, too. Like a movie, that whole mob, a bunch of people said. Afterwards, man, you didn't look at someone the wrong way. Those few white folks that lived in the Gray's Ferry area, they walked around apologizing—I ain't one of them, their eyes said— being extra nice to you like you were close friends. Of course, the law did shit. The ten guys—all but one—got community service.

If ten black kids had cornered a couple of white people, they'd be swinging from the power lines. But that was 15 years ago, and Nathan had no time to be angry at people who'd left him alone. Since he didn't ride a bike, he was safe from any white people with road rage. He had more important things on his mind. He opened a new window and Googled. Would something have changed since his last search? One out of every 733 kids born every year has this extra chromosome. *Extra.* The first fucking time having more made you worse off. Well, maybe if you were on a boat that was taking on extra water. Maybe he *was* on that ship. He imagined the water climbing his calves, the boat sinking. Why jump out of such a boat when you're surrounded by an ocean? He needed a fucking life preserver. His mounting bills, this house, his life. How could he provide for Darian's future? *Group home.* His neck tightened.

His paycheck. If the union voted to strike, how was he supposed to live on unemployment? Would he even get unemployment? Before Darian came along, he would've sided with the union refusing to allow the employees to contribute more for their benefits. Fuck it, strike. But part of him remembered the 1998 Septa strike, which lasted 40 days. He counted every block he had had to trudge to the market and back. His back ached all the way home as he clutched those bags. People count on you, man, whether it's convenient or not, you have to pull through. *You can't just bail.* His stomach knotted thinking about staring at his walls every day. He couldn't handle watching his boy's arms flail through all of his daily exercises.

Darian sneezed. Nathan listened for a cry. He scratched a phantom itch on his arm. After easing the chair back, he walked to the hall. With his hand on the door, he inched his ear closer. Silence. The cold floor stung. *You can't just bail.* He closed his eyes. He thought about those group homes, with their vaguely Biblical write-ups and fortune-cookie ad lines. Sooner than later, would he have to surrender? He thought about the special hands-on teaching the school district couldn't afford, even if they were required to. The tears threatened. He was a free agent without a team. Undiscovered talent didn't matter if no one noticed. How much more could he take? *Erica, I hope you rot for leaving me saddled with this.*

He returned to the office and turned off the monitor. Standing there, he noticed the folded piece of paper that woman had given him. He opened it and read: community meeting, about the accident. Man, did that woman Ms. Rose think talk would really solve anything? But instead of throwing the paper into the trash, he tossed it onto the desk. He couldn't be sure, but maybe he would feel differently in the morning.

12

The next morning, Nathan awoke to the light piercing his sun-bled blinds. His head in a fog, he put on his pressed uniform. Downstairs, his mother was sipping tea, watching her morning show. "Have a good day, Nathan." He patted her shoulder. She'd been happy to babysit for him once "that bitch" was gone.

"Mom, do you know a Ms. Rose that lives around here?" His mother eyed him. "She was at the field yesterday, talked to me."

"Hmm, Ms. Rose. Older woman, grey dreads?" Nathan nodded. "Yes, I knew her and her husband. Haven't seen her since she stopped coming to church." She blew her tea and narrowed her eyes. "Why?"

Nathan thought of the flyer she gave him. "She seemed nice." She nodded, waiting for the rest of the story, that, for some reason he didn't feel like offering. After a weird silence, he excused himself.

She called out as he was closing the front door behind him: "You be careful driving that bus today, what with that accident and all." It was Friday, and he'd never told her what this day meant to him, what his afternoon shift promised him, and today, that outweighed any of this accident nonsense.

At the bus station, he fetched his run batch and his bus assignment. Outside, he ran through his CDL list, scouring every inch of the bus like he was returning a rental car. Once, he'd almost hit a car because his mirrors were caked in dirt. Now his windows sparkled, his mirrors gleamed, and his schedule holders were full. He finished his sweep and bagged his cleaning rags. *Fourteen minutes to enjoy my coffee.*

After the last drop of his coffee, he cranked the engine. For the 8 minutes he dead-headed to his first stop, he swam in the quiet.

At the day's first red light, the idling engine chugged. Maybe one day he would get to drive one of the new, smoother natural-gas powered buses. Then he pictured the afternoon, their rowdiness on his bus: the school kids waiting at his 3:01 stop at Broad and Washington. To his left, a woman pushed a stroller down the street. A puffy Baby Phat jacket, boots to match, with fake fur around the tops, and chunky sunglasses. Her head raised, she strutted behind that stroller. He looked away. From the stroller, little legs kicked. Once the light changed to green, he hit the gas, and the bus lurched forward.

From his side mirror, he could still make her out, that confident, I-don't-have-a-care-in-the-world stride. He checked her in his side mirror. He thought of Erica. While she had carried Darian, she wouldn't shut up about what kind of a bad ass mother she was going to be. Her belly swelled, her smile widened.

Then she delivered. The patience, the exercises, how her boy was going to end up, that all wasn't for her. For three and a half years, she'd made a go of it, and then packed her shit. This is not how she wanted her life to be, she announced, one eye aimed at Darian's room, bullshit tears dropping.

What she really meant: *I won't have a son that don't look like other people.* It seared her insides that people viewed him as trash. She'd had it with the state's inept "Intervention" program, and all those coping counseling sessions. He nudged her bag across the threshold.

Her friends had talked about how getting stuck would get you a check. *You still gotta change those fucking diapers*, he'd wanted to say. *Ain't no fun dragging your ass out the bed at four in the morning to pick up your kid and quiet him when he cries*, thought of that? But those girls, man, they dolled up their babies in all kinds of expensive crap when their checks arrived. Of course, when your baby's daddy didn't man up, Nathan guessed they needed something.

That day, once she left, with her perfume still lingering, he'd mounted the stairs two at a time, and rushed to Darian's room. He picked up his son, who'd been sleeping. "I ain't going anywhere, son," he whispered. Swaying him back and forth, little man's hot breath on his neck, he couldn't accept, not ever, that one day he'd maybe have to break his word. And maybe he'd been a stubborn fool, taking any shift he could, become a kind of hermit, guarding his money, shutting himself off to friends, the only real social life being his time with a few guys at the station. *People will let you down, when given the chance, right?* For now, he had his mother, a strong woman, and that was good enough, for him, for his son.

The light changed and he lurched forward until catching yet another red. Slowly, she returned to his mirror. He leaned towards that mirror, focused his eyes; her face eventually gelled. *Holy hell. Erica.* She had a new weave and looked like she'd lost some weight. Whose fucking stroller was she pushing? He heard honking. The light had changed and he hit the gas. Traffic slowed him before he could make the next light. In his side mirror, she showed. Traffic crept. He moved. She closed on the bus. The light changed to red. She reached the back of the bus. In the stroller, the baby's legs kicked. Considering opening the door to shout her down, he eyed the mounted windshield camera. Clenching his teeth, he worried he'd break a crown. She passed the doors and kept on, not even noticing the bus. Gunning the bus onto the sidewalk and right over her seemed a perfectly acceptable idea until the light changed and he eased forward.

• • •

Throughout the morning, his anger guided him through traffic, insulated him against obnoxious riders eating their food and leaving their trash behind, and entitled jerks walking right past him without paying their fare, knowing he was not empowered to force them to pay. During his break, he would sit in the corner of the break room, ignore the checker and poker games, the pool match. But when he swept the crumbs from his table and gathered his trash, he knew he'd feel that first drop of sweat in his armpits. Why today of all days did he have to see her, her image seared into his brain like the horror movie he'd turned off too late? Then, to cap the perfect morning shift, he noticed Brenda, Erica's friend, waiting for his bus on the next block. Even better: with a packed bus, she'd be stuck close enough to feel. Considering blowing right past her, he eyed the mounted camera. He took a deep breath as he slowed the bus along the curb. The doors opened without earning her attention. Why was he not surprised?

"Coming out, coming *out*!" People surged towards the front, goaded forward by the woman who had been consumed by her cell phone since she'd boarded. She lurched out of the bus as Brenda stepped on. "Can't you wait for people to get off the fucking bus?" she barked real close to Brenda's face. Bracing, Nathan waited for the Brenda he knew all too well to unload.

Instead, she stepped aside. With a hand on the rail, she breathed deeply, as if she were about to jump into a cold shower. He lowered the bus. Since it had been a year since they'd seen one another, she might not have recognized him, but then he realized she was an entire world away in her head, which, as he studied it, he noticed had far more grey hairs than someone their age should have. In the rearview mirror, he watched a guy clear space on the bag area for her laundry baskets. After settling them, she opened her purse. She eyed the floor as she fumbled inside; he eyed her as he entered traffic. At least she was pretending to have the fare he knew she didn't.

"I got it, I got it." She must have thought he was coughing for her. Opening her wallet, she produced last week's Trans Pass, the one decorated with the Art Museum. The reader beeped twice. "Shit." She looked at it as if it were written in Spanish.

"Give it another go, Brenda," he said. *When had her eyes looked so defeated?*

"Hey, Nathan," she muttered. Her face drooped as she searched her wallet real slow. She swiped the card again and the reader beeped twice.

He nodded, and she leaned against her laundry. She crossed her arms and then massaged her head. *Yeah, he knew the feeling.* He wished he could have asked her what she'd heard about that bitch, but instead, he coasted through the next yellow light and didn't bother. At her stop, she put a hand on his shoulder. "Thanks, Nathan," she almost whispered, to which he nodded. For some reason, a little sting dissipated from his stomach.

• • •

At the station, the smell of fresh coffee deceived Nathan into thinking he could relax. Nathan hoped nobody had swiped his sandwich out of the fridge. Rick didn't normally work Fridays, so he should have been fine. *Unless he traded shifts.* Pushing through the doors, he couldn't wait to unwind by himself.

To Terry and Lou, he nodded. Engrossed with their pool game, he knew better than to disturb them, for they'd be on a short fuse that weekend without their seven games, seeing as how they'd nearly bribed the scheduling manager to give them at least one swing shift together a week. Scanning the rest of the room, he noticed Rick in the corner. Grinding his teeth, he prayed his lunch was still where he left it. He eased open the fridge while his stomach rumbled like a low bass hum. Mr.-sticky-fingers Rick buried his nose in a magazine. Snatching his brown bag, he almost walked to the only open chair, which happened to be next to Rick. He took one step in that direction and Rick dropped the magazine on the table and eased back, primed for small talk. He spun around towards Russell and Carl's dominoes game, his need for solitude evaporating, and as he approached them, he felt a sudden surge of vigor.

"Hey Russell."

"Nathan." He tapped his fingers to a rhythm without peeling his eyes from the table. He was about to fuck up.

"You boys done with your practice rounds and ready for a beat down?" Nathan said. His chair was still warm, so he must've just missed Steve.

"Son, the only beat down I'm getting ready for is the one I am about to throw your way." Carl surveyed his tiles then locked eyes with Russell's forehead, for he was studying and studying but, as usual, coming up empty. "You can toss something down, Russell, or not. I ain't got all day for this game."

"In a minute, in a minute. I'm thinking over here, can't you see that?" he said.

Nathan pulled his sandwich out, his fingers trembling. How did he get so hungry?

"What you got there?" Carl asked.

"Turkey, little spicy jack, mustard, couple onions."

Carl leaned in. "Good?"

"Don't know yet." Carl's lunch money went to the track. Saving for a house, his wife locked up their finances. He would've rather sponged food than give up those horses. Somehow he managed to piece together a meal. But he wouldn't take something that wasn't offered.

"They still haven't settled our contract, in case you're curious."

"Figures," Nathan said. Crumbs dropped to the table. He brushed them to the floor.

"They almost sealed the deal last night but the shit fell through at the last minute."

"Great." His neck tensed. Payday was next Friday. Russell eyed Nathan and then Carl. He had missed something.

"Go ahead and tell him, you know it's killing you?" Russell's eyes panned his seven tiles, hoping one of them would tell him what he should've played.

"Tell me what?" he asked through a full mouth.

"Tom and Steve are taking early retirement, can't deal with this contract shit anymore."

"No shit?" Tom and Steve had seniority. With them gone, he could get better shifts. His sandwich lost all flavor; his toes tingled. *Darian.*

"No shit." Carl rotated his pieces.

Better routes meant maybe five more hours a week, twenty more hours a month. Like $300 a month, after taxes. *Darian.* Less swings, no more... He dropped his sandwich. He was a little light headed. Of course, this meant shit if the strike happened. Would the money from the new routes rescue him from whatever financial hole being out of work created? He watched Russell and Carl and felt the warm seat underneath him. "And if this motherfucker ever gets around to playing something, we might be able to move on with our day."

Russell rearranged his tiles like a street hustler working a shell game.

Under the table, Nathan socked his knees with his fists, like he used to do before a big game.

With Tom leaving, would Nathan have the discipline to maintain his positive attitude? Man, if Tom threw in the towel, what did that mean for people like him? "When are they done here?" he asked.

Carl lifted his head. "Tom's done in two weeks. Steve, a couple months or so." He squinted for a moment. Being under Nathan in terms of seniority, his opportunities wouldn't change much; not yet, anyway. Maybe that's why he wasn't so excited. "What do you think about that, Russell? Or should I keep my mouth shut so you can concentrate?"

"Do as you like, Carl, but I won't go until I'm ready, so you might as well just cool your heels." In a moment or two, he would play a tile; then, he would want to take it back, saying he noticed something else he should've played.

"One of these days, man, I ain't gonna play your ass anymore because you drag it out too much." He shook his head then turned to Nathan. His tone softened. Nathan hadn't taken another bite of his sandwich. His mind was awash in number crunching and processing Tom leaving. *Darian.* "So you lucky, man, you stepping into some better routes. You gonna be in the money now, son. Looks like someone watching out for you. You're one step closer, my friend, one step closer. Soon enough, it'll be me." He turned his head to Russell, who was scratching his chin's three-day growth. In a few months' time Nathan wouldn't be sitting there watching them rib one another. This took a moment to register.

When Darian was born, they were there; when Erica bounced, they listened. Before all that and every week in between, they had this table. He looked at Carl. You could always tell when his wife had headed to the shore for the week because she wasn't around to demand he shave. Would he stop noticing those subtle things in his friend?

"Now if only I could get help with this, I would be better off too."

"If you got nothing better to do, tell Nathan your story?"

"What now?" Nathan switched off the calculator in his head. Carl could really rub a person wrong with his mouth. Rick dropped his magazine and leaned forward.

"Oh man, on my early route, this white woman gets on, and she's wearing this sun dress and, you know, it's not hugging her, so it looks like she got a belly, right? To be polite, I asked how far along she was." The way he smiled, he'd found his zone.

Shaking his head, Russell chuckled. Laughing, Carl rolled his eyes. "All right, I'll bite, what happened next?" Nathan asked.

"So, she looks at me from over her sunglasses and snaps, 'I'm not pregnant.' You could tell I had just about ruined her day. But you know how you can say stuff to white people and they don't get up in your face like a sister? Well, I should've apologized, but I wanted to save a bit of face. So I turned my attention to the window and say to her, 'Well, I guess it must have been a big dinner last night.'" Nathan imagined this perfectly nice woman boarding the bus and wishing she'd stayed home. Still, he felt a laugh coming. "I swear, I've never seen somebody walk so fast to the back of my bus." Carl slapped the table.

Russell set a double one in place. "Your move, Carl." He was smiling wide, for some reason. Nathan looked at Carl's tiles. He was gonna have to draw.

"Great, man I knew we should have played cards today."

"That mean you can't play that?"

"Yes, Russell, that's what that means."

"So Nathan, what do you think about that accident?"

"Shit, look at the time." Carl checked his watch and stood. "Gotta get to my route."

Russell frowned as Carl bolted for the door. In his neighborhood, Carl noticed nicer cars owned by people who paid for them without drug money, smelled strange food cooking on the grills from behind high fenced yards. In the recycling bins left out on trash day, beer bottles of brands he'd never heard of. Combined, this made him—and perhaps the other old timers—bitter. Nathan was sure it was an ego thing but he let them have their resentment. They had to make a stand somewhere, as if they would be chased out sooner or later—feeling like they didn't belong anymore, that their tax bills were climbing—and they were tired of feeling like the walls were closing in on the home that they'd lived in before people made it trendy.

Whites weren't the only ones buying those houses, Nathan had tried to tell him. Bring on the whites, bring anyone with clout. Darian needed their resources. When enough of them lived in the neighborhood, those more affluent people would force change. The higher property taxes would boost what the schools could do. People with money, they demanded things. If having people with more money moving into the neighborhood raised his house value, he might offer a hand when the moving truck parked.

"What was that about?" Nathan asked.

Watching the door close, Russell said, "You know how he gets. He can't get worked up before his shift." He looked at the table, as if the answer might be waiting. "So anyway, the accident. You headed to that meeting on Monday?"

He paused here. If he volunteered yes, they might wonder which side he was on. "I heard about it. Wasn't sure."

"Not sure how *I* feel about it. Heard it's about protecting that white driver. Wonder when the meeting about the black kid getting hit is going to be, know what I mean?" Nathan shook his head, though he hadn't thought about that. He thought about Miss Rose. He couldn't imagine a woman like that sticking her neck out for some random white guy; once Mom had mentioned how they knew each other, he remembered her, seeing her every week at Church, always smiling, patting people on the back, settling rowdy kids down on the sidewalk. What was her angle? Then he imagined sitting around a bar with a bunch of strangers complaining all night. He got enough of that on his routes. Those would be the people he would look to build a community. He needed doers, not whiners. He was sure he would pass on that. Since Russell was looking to buy a house soon, he would probably pass. He didn't want to give his wife any opportunity to shoot his house decision down.

"Anyway, you want to pick up where Carl left off?" He motioned to the remaining tiles.

• • •

Man, what a day. Once Russel left, Nathan swiped the crumbs from the table and gathered his trash. His head was swimming, and back in the driver's seat, he buckled up. On autopilot, he dead-headed to his first stop. There, he greeted every rider that boarded, and it wasn't until he exited the Wal-Mart parking lot, coasted up Columbus Boulevard and approached Washington Avenue that he felt the first bead of sweat drop down his side. The green arrow lit and his stomach turned.

On Washington, traffic thinned. With three empty stops, he crept a minute ahead of schedule. He slowed for the next yellow. A passenger bitched. Eyeing the guy in his rearview mirror, he stretched his tightening back. Before he finished his deep breath, the light changed and he hit the gas. At 12th, his sight line opened. They were there. Huddled, waiting, like a bunch of worms when you pull back a patch of soil, they were being their typical rowdy, obnoxious selves. Them, with their backpacks, pushing and shoving one another. His throat tightened. As the light changed, he blew past 13th street and slowed as he approached Broad.

His hand vibrating, he opened the door, and in a flash, the mob clogged his steps. They yelled and screamed, like children should when they're free for the day. Their buoyant voices grated. In the aisle, they nudged one another. The last kid, maybe 10, was tossing a football to himself. Nathan shut the door and, seeing that kid a bit off balance, when the light changed, he floored the pedal, lurching everyone back. In his rearview mirror, he watched the kid struggle to gain his balance. Nathan smiled.

• • •

At day's end, Nathan could not stretch out the kinks in his back, the knot in his jaw. Still, he could be wrong but he felt a bit of a spring in his step, and once home, he dumped his wallet, his keys, and the plastic shopping bag on his entry-way table. In the kitchen, he snagged an ice pack from the fridge.

"We're upstairs, Nate." Mom sounded tired.

"Be up in a minute," he said.

He tucked the pack under his belt. The cool soothed and his mind raced. For every flash of Erica, those brats, he attempted to wedge thoughts of his new routes. Finally, a say in his own life. When they got pregnant, Erica made their choice. Erica wanted out of them, she left. When he'd started at Septa: "Here are the scraps." Now, man, thousands more a year. He grabbed the plastic bag and took the steps two at a time. As the steps creaked, he prayed he wasn't getting his own hopes up over nothing, but in the moment, this relief felt good. He was allowing himself to float in the hope that the new money would provide. The strike might not happen. Erica, gone; his neighborhood, improving, regardless of what happened with this accident business. Buoyant, he'd handed that sporting goods store cashier his credit card right before he headed home.

At the top of the stairs, he swung around the wobbly banister.

In the middle room Mom and Darian were parked on the small carpet in the room's center. Darian watched Mom, who sat forward with a dinosaur in her hand.

Keeping her eyes on her grandchild, she danced the toy. "Hi." She lowered the toy.

"Hey." He leaned against the doorjamb.

She lowered her eyes as she eased herself up like an aging athlete. How much longer could she help at this level? How much more challenging would Darian get? She patted his shoulder as she brushed past him towards the bathroom.

Darian raised his arms, babbling something that sounded like "Daddy."

Nathan grasped his little hands and eased to the floor. He dropped the bag. Darian bobbed his head a little. Nathan grabbed the toy Mom was holding. Taking Darian's hand, he placed the small rubber dinosaur in it, and then held his fingers closed around it. Darian looked at it with his saucer eyes. Nathan let go and the toy thudded on the carpet. "One day, buddy." He kissed his forehead. Smelling of Johnson's shampoo, the child gurgled. Nathan grabbed him and stood, having trouble balancing as he did so. He snagged the shopping bag on his way down the hall, towards the master bedroom. "Little man, I got you something."

In the bedroom he turned on the light. Darian scanned the room like he didn't know where he was. After sitting Darian on the edge of the bed, Nathan steadied him with a hand. Darian started tapping on Nathan's fingers. With his free hand, he pulled out a green Eagles jersey. He held it up.

"What do you think of this, buddy?"

Darian looked confused. Without clipping the tags, Nathan held it over Darian's head while the little man watched. "Okay, maybe not. Try this, little man, do like I do." Nathan crouched and raised his arms. Laughing, Darian raised his own arms. Nathan scrunched the bottom of the jersey in his hand and slipped it through Darian's arms. Scooting the jersey over his head, he pulled it down. He adjusted the material over the shoulders. *There.* The number was a bit hard to read but it would do. He'd meant to buy it a couple sizes too big.

"You like it?"

Darian half laughed, half squealed. Nathan lifted him and then stood by the front window. The bathroom door opened and his mother's feet thumped down the hall.

Holding Darian, he looked out the window. A loud car passed as he rocked his son. Four years ago there were three shells on this block and several houses with rickety doors, crooked address plates, busted windows. If you had a car, you could park it anywhere. Those shells had been gutted and renovated; and professionally dressed people, who never would've walked those streets ten years ago, had moved in. From several homes, tired paint had been power-washed away, mortar re-pointed, doors stripped and repainted. He didn't want to leave that window and he didn't want to let go of his boy. If he stayed like this forever, would he ever have to let go of his boy? In a few months' time, he would be able to pay bills down and then replace a couple windows, install a washer and dryer. The neighborhood around him might continue to evolve, property values continue to rise, and if he was lucky, some of that increased tax revenue would fund their school. Darian's school. If even more people retired, he might step into even more cash. But for now, this was what he had.

"How was your day, son?"

He felt his mother's warmth. "Some interesting stuff at work." He took a deep breath. "I saw her on my early route, walking down the street." His mother rubbed his shoulder. "She was pushing a stroller." In the window's reflection, he could see his mother's eyes tighten.

"She came by." His grip on Darian constricted. "I didn't let her in. She said you two had to talk. She was wearing a ring."

"Oh."

He felt hollow. *That stroller.* "The papers have gone through. What if she comes for this house, for Darian? I ain't letting her take him."

An eerie calm descended on his mother. "Oh, don't worry, Son. She won't get anything from us. She's made so many mis-steps, she hasn't a leg to stand on. We have friends, dear." She put her hands on his shoulders. "Don't worry."

Friends. He watched a white couple walk down the sidewalk. Something about them seemed familiar. They stopped, chatted with a black person, who seemed to be about their age, someone he didn't recognize, and then both went their separate ways. He thought about that meeting. There were bound to be people from both sides of this thing, but if he went, which side would he choose? He knew what happened if you signed to the wrong team. But maybe it was about time he got to know who his neighbors were, hear how they saw things. If things went south, he could use some backup. Then again, maybe he should avoid this nonsense at all costs.

He imagined he was crouching at the line of scrimmage, waiting for the ball to be snapped. Hearing that homefield crowd roaring, he didn't want to see the scoreboard or the clock. He wondered if this was what players on a losing team felt at the end of their losing season when their contract was expiring and they had to make a big decision: re-up with the team who'd drafted you or jump ship for a chance at more money, winning, or both.

13

Brenda's eyes narrowed, targeting those motherfuckers who needed to find themselves a motherfucking job and get the fuck off of her corner. They slapped their knees, carrying on like they were sitting in a comedy club; she scraped her front teeth with a fingernail. Against the wall went those dice. In paper bags at their feet, 40s of liquor. When people with money hunted for their houses, they'd see those idiots, rethink their location, and then reconsider buying up her neighborhood. She used to believe this, taking pride in their freedom to do as they please in public—*why start giving a shit about us now*? Then, as her boys got older, she noticed their little eyes watching those clowns more and more, mimicking their dice tossing gestures. And if that wasn't bad enough, she knew the city was planning to reassess all their properties, "adjust" their taxes—they all knew this day was coming once the white people started buying up places around them. Not only could she not afford that bullshit—a white tax, it sure felt like—but if they were moving up, perhaps what she chose to ignore might become something worth caring about. She wasn't judging those men there, but damned if she wasn't wishing they'd go be themselves somewhere she didn't have to see. What made this worse: white people taking over her neighborhood felt this way, and this made her teeth hurt. She counted to ten, and then exhaled through her nose. *Fucking anger management classes were good for something.* She cracked her knuckles. *Where was the damn bus?*

"Hey Miss Brenda. How you been, girl?" That high pitched, ratty voice. Damn Miss Marcy always lurking, spreading her infectious lies. Brenda didn't need that woman begging for cigarettes today. She hated lying, but she only had four left and was not about to share.

When the dragging feet slowed, Brenda faced her. You never knew where that woman's hands might go. Covering her purse, she scrunched her nose because of the stench of tequila that escaped that woman's smacking gums. *Woman, why can't you put your teeth in when you walking around?*

"Hey Miss Marcy." She used a dry tone.

"I seen you out here waiting on your bus. How you been?"

"I'll be better when this bus shows."

"Uh-huh, say..."

"You know I don't smoke."

"Oh, ah, that wasn't what I was going to... You hear about the accident?" She stepped far too close, and Brenda had half a mind to move her back. "That white man done run a black kid right over." *Oh, here we go.* It was Saturday and part of her was surprised people still pretended to care, but then again, this was Miss Marcy. "Even worse, Ms. Rose, she stirring up all kinds of trouble, picking the wrong side, if you ask me." Brenda bore her eyes into this woman. "You heard about that meeting she organizing. Everyone know it about taking that white man's side."

Brenda took a slow breath. Sure, she was inclined to believe that although that white man probably didn't set out to run down that black man, he probably wasn't losing too much sleep over doing it neither. Of all the bullshit happening in the neighborhood—people getting forced out, city finally going after people for not paying their property taxes (the people too old to do anything about it)—why finally get worked up over this small detail? Getting annoyed was bringing her over to Rose's side. Looking at Miss Marcy, Brenda could not decide how seriously she should take this warning though. "That a new rag you wearing, Miss Marcy? Look new, nice and tight round your head like that." Please, simple woman, believe this fake compliment.

She jabbed her head. Brenda looked over Miss Marcy's shoulder. *Pieces of shit still slanging those dice.* She had two jobs and those punks couldn't get one? Brenda heard the brakes and familiar droning of the bus lowering. The bus was one block away.

"Here comes my bus, Miss Marcy."

"You might want to go talk with Ms. Rose, now, remind her who her side is," Miss Marcy mumbled.

Brenda didn't wave back before boarding the bus. If the driver hauled ass, she might arrive at work on time for a change.

Wedging herself next to a fat person occupying too much room, Brenda exhaled a sigh of relief. At least Nathan wasn't driving today. Seeing him yesterday brought all kinds of shit back to her, namely that I-don't-take-care-of-my-kid bitch, Erica. And to think, they used to have shit in common. Her muscles tensed picturing that woman abandoning her responsibilities like they were clothes she'd grown out of. What she wouldn't have given for a responsible man. Her neck stiffened. Then she noticed that half the bus was filled with white people.

These fake-ass rich, white people, with their leather briefcases and Starbucks this and that. Ms Rose always saying how it ain't just white folks buying, but they all looked the same to Brenda. People with money only came in one shade. They didn't want to be neighbors. They wanted to isolate themselves in the space next to you, like this guy occupying the middle of the aisle, who got annoyed when someone squeezed by. Not everyone was worth knowing, but you never knew when you'd need a neighbor to keep your back. If her children grew up around these people, would they understand what a community meant, to feel like you and the people living around you were all in this together? Then she thought about the changes to the grocery store up the street, how the run-down place, which had been that way for decades, all of sudden discovered money for new freezers, better produce selection and better dressed employees to stock it all. Now, you couldn't find an expired carton of milk if you tried. Walking to the checkout, you passed a fancy cheese display that looked like it might just melt in your mouth right there, but then you checked the prices—like all the prices—and you felt like you were in the wrong store. *Why fresh gotta cost so much?* Knowing that the store only started caring once more white dollars was being spent there inflamed her rage. Who cared if they were "safer" walking around at night if soon you couldn't afford to buy food where you lived?

At the next stop, more people boarded the bus and she pressed her way back. By the back row, a white man stood blocking an empty seat, his face consumed by his little smart phone. Sit or move, she almost said, but she resented being the one to have to point this out. After all, he would probably just think her another angry black woman.

• • •

On her afternoon break, Brenda paced outside her office building. Leaving her flimsy headset by her computer, she'd grabbed a cup of coffee and wished she'd had enough change to buy chips. A little hungry, she expected peace and quiet, since smokers were generally the only ones who bothered riding the elevator, crossing the lobby, and signing out at the front desk. Thankfully, too much chatter cut into their puffing.

Tina groaned as she stretched. "Hey, girl," Brenda said. She'd anticipated at least one intrusion, and it might as well have been Tina.

"You as tired as me today? I need a vacation, I am telling you." Tina lit her cigarette. "Customers is all kinds of crazy today, talking about someone stole the check they sent in. Motherfucker, please, you know you didn't pay your shit. Man, just once I would like to tell a customer the truth. Must be a full moon." Tina tilted her head and blew a stream of smoke like a train engine. "I thought you quit smoking, what are you doing out here?"

"I can't handle them complaints, not today." Brenda studied the fragrant cigarette and wondered if maybe she should cave and have one of her four cigarettes, which had to last through tomorrow night.

"Mmm," Tina sucked on her cigarette. "I thought you might have been worried about that accident that happened down your way."

Brenda nodded. In the trail of a passing car, a small cloud of exhaust assaulted her. She swatted it.

"Well, I wish my neighborhood had something so small to bitch about."

Brenda cocked an eyebrow.

She took a long drag, held it, and then forced the smoke out. "A couple blocks away from us, neighbors got letters this week, talking about how the city needs to put forward community planning shit, get rid of the blight. Too many blocks have one house standing for every three or four empty lots, apparently."

Brenda wasn't following.

"They're talking about kicking people out of their houses with eminent domain bullshit. City wants to snatch these people's homes right out from under them, talking about giving them 'fair market value'. Please, in North Philly, what they going to offer? And where those people supposed to go? A bunch of places on the block over from them, the government already seized; knocked them down, leveled the ground, fenced the area. Developers were supposed to arrive, bring businesses, jobs." She examined the fire scaling her cigarette, turning to ash. "We're waiting for ours to come. Maybe it will, maybe it won't."

"You really think the city is going to take over everything? What would they do with it?"

"Whatever the fuck they want. You know what they did down by you, back when they were extending 76 to meet up with 95? Sent letters, booted 'em out, cleared the way. Ask some of the old heads round you. They'll tell you."

Brenda thought of Ms. Rose.

"We're thinking of selling before we don't have a say."

"Sell?"

"Move it or lose it. Down by you, things heating up the way they are with property value and taxes rising, you might as well cash out while you can." She dropped her cigarette and stubbed it with her high heel. "See you inside."

Move? Maybe she *should* take care of her business before someone forced her hand. Fuck it, let these white folks have her neighborhood. She wouldn't let some law snatch her house with some bullshit buyout price. Maybe her boys would learn what it meant to take your life into your own hands.

Jane, from accounting, bounded out of the front door, with her fake-ass blond hair and tits popping out of her blouse. It must have been Girl Scout Cookie season, for she had that fake smile plastered on her face as she approached Brenda. Her head throbbed.

• • •

When Brenda was little, about five, her mother had taken her to Wawa to get money orders for their bills. Brenda wandered to the refrigerators. She saw her favorite can of strawberry soda and touched the door. She gazed at her mom as the man printed their slips. "None of that, Brenda. We ain't got the money for no soda." Her mama turned while Brenda gazed at those lined-up soda cans. A big white man with thick black glasses crouched, removed his wallet, and took out a dollar.

"Here you go, little lady. Get your soda." Then he opened the door for her.

Brenda reached, but her mama had her by the shoulder the moment before she could touch that can. "You give that money back now, you hear?"

"No, miss, it's okay."

"Sir, let me handle my business," her mama said. "Give this man back his money and we can leave."

Brenda returned the money and the man waited a moment before he took it. He dipped his hat as he left. On the bus home, as her mama adjusted Brenda's coat, Brenda sniffled instead of crying, for her mama didn't stand for any public attention nonsense.

"That money wasn't yours to take. We don't need charity, especially from some strange white man." Her mama zipped the jacket, then stared out the window, perhaps wondering about Brenda's father. He'd taken off to Baltimore with that bitch of a friend of her mama's; no phone call, no letter; that friend's husband conveyed the information. Until their stop came, her mama didn't turn from that window.

• • •

She'd impressed herself by how calmly she'd jumped on Tina's advice, but she was surprised—and a little leery—at how quickly that realtor appeared on her doorstep. She'd picked a white one, one with signs all over her neighborhood, against her better judgment—but she accepted that he would have the contacts she needed. She did, however, expect him to be fat, with big, thick black glasses. Neither impression was correct.

"Hi, Brenda?" He extended his pale hand. "I'm Walter." And without being invited in, he moved inside, as if they were old friends. Once he had finished picking apart the first floor, they were standing outside her boys' room on the second, his eyes looking like he was searching for the right words. That was the moment that let her know she'd messed up picking a man who wasn't going to speak his mind. Why were white people like this? But she felt a warmth from this man she hadn't expected, or maybe she'd been fucked over so many times she didn't know what decency looked like.

"Brenda, it's none of my business, but why are you selling this house?"

"Excuse me?" She checked her tone so she didn't sound like those black actresses; the bitches who cocked their heads and flung their weaves when they got pissed. For once, she was glad she learned so much in her time in billing.

"I see a lot of homes, and I meet a lot of families. Especially in this area, I see people who are unloading houses because they either want to cash in or they can't afford tax hikes or the upkeep on their houses. Are there other reasons? Sure, but those seem to come up the most often. Again, if you don't mind me asking, why sell?"

His eyes were soft, and although they might just be concerned, she felt his pity. This made her want to shake.

He waited for her answer.

"I'm not sure. I guess I'm looking to avoid those big ass tax hikes I hear are coming our way." He'd probably tell her she was crazy for thinking the city would use eminent domain on her. Besides, he didn't need to hear what she thought about the neighborhood changing over, because he'd feed her the line about how things were changing for the better. People dressed like him all seemed to think that way, at least the ones chatting on the bus did. She hated them for celebrating her community being torn apart. Course, Ms. Rose wasn't no different in that regard.

"Well, if I can be frank, because you might not be hearing this from someone else, those are going to hit you wherever they are going to hit you. Yeah, you will pay a bit more, but if you can put a little more away each month, the pinch won't be so bad." While he waited for those words to settle, he studied her eyes, which she kept flat. "Taxes are going to go up everywhere in the city, and if you have good roots here, with your kids and all, you might as well stay here, take advantage of the rising property values."

Like he knew what a pinch felt like. She resisted shaking again. "Plus, work has to get done around here, stuff I don't want to blow my savings on. The roof, some of these windows. I want to make money on this place not dump money into it." She didn't want to think too much about what needed to be done, just like when she had kicked DeSean out: get the fuck out, move on. *That worked, why wouldn't this?*

"Well, some of what you need to have done might have to be done anyway for the place to sell. But if you're interested, there are programs in place to help..."—he bit at his lip. His eyes were anchored to her face—"...certain income levels maintain their homes. They can give you grants to give the roof a new coating, rebates towards new energy efficient windows."

She heard "program" and couldn't handle any more, especially after he struggled to stop from saying fucking "poor people." She was no fucking charity case. Her children weren't charity cases. She pictured her mother listening, her folded arms. "That's something, but I think I want to go ahead and list it." If she said this over and over, he might stop talking. Her kids would adjust, just like her. That's life.

• • •

The day since his visit had not removed the rawness of his words, and like wet cement finally firming, her resolve had hardened. Or had it? She sat on her couch in her front room, the delivered papers arranged on her coffee table. Through the stereo speakers, jazz crackled, like a record. Along with those papers, brochures on the assistance programs he'd mentioned. All this paper, all these applications, questions. Brenda gnawed her fingernails. Her house had been reduced to a bunch of measurements, checked boxes, and a price. Her memories, the only home her children have ever known, reduced to $162,500. She pictured the strangers perusing her home while she was at work, the ones who would judge, scratch their heads, think *well, maybe*. Her stomach growled. Pressure built on the side of her fucking head. That comparables sheet told her that people weren't getting what people thought they were getting for their homes. Walter even listed choices, asking her how long she wanted to have her house on the market. If she wanted out quick, she should slash the price so someone could snatch it from her. This was what "giving someone a good, tempting deal" meant. If she was patient—if she actually wanted what he said her home was worth—then on the market it would sit. If you asked people to pay you what you were worth, you had to hold out, like you were striking or something. She could taste those tobacco flakes on her tongue, hear the paper crumbling with the flame. Did she have any cigarette packs stashed anywhere?

In the kitchen she rummaged through the basket on top of the fridge.

"Ma?" She didn't even hear her son Ray use the stairs. Where was her head? She turned. His soft four-year-old brown eyes pleaded as he stood by the dining room table.

"Yeah, honey, what do you need?" In his left hand, he clutched his raggedy-ass teddy bear, the one his father bought him two years ago, the one Ray wouldn't let her trash even though it stunk and probably couldn't take any more stitches.

"I'm hungry." He had just eaten lunch, so she knew he was looking to talk until he found his point. His fucking father did this.

Next to him, she crouched. "Now, you know I know that you ate and didn't clear your plate, so I know that ain't what's on your mind, son." His eyes meandered, so she lifted his chin to meet her stare. "One more time, what do you need?"

"What are you reading, Mom?" He'd turned his head towards the coffee table.

"Mom's going through paper work that white man sent over for me to read."

"Is that man going to sell our house and we're going to move?" She wished she could trample that sadness in his voice all over that carpet, like that time she'd heard that little punk was bullying him at school. Not like this would have helped, but she told him he had to fight his own battles, fight that crap. Life wasn't going to make things easy, never.

"If I sell the house, yes, we're going to have to move." Her finger throbbed, right where she had chewed the nail.

"But I don't want to move, Mom." He whined like she had taught him never to do. Never let no one see that they affected you, she wanted to say, but the effort was too much.

"There's plenty of stuff that I don't want to do but I got to get it done, you understand? Now go back upstairs and play with your brother." He sulked up those stairs and her heart tugged. She could fix 'em up quick when they scraped their knees, but not help them with the school subjects they didn't understand. They had to settle their own issues and pass their own tests. But could she control this? Was she doing the right thing? She leaned against the kitchen counter. Did she have any cigarettes in the freezer? *Mom, what would you do?*

Once, when Brenda came home from school, her mother was at the kitchen table, her head against her hand. The house smelled all burnt. Brenda didn't remember why her mom, who looked like she hadn't had much sleep, wasn't at work. That might have been one of the times she had gotten laid off. In front of her, a plate of dark brown cookies. Whirring in the kitchen window, the dirty box fan wobbled. Brenda was 11.

"Cookie?" Her mom offered in that voice that meant take one and don't question.

But Brenda was feeling something in her veins that day, so she asked, "Momma, if you burned 'em, why didn't you throw them in the trash?" Brenda sat.

Her mother took a cookie. "Well," her mom said, chomping, the crumbs spilling, "if I threw out all of my mistakes, I wouldn't have no reminders to make sure I didn't mess them up the next time." She gulped her milk.

"But why I got to eat your mistakes?"

Her eyes softened, like she were reading her a bedtime story. "Because you under my roof, and when I make a mistake, you got to live with it. And the sooner we make it through this batch, the sooner we can make another one. Do you want a cookie or don't you?" Brenda remembered grabbing a cookie but not eating it. Her mom sat at that table at least another hour, not even looking up when Brenda plopped on the couch to watch cartoons.

Mom, I could use you now, she thought, as she looked out her kitchen window. Studying the cracked cement backyard, Brenda wanted to cry. Was she just abandoning that place because it was easier than staying, putting in the work, the money to fix it? She chewed on this. What was she really running from? She thought about Nathan and how Erica quit her family, left her man holding that child—the one that had no future. *You don't ditch your blood like that*. She leaned into her anger and felt charged.

Years ago, when Brenda found out she was carrying Ray, she had wanted nothing to do with a second child. But she stuck it out. When she rocked her son for the first time, watched his little face contort when he coughed, she knew there wasn't nothing in the world she wouldn't do for that new life. She would protect her boys, give them everything in the world. She'd be doing it on her own, too; she'd been down that road and back again. DeSean said he was going to be there every step of the way. *Nope*. She held her head high, got herself a second job, had a long talk with her aunt about her plans, how she was fixing to manage her kids. She needed help with watching them, though. When her uncle passed, her aunt got Brenda that house—her aunt wouldn't be living with any ghosts, thank you.

Brenda's eyes sparkled when they moved in. "This is yours now, can't nobody take it from you but yourself," her aunt said, as she removed the blue painter's tape from the walls they'd painted together.

Those words returned to her as she stood there in that kitchen, looking at the old-ass tree in the access alley. Its roots would continue to crack the concrete, and what would happen if that big ass tree fell during a storm? Would her sons be the ones to handle it?

Mine.

Can't nobody take this from you but yourself.

Mine.

Worse shit than this had found her; would in the future, too. An address wouldn't change that. She looked at the front room. From where she stood, she could make out those "assistance" pamphlets she couldn't bring herself to open.

Can't nobody take this from you but yourself.

Erica. Brenda pictured that fake-ass smile Erica could muster even when she was knee-deep in bullshit. But now Brenda was starting to appreciate that whenever things got too much for her, Erica'd just walk away, go find joy. Brenda had always resented her for being such a cold bitch, but now, maybe she'd been jealous of her all along. *Jealous? Could that really be?* She poked at this idea from every angle, and then something opened in her, something with which she wasn't all that comfortable. No, she would not let this sit with her. A strange idea surfaced then: she had to find Erica, see her in person, read her face, search for something—Brenda wasn't sure what, but she'd know it when she found it—and then put this to rest. Maybe she could decide when she let somebody—a stranger even—help her through this, keep her on her feet. She was not off her feet, just teetering. She'd been creative enough with the bills, but could she keep juggling? *Fuck it, maybe it was easier to walk away.* She had to find her.

"Momma, are we really moving?" Anthony asked as he thumped down the steps.

Brenda exited the kitchen. "What makes you ask that?" She'd never lied to her child.

"That man that was over here the other day, he fixing to help you sell this place?" He steadied his voice like his father used to when he was negotiating with bill collectors. He hadn't believed the brother he'd probably dispatched. Her seven-year-old boy was becoming a man.

"Come here, honey, sit by your mother." She swiped crumbs off the fucking couch. Why were they eating up there? But she couldn't touch her anger now, it was so far away from her that she couldn't even taste it. After she sat, he muscled next to her, his fist clenched. His legs hung a little lower than she'd ever noticed. This house, this neighborhood should witness them become men. Maybe new neighbors would shape them better than the people who'd guided their fathers. "I did have that man come over to see about maybe selling this place. But I don't know what I'm going to do." It was scarier to stay and fight than pull up stakes and start somewhere new. She thought of her sons' fathers. Sometimes it was worth giving things up, but she wasn't surrendering now.

"Why would you have him come here, Momma?" When his voice sagged, she wanted to tell him to cut that shit, strengthen his voice, but she didn't.

Maybe he was going be a man who could feel a bit, not ashamed to let a little pain show. He was going to have to learn to control it a little better than that though.

"Times get hard. And sometimes, to make those hard times go away, you gotta do things you didn't want to do just to make it. If we move, we could make those hard times disappear. But this man gave me ideas; he might be able to help us stay here and take care of our business." She pulled his head to her chest and held it there. She wondered if he could hear her thumping heart.

"That white man is going to do that for us?" Judgment had infected his words.

When she recognized that those were her words out of his young mouth, she cringed. This white man, this *man* had extended a hand to her, to her boys, and she didn't want to see his color. "He's just a man, sweetheart. Don't matter that he white. Only matter that he helping us." She held his head to her chest and closed her eyes. She could feel his little heartbeat. "Now, you and your brother stay out of trouble. Janet is coming over and keep an eye on you two. Momma has to do something."

• • •

Thankfully, Janet was around to help, and when she showed, Brenda bolted. Probably walking like a crazy woman, or perhaps like Miss Marcy looking to score, she slowed herself. Ms. Rose would know where Erica lived, so she headed towards the Laundromat. The last thing she wanted to do was knock on the wrong place and have some recent neighbor—some white person—get all paranoid that some black woman was coming for them.

When she reached the front window, she couldn't see Rose, just that Asian woman talking to some Mexican woman. *Hmm, now what? Nathan.* Did she dare ask? It'd be too cold on the phone, though, and he could always hang up on her. They had to still be cool, otherwise why would he have let her on the bus, knowing she had an expired pass? Before she could convince herself how bad of an idea it was, her feet had her moving towards his house.

Nathan answered the door with Darian in his arms. "Hey, Nathan." She kept her tone simple and not too happy. The last thing she needed was him to think she was being fake. He was tired and the boy's bib was covered with food. She'd make this quick.

"Brenda." He was confused and not thrilled to see her, otherwise he probably would have stepped aside and asked her in. Did she blame him?

"I know you haven't got any time for bullshit, Nathan, but—and I hate to ask—do you know where I can find Erica?"

He flinched and then studied her face like he was waiting for a mirage to vanish. Then he curled his mouth, like he'd been asked a question he'd been waiting to answer all day. "Come on in; let me tell you what Erica is up to." He stepped aside.

There, in his front room, he told her about the stroller Erica had been pushing, the visit to the house, the letter, her designs. "But no, I don't know where the bitch is." He paused. "Pardon my language." Why or how he could be so calm bewildered her. Maybe she'd been seeking out the wrong person. He bounced his boy on his knee.

Darian reached for her, and she held out her finger. He tugged it back and forth like it was a video game controller. He let it go, looked at her, and held out his arms. Brenda looked at Nathan. "He gets restless after he eats. Sorry."

"You look like you could use a hand," and she reached for the boy.

He looked at Darian, who squirmed. "Okay, buddy." He eased him towards her. In her arms, he was heavy and she adjusted her grip, but holding this child whose mother abandoned him warmed her in a way she assumed being able to donate lots of money to a worthy cause would. His tugging on her earring felt good.

"Sorry she bounced on you, Nathan. No man, no child deserves what she did to you all." She realized that she should have led with this. She bobbed the boy and he dove his head into her shoulder a couple times, like he was trying to break a wall. She hated that she hadn't come by sooner, and for no other reason than just to do it.

Nathan nodded. He was over talking about Erica, she could tell. She felt a pang of shame for considering that bitch for any reason, much less for advice, good or bad. She felt his pain, and why she never reached out to him—given how she'd been stuck twice before—she wished she'd known. Not just as a friend but as a member of the community. She'd been too lost in her own shit to worry about someone else's, and as she held that child to her, she could see a little relief come over Nathan's face. She could also feel something knowing in the child, like he needed someone like her to hold him.

She swung slowly towards Nathan so she could see his face better. "You know about some community programs that can help us get our houses fixed?"

"Nope."

"I got the materials back at my house. This realtor sent them to me. I'll get them to you." The boy spit up on her shoulder and she patted his back. Then it occurred to her. Sure, she could go warn Ms. Rose about all this supposed animosity towards her, but in that moment, she got a better idea. "You going to that meeting?"

His mouth open and his tongue flexed, but then he clamped his mouth shut as he watched her holding his boy. "Wasn't planning on it."

"Might be a good idea to go."

"I thought so too, but then I realized I got my hands full here, as you can see." He was too guarded. She understood that determination to go it alone because so many people had bailed on you. But she needed him, and she needed him to believe he was worth something. Because if she could convince him of this, she could convince herself. And she knew she needed that push. She thought of the campaign posters that had been spread throughout the neighborhood in 2008: Hope. She'd believed, and now she understood hope will get you over the hump, but it won't get you home. She was done with hope, with waiting. She needed to *do*, and she needed a community behind her, and if she were friends with those in the community, there was a better chance that would last. But she needed that first brick in place, and she wasn't sure if she was about to secure it or break it.

"Sounds like something Erica would say." She held her breath, bracing. The words looked like they cut through him and then doubled back to smack him through anger and then to a tinge of sadness. She was glad she was the one holding the child. "This neighborhood, this is all we got right now. We can make it work better if we do it together. We can't keep going at this shit alone."

He caressed his son's head and she could tell he was fighting back tears, but she knew he was with her. She couldn't believe for a moment that she had even considered selling her home.

14

The book Michael had been reading had a plot that was going absolutely nowhere, and he was moments from putting it down—tossing it against the wall, actually—when he found himself soldiering through. He'd already given up on the dinner he'd burned as well as the TV that lacked anything worth watching, and, to be honest, he needed something to accomplish. There, in his home, he'd already swept the basement floor, cleaned the barren refrigerator, and scrubbed the bathtub. If the empty guest bedroom closet mocked him anymore he might bash his head into the door. He turned the page, and as each word seemed to say "accident," he admitted defeat and tossed the book aside. He went to the window and lowered a blind. Dead leaves danced down the sidewalk. The mechanic said that the insurance company had decided it was better to junk the car than pay to repair it. *What did he want to do about the car?* He hadn't returned the call. He turned.

On the couch's armrest, Fitzgerald, his eight-year-old tabby, appeared bored as he watched Michael. "If I don't leave this house tonight, cat, I might never leave again." He could wash his face, find an outfit, maybe even run product through his hair. His armpits started sweating. It was, after all, Karaoke night at Voyeur--and no windows downstairs. What if Aiden showed up? He looked at his framed photos of Niagara Falls, the Eiffel Tower, the Space Needle. Near the end of the wall, dust made a square. In the middle of that square, a nail.

On the table, a candle flickered and crackled. Through a gash on the side, a river of vanilla scented wax dripped. He blew the wick out and cooled the wax. He watched as it firmed. *Fuck it*, and he went upstairs and opened his closet.

Outside, walking at a brisk clip, he reached the open French doors of the Turkish restaurant on the corner. Middle Eastern music jingled. A few people looked from their plates as he dawdled by their sidewalk tables. After a few moments, the conversations resumed. In the street, two cars slowed as they approached the intersection simultaneously. The station wagon laid on its horn. Michael flinched. After a few false starts, one car eventually crossed, followed by the station wagon, whose driver shook his head.

That little girl had nodded as she passed. I was *paying attention.* He remembered her timid smile, the wind blowing through the sun roof, the Beach Walk Yankee Candle scent wafting through the car. For a moment on that day, he'd almost forgotten how depressed he was. The conversations died again and he took his cue.

Smoking a cigarette as he stood outside the kitchen's basement door, a cook nodded to him as he passed. Did he recognize him? He flagged a cab and trotted over when it slowed.

The driver lowered his window. "13th and Locust?" He nodded and Michael got in. When the cab entered traffic, he rolled down the window and nosed closer to the fresh air whizzing by.

At the club, with his wristband freshly fastened, he breezed towards the music drifting up the felted stairwell. Someone was busy butchering a song. The tension in his neck soothed. Each step on the worn carpet released sweat, alcohol and cigarettes. His scalp tingled, thinking about how much Aiden hated that place. Everyone was going to ask about him, weren't they? Or would the accident dominate conversations? He stopped three steps from the bottom, before anyone would see him. He gripped the stair railing. He took a deep breath, counted to five, and then exhaled. He stepped down and rounded the corner. Crossing the carpet, he took an empty barstool.

"Good morning!" Frankie held a cocktail napkin.

"Hey Frankie, how are you?"

"Good, good. You?"

"Eh, you know."

Frankie squeezed his hand the way his grandmother used to when she wanted to say something but had forgotten what it was once her mouth opened. "Manhattan or a beer?" The hand stayed.

"Manhattan." Michael edged a sad twenty across the bar. Frankie drained an 8-count pour into a shaker. Michael squirmed. With his peripheral vision, he saw friends, fellow regulars—the couples who'd also been in their circle—

at the bar's end. He warmed and then shivered. He couldn't get his drink fast enough. Frankie dropped a cherry over the chilled martini glass, parked the drink in front of him, and then snagged the twenty. He slurped and the burn soothed.

On stage, Natasha introduced the next singer, who jumped on stage. Pointlessly, he flipped the pages of the song book while feeling his friends' eyes on him. Why couldn't people let these songs die? From the stage, the melody kicked in. Moments later, the singing. Clapton's ears weren't so much ringing as they were bleeding about that time. This would have sent Aiden into a tizzy. Michael would then shift in his seat and check his watch to see how much time they would be allowed to stay. He inhaled half his drink.

The night he had met Aiden, Michael got trapped by those soft hazel eyes that reminded him of a stone in one of his mother's rings. They were at Richard and Jeff's housewarming party. Aiden was a friend's plus one. With each glance, Michael filled in more of the picture: A nice charcoal Banana Republic sweater, bangs (that were just losing their highlights) slid off his eyebrows with each drink he took; a chin cleft quivered when he chuckled. When Aiden nodded to acknowledge Michael's "excuse me" on the way to the bathroom, Michael was, in a word that normally elicited an eye roll, smitten. *Always check under the hood, he could hear his father say.* Now, he wished he'd better heeded Dad's advice. *God damn you, Aiden.* He emptied his drink. Frankie grabbed the glass, swapped out the used napkin, and set down a water. He filled the shaker with some ice.

The song ended and someone new took the stage. Matty patted the exiting singer on the back as he settled into his stool. Who was that guy that just sang?

"You going to say hello?" Jeff yelled from the end of the bar. He handed a card to Natasha as she went on stage. Michael raised his glass. Jeff lifted his beer. Next to him, Richard dipped his cocktail. Couples. His heart welled up.

A Journey song started. Neither Steve Perry nor Mariah Carey would be proud.

The night Michael knew he and Aiden were done, he had peeled Aiden out of a cab. Soused to hell from Ben's party, Aiden could barely reach the front door. Inside, Michael steadied him against the couch so he could untie Aiden's shoes. After easing him out of his shirt, Michael guided him up the stairs. Aiden crawled each step. He blew chunks in the bathroom and Michael wiped the side of his face. After maneuvering him to the bed,

Michael scrubbed the hunks of pasta and jelly beans from around the toilet's base. Sprawled on the bed, Aiden had only gotten halfway out of his jeans. Aiden babbled until he passed out. Michael set a full glass of water on the nightstand and he watched Aiden breathe. Finally at peace, he looked fragile, and quieter than he had in months. How much more could the two of them take with all the fighting and the stress? Michael couldn't have imagined that Aiden's ticket out was Sean. *Him.*

Frankie presented a fresh glass. He took cash from the twenty's change. Michael slurped his drink while a girl with frizzy hair sang a song from *Wicked. Hmm, better than I expected.* His eyes drifted towards the end of the bar and noticed Jeff.

"Go say hello before she throws a cigarette at you." Frankie nodded in Jeff's direction. "Everyone misses you but doesn't know what to say. So go."

Drink in hand, he left his stool and walked to the bar's end.

"Don't say hello anymore, you bitch?" Jeff exhaled and they exchanged kisses.

Richard leaned in. "You doing okay?" He patted Michael's shoulder. His shoulders eased.

"Eh, you know." Michael set his drink in the space they'd cleared on the bar.

"Well, you're safe here." He blew smoke and sent Jeff a look. "For now." Michael's stomach knotted. "Todd was here earlier, said hi, then headed to Tavern. Said he might be back." He took a drag from his cigarette. "Thought you should know."

Great, another ex. Was he moving back from Chicago? Their eyes searched for a reaction. Michael shrugged. The girl on stage was belting out the song's end. From behind her computer at the back of the stage, Natasha waved. "Next up, Phillip," she shouted. The opening to Janet Jackson's "Just a Little While" thumped.

Aiden's one dance song. This one night, when the DJ segued into the opening guitar riff, Aiden, who avoided dancing like most people avoid the dentist, yanked Michael to the edge of the crowd. Mouthing every word, he had moved closer to him than he'd yet to do in public. His heart fluttered. Aiden watched him move, pointing at him as he sang, "*and how it feels making love to you*," as if he had written the words himself. He smiled at the end of the line and moved in for a long succession of kisses.

Those moments had proven that they could be happy. The sting was that was the best it would ever get.

Richard grabbed Michael's shoulder. "Just keep drinking, it will get better. Frankie, get the man another." Michael emptied his glass. *So much for the brakes.* A lump developed in his throat. It wouldn't be starting smoking unless he had a second, right?

Phillip finished his song and someone took the stage. Something sounding like Coldplay blared out of the speakers. Blue? Red? Yellow? Why couldn't he pick and choose what he was able to forget? As the guitar chords chugged, he could hear that little girl scream.

Richard had his hand on Michael's shoulder. "Take this seat; I have to use the bathroom." The warm cushion soothed Michael, though his body slumped.

Frankie drained a shaker into a fresh glass, then plopped in the cherry. The edges of his eyesight fuzzed. Richard was back. "Nope, keep the chair. I'll stand." Richard was looking away but Michael could feel his pity. His limbs lightened. He slurped his drink. Richard still avoided eye contact. He lit a cigarette. The end glowed bright and then gave way to ash. He wanted to touch it. Michael returned to his drink.

On stage, a new song started.

"Hello," Josh brushed his shoulder. He's the type of guy who, if his basement got a few inches of water, he was happy that his concrete floor would get cleaned. Michael smiled.

"Hey."

"How are you?"

"I've been better."

Josh shook his head somewhere between understanding and not knowing what to say. "You singing tonight?" he sucked the top off his fresh drink.

"I sang earlier." He grabbed the glass filled with matchbooks. He removed the top row, set it aside, then tipped the glass and emptied the bottom row into his palm. He alternated each book then returned them to the glass. Then the top row. He pushed the glass towards Frankie, who'd moved the glass with the pencils to the other end of the bar months ago.

Was someone singing a Ben Folds Five song? Why couldn't people let certain songs die? Dead. Was that guy still alive? Aiden. *Why haven't you tried to contact me once through this whole mess? Too busy with your head being in Sean's pillow, perhaps. Prick.* From the stage, if he heard about that fucking brick one more time he was going to hurl his drink at someone, preferably someone on stage. Why were people allowed to butcher any song they chose?

"Still with us?" Josh asked.

"Yeah, I need to piss."

Moments later, with wet hands because hand dryers suck, Michael returned to empty chairs. At the other end of the bar, Natasha was talking to the second bartender. As he sat down, his eyes settled on Josh's glass of immaculately organized matches. He wanted to throw it across the fucking room.

"You okay, honey?" Frankie was stacking clean glasses.

A Queen song on stage. Freddy Mercury would be impressed. "Yeah, can I grab a water?" He made sure his words sounded slow and crisp. His tongue was heavy.

"Sure."

As his eyes scanned the room, the walls drifted. When the sound got a little hollow, he grabbed the end of the bar. *Breathe*. Long, deliberate breaths that don't look like you are huffing. *Flashes.* His eyes followed the light, to a corner on the other end of the room, where four people, all draped around each other, smiled, packing themselves tight for the camera. When they passed the camera around to see, he wanted to rip it out of their hands and smash it.

Pressure on his left shoulder. A whiff of Curve. *Todd.*

"I thought you might be hiding here tonight." His voice bounced. *Why was he so chipper*? Michael looked to see how much his ex had changed. "Mind if I sit?" Michael hoped for a receding hair line, crow's feet and a second chin. Instead he saw a full head of thick hair, now greyer than the brown it once was, flawless skin and less puffy cheeks.

"Not my stool to offer." Michael turned.

"You're going through some shit, so I'm going to pretend you're not being a cunt."

"Yeah, what do you know?"

"Well, since I have the Internet and Facebook, I know about Aiden. Also, Richard mentioned the accident. Sorry. He said you'd been dodging people, like no one had seen or heard from you in weeks."

"I always bounce back, don't I?" Michael had come home to packed bags one day, Todd's apartment key left next to a note: "Sorry, I tried. I also can't pass up Chicago."

"At least you're not still bitter." Why was it the ones who leave who seem to be in such control of their emotions? The other bartender appeared. Where'd Frankie go? "Citron and soda." Todd set a twenty on the bar. "You know, people move on; it wasn't just me." He must have been waiting for Michael to turn towards him. He made it seem so clean, so easy. They'd had a good group of friends, a bunch of couples with whom they would alternate hosting dinners, where they'd laugh, Scattergories, swallowing wine. So what if they were at their best when they were among company? Why did they end up fighting over what brand of toilet paper to buy, whether to use Shake 'n Bake or "real" bread crumbs? When they split, the group of friends drifted, held together by the occasional Christmas card from the one couple who was still together, whose personal message shortened each year. He wondered what Aiden and Sean's Christmas card would look like. His cherry kept slipping from his fingers. Perhaps he should try the stem. "Try a straw," Todd said. The bartender delivered the drink and grabbed the twenty. Todd took his glass. Michael eyed that uncooperative damn cherry. "Stab it and you'll get it."

Michael reached for a straw. After jabbing the cherry on the first try, he plopped it into his mouth. "Thanks," he said, while chomping. He dropped the straw in the glass.

"You have to stop letting the past get in the way of your future." Todd fumbled in his pocket like he was checking for his keys. Michael gulped the rest of the drink. Todd scrolled on his phone. "Richard and everyone are at Venture. Come over with me?" Michael watched him. His button-down hung a little funny off his shoulders, like he'd bought it a size too big or lost some weight. He almost aligned it for him across his shoulders. His head was fogging.

"Who is everyone?" A little after midnight, there would be too many people.

Todd checked his phone. "Richard, Jeff, Josh, Chris…hold on… Brian, Kirsten. Oh, and look, John's gonna be there. You can talk to someone who actually has a reason to mope."

He swirled the straw in his empty glass. "The man's boyfriend was killed. You act like his dry cleaner lost his shirts."

"See, got you worked up just like that. No, seriously, maybe talking to him about what a real problem is will help you out."

"I may have killed someone, Todd. I know what a real problem is." He needed another cherry to stab.

"Look, you *may* have. You don't know what is going to happen to him. It was an accident, right? The guy wasn't wearing a helmet. These things are beyond your control. Plus, you can't tell me that Aiden is not in your head, too. I know you, and you have to be able to put it aside, at least for a night, because usually you can't. You get through one day, there'll be another." At this point, his hand rested on Michael's shoulder. Michael felt nauseous.

"Why are you trying to be so nice to me?"

"I'm not trying. Come on, finish your drink." He chugged his. "Besides, not like there's any more of your Karaoke going on." The music had stopped. At the end of the stage, Natasha was packing up her computer. She blew a kiss. When Michael turned around, Todd was by the stairs.

They stepped through the double doors into the breezy night. He nearly tripped off the bottom step. Water, he needed more water. Todd steadied him and then they walked.

"So I guess I should ask: what are you doing in town?" The night air danced on the back of his neck and pricked his forearms. His tongue felt thick.

"I came out to see my niece's little league game."

"You came to watch kids play baseball?"

"Yeah, although, half-way through, I got a little sad." Todd paused the way people do when they want to be goaded into continuing. Michael wondered if the sidewalk would be better than the cobblestones. "Yeah, so anyway, I started to feel a little sad that this would never be my life, that I would never have a kid; and I wouldn't be able to bring this child to one of these games, to cheer for him or her." Todd had always wanted kids. When a friend got pregnant, he jumped at the chance to shop for kids clothes, always spending more than most people would.

"So why can't you have kids now?"

"Being practical. When you hit your mid-thirties and aren't dating anyone seriously, odds are against it. Not something I want to do alone. And by the time I reached the right point with a partner, it would take longer than would be fair to us or the child."

"Sounds like you're making excuses for ditching a life goal." The uneven sidewalk challenged his feet to stay level.

Todd exhaled. "Look, that's not the point of the story. My point was that, at some point, the sadness passed." His hands were tucked in his pockets and he looked downright contemplative, the way he used to when he'd just finished an Oprah book selection, as if something profound had just been unloaded on him and he was forced to take stock of his life. They rounded the corner and Michael's numb limbs felt good.

"So you might as well tell me what caused the sadness to pass." The alley opened to Locust Street. Crossing, they passed U-bar, whose windows were opened and a bunch of guys crowded by the railing. Michael was sure they were talking about him and Todd. A few steps later, their chatter had merged with the cranked music escaping the windows.

"What happened here?" Todd motioned to the boarded-up Lincoln building.

"Fire gutted it. They're working on restoring it. Did your story ever reach a point?" He felt his nostrils expanding and contracting. He was a fish plucked from the water.

Clearly miffed, he continued. "Yeah, so I figured I could be bitter about not having something or I could focus on what I do have; you know, look forward instead of back." They stopped short once they hit Tavern, the kind of stop one member of a couple makes before he says "I love you" for the first time or *There's something I need to tell you.*

"And so you thought of me? How sweet."

Todd reached for Michael, who brushed past him. Somehow, Todd caught him by the upper arm.

"I thought of you because I heard about all you were going through. Since I know how you are, I figured you needed somebody to talk to. Watching Tiffany play, I realized I was doing the same thing: holding on to something I wasn't in a position to change."

"You think me having a cheating boyfriend leave me and then me maybe killing somebody is on par with you wanting to be a dad?" He looked at the fingers clutching his arm. The firm grip felt good. "Can I go now?"

"None of it is your fault, Mike. You gotta let it go, all of it." He drew him close and hugged his neck, the way he used to do when they'd be at Penn's Landing. During the summer nights when the Camden Riversharks were home, they'd wait for the fireworks over the river at the game's end. Thinking about those tucked away moments made him sad and angry, though he couldn't finger the anger that he was sure was within reach. Todd's embrace tightened and warmed his neck. His head cleared as his eyes welled up. "Dig in your heels, Michael, and don't look back. Your whole life is in front of you,

you just have to want it to be there." He kissed his neck in that loving way good friends will, and then pulled away. "Come on." He tugged him down Camac Street. Michael's head swirled.

After weaving through the smokers perched outside Tavern, they passed the dumpsters and arrived at the steps of The Venture Inn. Outside smoking, Richard and Jeff tilted their heads as they exhaled. "Everyone's inside." Jeff's eyes bounced between them. He prayed Aiden wasn't among everyone.

The place was more crowded than a bar right before closing should be. Josh was locked in conversation with Christian and James in the middle of the bar while Brian and Kirsten fussed with the corner juke box. He kept slapping her hand when she went to punch something in. People mashed against the wall to let a guy pass. Pointing to his mouth and grimacing, Ben was holding court with Jeffrey (to whom he'd just gotten married), Jared, Phillip, Jack (who was snapping pictures), and Lindsey and Julianne. He'd probably had some patient with some freaky teeth. Near the end of the cluster, flanked by a few girls—who'd probably strolled in from a bachelorette party (by the looks of their tiaras and sashes and constant picture-taking)—sat John, who picked at the label on his Hoegarrden. Slouched shoulders, heavy eyes, slow finger movements on the beer bottle label. Michael's head grew heavy.

A rush of people swooped in—Dave and Byron, Vinny, Steve Z., Stephen, Brian E., Chuck and John, Freddie, Jim G. (and his ever-present Miller Lite), Julianne and Lindsey, and Pete among them. Hugs and kisses all around. John locked eyes on Pete, focusing perhaps on the green and white striped polo and blue and white striped shorts that stopped above the knee. But more than likely something deeper. The way he wore his spiked hair or perhaps he had that same clean-cut look that John's Kevin had had the day he died, the day John held him when he breathed his last breath. Even from this many feet away, Michael saw every moment of their love returning to him. That loss strangled him. Some things you might never overcome, they will stay with you if you allow them to, and only someone who has ever truly loved can feel this. *He had to let go.* The music sounded a bit richer.

But he had to find a way to handle his guilt. He didn't want to be that guy—like John—sitting at the bar, watching, waiting for the door to open and a trigger to walk in. Any dam was bound to break if you kept enough pressure on it. He needed to find a way out of this pain, this loss, this lack of control.

"You okay?" Todd asked.

"Yeah," he said. Todd put a hand on his shoulder.

He had an art conversation once with a painter friend. She believed that certain pieces of art find you when you were ready for them, not just for appreciation but for understanding. This applied to books, music, movies, anything that has the potential to inform, to instruct, to change you. Maybe this also applied to people, whether for the first time or after a long while. They open a door for which you lacked a key.

John ripped half the label off his beer, crumpled the thin paper, then stood. He staggered towards the bathroom. Michael flagged down Henry and ordered a drink for Todd and a beer and a water for himself. The life in the room soothed.

And as he sat on that bar stool, downing the water, he didn't know that a few paces from the door, Rick was getting ready to trot through it, having no clue that he would run into Todd and Michael, and in a perfectly casual way—because he had a tendency to leave his sense (probably from the weed he'd smoke on the way out of his apartment)—say "So, how about that meeting your neighborhood is having about you in a few days?"

Michael was still some time away from responding, "What?" in part confusion and part fear. No, before all that, he was almost done with his water and had tapped his pocket and realized he had some quarters, thinking, *hmm*. By the time he'd made his way to the juke box though, he realized that these new jukeboxes had grown past quarters and only took cards or cash. But he didn't mind as he swiped his card and searched for a specific Janet Jackson song. He felt okay smiling. Would this feeling be there when he eventually crashed and woke up in his own bed?

15

Michael had left (or, stumbled from) the bar's warmth wrapped in the feeling that he was part of a community of friends who were looking to support, nurture him through any bump in one of life's roads. He'd been bathed in hugs, kisses, knowing glances and just about any other friendly gesture encouraged between people sharing the same space while imbibing copious amounts of alcohol. As Michael was learning—or, perhaps, being reminded—as he'd crawled into his bed, alone, you don't often realize just how much you've had to drink until you try to close your eyes. There, at 4:37 in the morning, the bedsheets moist from his sweat, his eyes crept open, hoping that the headache he knew would find him would relent. He kicked the comforter off. He shivered a bit, then yanked the comforter back. The pulse in his neck throbbed. He reached across the bed to the empty side and tried to recall one of the many nice things his friends had said to him but, there, alone in his bed, silence threatened to strangle him. What he wouldn't have given to have a warm body next to him to cement the idea that he was, in fact, not as alone as he felt. *455 steps, 48 houses.* He had to piss. After he returned from an erratic stream, he crashed to the pillows. He wedged his head as far in as it would go. Outside, someone dragged shoes against the sidewalk. *Pick up your damn feet.* Michael turned on his side, and the dragging faded. *Damn it.* Michael stormed to the bathroom. At the sink, he ran cold water on his face, and then looked in the mirror. Water dripped from his cheeks. He was so pale, his eyes so droopy, like that sad ugly cartoon dog whose name he couldn't remember. Hairs that were probably grey jutted out above his ears. *Fuck.* Even in the dim light of the early, early morning light filtering through the bathroom window, he looked pathetic. The longer he stared, the more his image tilted in the mirror. He hiccupped and the back of his throat retched. He stared at the toilet. Yes, this would make him feel better. He crumbled to the floor, held his head over the bowl, and jammed a finger in his throat, back and to the right. He held it there until he gagged and then up came the flow of his evening. Two quick bursts and he was done. He spit and spit and then wiped his mouth with the back of his hand. He flushed and leaned his pathetic head against the cool porcelain toilet bowl.

Before he'd ventured out, he felt like his despair would consume him, but then he willed himself out his door, and, surprisingly, he'd been shown a teasing hope; he'd allowed himself to have fun, to let the night show him a good time; smiling, he fought the guilt over this, and when his friends had reinforced his mood, he let it stand. In the cab home, he tried the smile again, testing it. *Yes, it's there; yes, it's allowed to be there.* And then he hit the bed and expected to drift right to sleep, and maybe, just maybe, he would wake up to a new day.

But, now, here he was. Square one. His tear ducts felt like cardboard. He wanted to rip the fucking mirror off the bathroom wall and scream until his vocal cords snapped. He tried to remind himself of Todd's advice, the friendly embrace, the feeling of comfort in both. *You are not alone, there are people who care about you.* Gingerly, he pushed himself up.

From the faucet he drank water. He waited a minute and drank more. There, better. His head cleared a bit. Did he have any Gatorade in the fridge? He guided himself down the stairs and then crossed the dining room into the kitchen. The whoosh of cold air from the fridge felt wonderful against his bare skin. There, on the top shelf, behind the leftover Chinese food—half a bottle of Gatorade. He gulped it down, then walked to the dining room table, pulled a chair back, and slumped into it. His eyes landed on that ceramic pot and its cluster of worthless soil. The light coming through the blinds was shining off the lacquer, as if advertising how pretty something so worthless could be.

Wait.

He leaned forward and squinted. After a moment, he swayed to his feet, stumbled to the wall, where he turned on the dimmer—too strong at first, until he lowered it to where he could open his eyes without much pain—and then crept to the pot.

He leaned over the pot; reaching out of the dirt, a little green sprout.

Life.

My God. His legs lightened as if he was cresting on a roller coaster. He eased to his knees. He'd never seen such a lush green; so bright, so thin. Little yellow in its tiny veins. How could he possibly take care of something like this? That fragile sprout begged to be ruined. His chest tightened, his jaw flexed and his eyes strained. As his heart raced, his nose itched. He wanted to thrust open his front door and scream to the entire neighborhood: look what I did! He hopelessly believed that Aiden would be impressed—he *needed* him to be impressed.

455 steps, 48 houses.

He needed fresh air, to walk. He stood.

455 steps, 48 houses.

In the bedroom, he dropped to the bed's edge. His head dipped.

455 steps, 48 houses.

What time was it? No, don't ask, don't ask.

455 steps, 48 houses.

Just fresh air.

455 steps, 48 houses.

He fished his jeans from the floor, yanked socks from the pile in the corner and laced his shoes.

455 steps, 48 houses.

Just fresh air.

On the front steps, he eyed both directions of the quiet street. His hand trembled as he moved his keys to the door lock. *Go back inside and lock the door behind you.* He locked the door and stepped down. His body turned left but his feet pulled him right.

After 111 steps, he stopped. There, on the corner, he lagged. He looked at the corner house under construction. In the pre-dawn hints of light the wood looked wet. The plastic insulation billowed in the breeze, whacking the wood frame. He breathed deeply and crossed the street. In the gutter, a McDonald's bag rustled. The street light overhead buzzed like a mosquito lamp. Aiden was probably snoring.

The quiet gnawed at him.

In the middle of the block, he stopped. He dislodged a nail from his shoe's sole and tossed it into the street. With 87 more steps covered, he leaned forward but his feet resisted. He should've turned left, back to the house. He lumbered to the right.

As he walked, the sounds of a television escaped a window he passed.

How many times had he come downstairs, having been kept awake for hours by the TV, reluctant to say a word, given the soothing effect it had on Aiden. And when he'd come down those stairs or into their old apartment front room and there, in the glow of the TV, Aiden was sprawled on the couch, his mouth open, his body jerking with the rhythm of his emphatic snoring. Calm. He wanted to crouch by him, caress his cheek, remember him this way always. He'd cover him with that ratty purple blanket that he loved. After turning off the TV, he slunk back to bed.

His block.

Sweat trickled down his sides; the waistband of his boxers chafed. Saliva collected in his mouth. After a moment he realized that his mouth was open. His legs weakened. Taking a deep breath, he slinked to the curb. What was he doing?

455 steps, 48 houses; I am almost there.

He pinched his forearm; nothing. Repeat, this time harder. Still nothing. Gazing at the lightening sky, he put his fist to his forehead and leaned into it. *Walk away.*

He looked at the houses at the mouth of the street. One had just replaced its façade—nice intricate brick-work with fresh, immaculate pointing. How long would it last? The one next to it had its paint all chipped to shit, a crack as long as the window, taped. The vacant lot across the street, strewn with trash and boasting a new realtor's sign. He needed to get away from this, all of this rebuilding. He shifted his ass and heard paper crinkling. Confused, he retrieved the folded paper in his back pocket.

He unfolded it, and then he remembered Rose. Those warm eyes. Black letters on white paper. Guess someone wasn't concerned about design:

Neighbors,

As many of you know, there has been discontent over a recent car accident involving a bicyclist. Let's assemble and discuss this as a community rather than let rumors run us into the ground. Horizons, Monday, March 14th, at 6 pm.

Not the most inviting invitation. Where was the enticing use of language? Why had they used a serif font? Not even a picture for the background? Ms. Rose. Perhaps budget was the issue. But still. Then he recalled the little girl she took by the hand once she'd canvassed the crowd. That little girl. Why did he feel like he knew her? Did she live on his street?

The paper felt so frail in his hand. Maybe he should put some time in, punch this up a bit. If this meeting was really going to make a difference, maybe he could… His heart rate rocketed. He felt that weekly pitch meeting pressure swell in his joints. He could feel the canker sore forming on the inside of his lip. Could he find Ms. Rose somehow and put a stop to it? God, what should he do? For once in his life, sitting still and waiting for it to happen seemed like the wrong choice. He looked across the street. He'd lost track of how many steps he had left. He took a deep breath and clinched his fists until the threatening tears receded.

Pulling himself up, he sulked towards home. What would he have done at their door anyway?

He walked and walked. His feet stopped. The park's blazing lights.

At the park's fence, he jostled the sign hanging to the side. Water had bled the letters. "Stay off the germinating grass seeds. They are very vulnerable now and need time to root, grow into the park grass you will love." *Germinating.* Right there, teasing someone to trounce them while they got their shit together in public view. He took two deep breaths.

Aiden.

He moved his fingers and the sign swayed. *Look at the life waiting to flourish in that park.* To his left, on the block that hugged the park, a house was decaying; the windows slanted, the wood frames rotted out, the steps to the front door busted. Running his tongue over his teeth, he turned. He needed to get back inside.

As he walked, he heard his friend Elizabeth's advice: "Rebuild you from the inside out." Aiden wouldn't be there to see how it ended. What he wouldn't have given to make him smile again, and more than anything else, the fact that after everything this still mattered to him sunk him deeper into despair. *When will I get back on my feet and stay there*? Then he wondered about the guy he'd hit. *How was he doing*?

• • •

Back home in bed and again undressed, he counted the dots in the drop ceiling. He squeezed his eyelids shut. Turning on his stomach, he waited, then shifted to his side, counted to 20, then turned over. He took two deep breaths and tried to zero his mind. He could feel Aiden's hand on his bare skin, kneading his shoulders. He did this during his crazy weeks at the agency. He opened his eyes.

When the clock's 3 blinked into a 4, he turned away.

455 steps, 48 houses.

Outside, the sky was surrendering to a shade of purple. He needed to do something.

He walked to the empty front room. On the side table, Milton's business card.

Michael remembered Milton's eyes, the invitation. He looked at the clock and then out the window. *No.*

In the bedroom, Michael opened his closet. From the thick wood hangers hung his dress shirts, slacks and jeans. He shifted the hangers until he reached the Brooks Brothers jacket, Aiden's Christmas present. He rubbed its lapel. *Christmas.* Aiden's domain. Their place always looked like Santa's workshop had exploded. He chided him, but was the first to hang a bulb on a tree branch. On the last hanger, a tie, one his mother had bought him. When he asked her to stop buying him underwear, she'd moved on to ties.

When's the last time he'd tied a double Windsor knot?

Standing in front of the closet door mirror, his fingers sweat. Big end over thin end. Wide end up through the loop and flop over. *Breathe.* Throw over end again then through the loop again, tuck and that should be… something that looked like what a clown would do to a handkerchief. He looked at himself in the mirror. One more time.

He yanked it apart. Again. Big end over the thin end. Now, pull the big end up through the loop and tighten it; slide it, flip it over the thin end again and pull it back through the loop. Throw it over again, bring through the loop like that, tuck under the loop, straighten it a bit and snug it to the neck.

He'd taught himself to tie that knot. That's what you wear if you want to get ahead, he remembered thinking, seeing some suit wear it in a magazine. Hours and hours he spent in high school, following diagrams, perfecting the tightening (not too tight because that shrunk the knot), the positioning (perfectly centered), tugging the bottom to give it the perfect length. On his second ad agency interview, the top manager said, "Nice tie." He got hired the next day.

Now he was 31 and he couldn't tie a tie.

455 steps, 48 houses.

Outside, blue encroached on the sky's purple. He needed to see that sunrise, to appreciate a fresh, clean start. He'd always forgotten about his roof deck. "Who wants to sit up there and get eaten alive?" Aiden had always whined.

He made sure the door wasn't locked as he closed it.

Up there, the air was lighter. The breeze soothed his nerves, though he hadn't felt goose bumps like that in a while. That damn tie still dangled from his neck. If anyone peered out their windows, they'd see an idiot outside in a t-shirt, boxers and half-assed knotted tie around his neck standing on the roof.

Look at that sky.

His eyes swept the neighborhood buildings. All shades drawn. His eyes skipped the new properties in their odd perfection and studied the chipped paint and sagging bricks on the ones that haven't had a chance to catch up. All decay, waiting to infect the beauty around it. But damn if those refreshed properties weren't giving it their best shot.

He trotted back inside. There had to be something he could do—something positive for a change. His thoughts overwhelmed him. Maybe he was too tired to think this much. He walked to the computer, to the side table next to it. The folded flyer rested. He opened it and tacked it to the wall. He smoothed it over and stared at it, waiting for it to confirm something. He took deep breaths and stared, as if it were one of those obnoxious prints from the nineties, the ones that formed an image if you looked long enough. He looked into the dining room. *That little plant.* Would a plastic bag carry that well enough? He scoured his cabinets and drawers until he found one. Before scooping up the pot, he yanked off the tie. He should probably put pants on too.

16

The ventilator beeped, whooshed. Occasionally, if Carol were lucky, a sole would squeak in the hallway outside the hospital room. Whispers of conversations trailed by the door, only to evaporate in moments. Pricks of light pierced the beige curtains. Carol's crowded toes tingled. On the side of her big toe, a blister teased. She slipped off her shoe, let it fall, then stared at the pristine polished floor, considered her bare foot, and then tucked it under her thigh. Outside, a confused fly battered the window, as if it were escaping a predator. She put her hand to the glass, and the fly pulled away, hovered by her fingers, then dove for the corner and smacked the glass.

She scooted her heavy chair across the floor until, at Geoffrey's bedside, she could hold his hand without much effort. His fingers felt like wet, deflated balloons. Watching his chest swell and cave, she wondered how, with all that technology flowing to and from his body, he could appear so at peace. Was he dreaming? As a boy, sleeping in a bed for the first time, he flailed out his hands as far as they would go, searching his new environment, his body stationary. Standing by the dim nightlight watching her only child, she knew, somehow, that this child would forever test his limits. Was his hand cold or it was hers? What she wouldn't give for him to open his eyes. Or would she? She'd read the chart, knew the statistics, had consulted doctor friends of theirs, who, in well meaning, tentative voices, confirmed her fears. It had been six days. She squeezed.

"Geoffrey, can you hear me?" Her skin looked ghostly white gripping her son's hand. She eased her fingers and felt the blood flow return.

On the crowded side table, the flowers drooped but she could see the water was clear. Among them, Sherri's tulips, along with a little card promising to "Be there soon." *Mason.* Still, the flowers were pleasant, even if they would be gone soon. She nudged a limp petal.

"Good morning." Carol wondered why she hadn't heard the squeak of the rubber soles skidding on the floor. The nurse examined the chart in his hands, then checked the fluid in the IV before jotting notes. "Were you comfortable last night, Mrs. Stevenson?"

"Comfortable enough." She turned to the window. This nurse's comportment reminded her too much of her son. This nurse's hair was cleanly managed the way she'd wished Geoffrey's had been; taut chocolate skin, wrinkle-free; that smile, full of white teeth just like Geoffrey's; his shoulders, broad. Geoff, in that bed, broken. Her hand trembled when she brought it to her mouth. "Are there any changes today?" She turned to find the man's eyes, for the doctors avoided hers, and she would not let this one handle her as if she were a fragile dolt.

"When the doctor arrives, she can provide you with a more detailed work-up, but I don't see a change."

The nurse's words blanketed her. Carol remembered when she and Mason met Geoffrey's second grade teacher. At that back-to-school event, "ordinary" was how that woman described her son. Carol chaffed at that woman's obvious ineptitude. This nurse, handling her son's vitals so casually, smiled with such distanced concern she wanted to shake him.

"I'm sure at least someone else has recommended this, Mrs. Stevenson, but perhaps fresh air might do you good. His condition is not likely to change in the immediate future." His soft tone grated.

A walk? Does she really look like someone who *strolls*? And where would she walk around here? Better to drive. The sky was lightening. The buildings appeared slopped in places: struggling sadness. In the window's reflection, she tensed at the nurse's blank expression. She wanted to scream. Couldn't someone look alive for once? Had he brought any life into this world; cultivated it, nurtured it, then watched it stumble as well as thrive in the world; shedding old skin in favor of new, exploring interests at the expense of past loves? She strained her ears until she could hear his slow, patient breathing. She grabbed her purse.

In the elevator she fanned herself. Her hands trembled; her feet twitched. Her eyes teared when she blinked. How was she supposed to drive in this condition? When his eyes finally opened and her first moment of joy passed, how long would it take to learn the cost of his consciousness? Did she want him back whether or not he was a shadow of the man he was? To what degree would his personality be distorted? What strength of will could she muster to watch him suffer, to learn to walk, speak again. Would he ever regain the ability to care for himself, smile at a picture, read a book? This was not vanity. Sympathy, sympathy for her son, she told herself, for she would care for him until the end of days. But what happened when her time ran out? She would not raise a vegetable just so she could have him near.

Years ago, Natalie's two children had been in a wreck. Nick was killed instantly; Samantha lingered for months in the hospital, her body twisted in ways a child's never should be. At the time, Carol recalled thinking that Natalie was lucky to have had one survive so she could nourish hope, a hope that her child would live again—whatever the price, your child's life was to be cherished at whatever cost. But little, joyful Samantha succumbed to her injuries and Natalie crumbled.

Seeing Geoffrey surrounded with all that technology, she did not reach for hope right away. Sorrow would recede in time--maybe; seeing him suffer for a lifetime would destroy every step of every day. Today she was strong enough to know that sometimes if you love something you must set it free; and tomorrow? The elevator doors parted to an insulting, quick ping. Carol took a deep breath. Sherri would arrive soon, land with her cheer and her hope. Mason pestered her with his lawsuit fantasy but he didn't ask if he should reach out to Sherri?

In the still lobby, a floor polisher hummed an obnoxiously cheery tune as he maneuvered his cumbersome machine. Her rubbery legs wobbled. Would walking steady her trembling feet? The front doors opened to the crisp morning. She cinched in her coat. Her chin quivered. There would be no driving, but she would be a fool to bring her purse. She walked towards the parking garage. Coffee beckoned, so she took a ten from her wallet before putting it back into her purse, which she secured in the trunk. She set the car's alarm and tucked her cell phone in her coat. On the sidewalk, she felt a light breeze, then a cyclist raced past her. *Geoffrey.* Her right leg went numb. Against a tree she braced herself. The limbs over her head were sprouting buds. In-between deep breaths, she studied these infant leaves. Their pale colors needed the constant summer sun soon. She should have nestled behind the wheel of her car, locked the door, and screamed her head off. In a vacant garage—and with her car's padded interior—who would have heard her? Enough, she told herself, and she straightened her coat.

In a 7-11 two blocks away, the eight coffee warmers overwhelmed her. Behind the counter, an Indian gentleman paced. Each pot filled with coffee so thick it looked like Jell-O when it swished. She grabbed a bottled water from a cooler and approached the counter.

"The coffee is fresh, Ma'am, don't worry. It's good."

Carol looked over her shoulder. Steam rose from a few of the coffee pots. "Fine, but just the water, thank you."

"Are you sure, you should have some of our coffee. It is very good, I promise."

She handed him her crisp ten.

Back outside, she remembered the days she and Sherri would run to the corner store. The drug dealers tipped their hat to them on their way home. She couldn't remember their faces, or how she knew what they did when she was so young, but she could still hear the broken glass crunching under her saddle shoes. She could've done without these memories.

At the corner, the light turned red. While it remained red for what seemed an eternity, the silence ate at her. In the intersection, the cracked asphalt was pocked with shades of grey. She imagined Geoffrey sprawled there, his blood seeping into the asphalt's pores. The light changed. She checked traffic both ways and charged across the street. When she reached the curb, she checked the street sign. She was headed towards Geoffrey's apartment. Her mouth dried, she gritted her teeth, and then walked forward. Why had she listened to the inner voice that allowed Mason to go home? Where was the strength that she had cultivated for years?

• • •

She had accepted her college roommate Gwen's invitation to accompany her to the Whitney M. Young Memorial Conference. At that point in her college career, she had been driven to pursue any and all opportunities to maximize her chances for professional success. And although she was still undecided about what shape her professional life would take, she understood that whatever it was would then determine her personal satisfaction. She'd grown up among people who had settled in life, opted for a humble life in a "humble" neighborhood, and given all the trappings that accompanied such a decision—the crime, the scraping by—she was reaching beyond the life she thought she had perceived around her. So, in order to nudge her further down one particular professional path, what better way to enjoy an evening than networking with Wharton students who might become her classmates should she decide to enter their business program. As she walked into the downtown hotel ballroom, she'd hoped the evening might decide for her whether a law degree or an MBA would suit her vision for her future. Given the members of this particular group were also African Americans, she felt she would pick up professional pointers for moving in the professional world from some of her own, some of her *refined* own. This reasoning she kept from Gwen—she knew it would sound far too conceited. Raised on the Main Line, Gwen would not understand what it was like to grow up feeling cheated, but not one to make excuses, Carol understood that in order to get ahead you needed luck, but fortune favors the prepared, and mingling here brought her into the proper orbit. Perhaps foolishly—she would later understand—she believed that in order to evolve as a person in this world, she would have to abandon her past and all that it had entailed. The first layer she would shed would be any association with the neighborhood that had raised her, and she had prepared conversation changers should the question of her home arise.

Scanning the crowd, she knew immediately the man who would be her ticket. As if he had stepped out of a movie screen, the man she would soon know as Mason Stevenson crossed the ballroom floor, and in his wake, his Billy Dee Williams smile lingered. His immaculately pressed shirt collar jutted out from his crisp suit jacket; his glasses reflected the chandelier lights. He nodded as he passed her. He commanded the air around him, and she knew this was the man she needed to meet. Eventually working the room towards him, she waited for a pause in his conversation. She shifted one way, then dipped another to catch his gaze, for he seemed to want to look everywhere but at her. The other two men left.

When they were left alone, she spoke. "Is that a lack-of-control issue with your eyes or would you rather have someone else standing in front of you?" Her glass of wine was sweating for both of them.

"What's that," he said, chuckling in a condescending way. Finally, he met her gaze. Were it a handshake, it would have been limp.

"You haven't even given me a chance to fail to impress you."

"I am sorry, Miss…?" He prolonged the last "s" and the charm rose in his face, softened his dazzling brown eyes and colored his delicate milk chocolate cheeks.

"Jones, Carol Irene Jones." Like most people, she rarely used her full name, but hoped the amount of syllables would impress the blue blood she sensed in his veins. Clearly, his name ended with a III or a IV.

"Well, Miss Carol Irene Jones, what brings you here tonight? I mean, besides the organization itself? Any particular speaker? Simply networking like the rest of us?"

"I was hoping to be swayed between a business or law degree. Either one would do."

"And what would you do with a law degree, Miss Jones?" His attention hardened.

"Work for the public defender's office, perhaps."

He chuckled. "Why invest all of that time and money into a career that won't support you? At least not in the way that a lady like you should be." In his eyes, she felt secure, safe. In that moment, she sensed the dawn of her future, and what better luck than encountering an opportunity that would also please her? Casually, their conversation touched on the arts, conservative politics, and fine wine—waking next to this man every morning for the rest of her life would not be the chore she had prepared herself to endure. Yes, they would be a true team, and given his business background, they would need balance. After she graduated law school, she accepted a position at a private firm. After a few years, she entertained the idea of availing herself once a quarter to the community center near her old neighborhood. She would be a beacon of hope for others, she told herself, oblivious to the fact that those who benefitted from her free legal advice and occasional representation recognized how she looked down on them from her privileged position, but accepted her as a necessary evil, one required to help them navigate a system so heavily stacked against them.

Now, walking these neighborhood blocks, that driven, determined young woman seemed very far from her. How much of what she was seeing on these streets was truly new and how much revealed to her for the first time? The barred windows—disappeared. Where once a jazz club sat, now a coffee shop. Here she stopped. Those great big windows would have begged to be smashed when she was a child. She stepped closer. Inside, a young woman was casually lining coffee cups behind the counter. The sign on the door said she had ten minutes until they opened. Should she knock? She walked. At the corner of 22nd street, she slowed.

Geoffrey's apartment was on the second floor of one of these row homes, only down a few blocks. She had the address correct, yes? What would she do when she reached his door?

The sky brightened. Her eyes traced the rooflines. The gutters appeared clutter-free. When she was a kid, they were usually so clogged that the rain created waterfalls from them. Perhaps the trees had nothing yet to shed, nothing to clutter the ground. She looked left. Didn't a store used to be there, the one where she and her friends would run to after school and buy gum with their allowance? My, condos now, by the looks of the realtor's sign swinging in the breeze along the new stone façade.

Hadn't she seen that stone work on a neighbor's house? Those angular stones layered, looking like late night TV static. In this neighborhood, people used to fix their facades with paint. Why spend the money re-pointing the grout when you can coat with paint cheaper? When the molding by your roof line was no longer sealed, why have someone strip it down, seal it up? Nothing a little plastic siding wouldn't fix. Now, those quick, functional but ugly fixes had been removed and the ornate, original wood workings restored. Had they always looked so glorious?

Geoffrey had noticed. You had probably read up on this neighborhood's past and realized what was hidden, waiting to be restored. Did you watch people strip that junk, like you used to watch the dryer being emptied so you could inspect the drum for surrendered change? She imagined him on those sidewalks, watching crews restore life.

Life.

She reached Geoffrey's block.

In the sky, purple was giving way to blue in patches. She faced his row home, his apartment. When she'd heard the address, an image of the street flooded to her. Standing there, she must have looked like a street person, but her feet wouldn't move.

Shondra had lived on this block. Head-strong, always-looking-for-a-fight Shondra. Once she became pregnant, she'd dropped out of high school. Although Carol couldn't comprehend wanting a child at their age, Shondra beamed. "What else am I gonna do?" she said, stroking her stomach with all the hope that carrying a child can bring. Of course, she believed the father would help care for the child, and her. Carol cut off all communication from her long-time friend, as if she had been harboring a deadly communicable disease.

She remembered all the notes they used to pass to one another in algebra, the times they studied for their *A Tale of Two Cities* exam, the days they would skip their PE class because they didn't want to undress in front of their peers. Improvising on her grandmother's recipe, Shondra mixed a mean egg nog. Egg nog to which, during holiday parties, they helped themselves, sipping, giggling, and mimicking badly the gestures of the adults around them. During the holidays, her parents allowed this. Why they let 14-year olds imbibe alcohol was beyond her, but now she understood that they simply trusted their kids not to get out of hand. She could feel that moment now, the honey-baked ham smell filling that house; the taste of sugar cookies as she nibbled on them in the kitchen, lightheaded from the egg nog; the sounds of Marvin Gaye's "I Want to Come Home for Christmas" playing on the record player, the vinyl crackling as the song faded. She hadn't lived those joys in decades, and as these memories found her, they felt awkward. Strange how those moments had been lost to a time she'd felt had been plagued by longing and despair. Why had she not allowed herself to lean on these moments rather than the ones that sent her fleeing? *Shondra, how could I have ever shut you out?*

Shondra, were you able to escape this place the way I did?

Fingering the keys on her ring, she was relieved to know that she had added Geoffrey's spare, the one he'd sent, along with a note that said, "just in case." In his home, would she smell him when she entered? She approached the front steps. In the lock, the key turned too easily. The stained carpeted stairs led her to the second story landing and the sole door. That lock also turned too easily. The door hinges creaked; hollow air beckoned her. She crossed the threshold and closed the door. The latch settling echoed in the stillness. She flipped a switch, and the light blasted the white walls. Underneath the permeating musty grime, she detected his cologne. Her lips quivered.

Across a ratty couch a thin folded blanket was draped. A glass coffee table, covered in design magazines, gleamed. In the corner, his desk; on the top shelf, a pencil holder stocked with tall pencils. To her right, a kitchen with a dirty glass in the sink. To her left, a closed door. His bedroom? She touched that cold wood door, lacquered with coats and coats of white paint, waiting for a pulse. Her hand dropped. She turned. Where was his television? Where it should've been, a framed Ansel Adams print.

Growing up, he'd lined the tops of his bookcases with his basketball trophies. On his floor, a few weeks' worth of laundry. Rap posters tacked into their beautiful wallpaper. The stereo always playing. The video game system paused until a friend arrived to begin the newly discovered level. That black desk lamp on while he studied. Before bed, he'd be hunched over his desk, scribbling away, so engrossed in his studies he didn't even notice she was watching.

When did *this* become his taste? She looked at the worn carpet under her shoes.

On the wall next to the desk, on the bulletin board, pictures. She crouched. Decrepit buildings, vacant lots, decayed concrete sidewalks. This neighborhood, no doubt.

She stepped closer to the desk. On the hutch, a framed family picture. When was that taken? Her hand hovered over the finger print smudges on the closed laptop. Her throat tightened.

Next to the computer, a composition notebook. She flipped through its pages crusted in black ink scribbling, the pages crinkling as they shifted. Street corners penned with trees in the median, boxes near the stop lights. Next to these boxes, in impeccable letters "solar powered trash compactors." She flipped. Multi-storied buildings. On the ground floor, businesses. Above, housing with terraces and plants and seating. On top, penthouses? He even drew someone walking a dog down the sidewalk. She flipped. Buildings, houses, streets, sidewalks, crosswalks, trashcans, people. She closed the book. This is what became of the imagination that used to sketch comic book characters over his textbook covers.

What would you think of all the chatter in the papers about you, the ones your father probably thinks I haven't seen? Would you slough it off, taking a nod from your grandmother's book, that old tired yarn that "this too shall pass"? Will the glass still appear half full when you see your scarred face in the mirror? Will you understand hope in the same way when you attempt to recall words you once knew but can no longer articulate?

She heard something—feet maybe, dragging on carpet, coming from behind the closed door. Carol stepped against the wall. Why hadn't Geoffrey mentioned a roommate? The door opened a crack. Through the dark, a pair of eyes.

"Hello?" A weary voice asked.

"Hello. My son lives here. And you are?"

The labored breathing of someone just roused from sleep. The door swung. Dressed in a U Penn t-shirt and gym shorts, out stepped a broad shouldered man with tightly cropped dark hair and lovely milky brown skin that almost glistened in the early morning light. “Hi, Mrs. Stevenson,” the voice half-whispered, in a strange, apologetic tone. She almost corrected this young man for using her husband’s last name. There was something so defeated in this young man that she resisted walking in and hugging him.

“I’m sorry to have woken you. I didn’t know Geoffrey had a roommate.”

“Huh? Oh, a roommate…” he eyed the floor and then stretched his arms. “Yeah, roommate.” His sapphire eyes swimming in bloodshot puffy eye sockets, he wore sadness as if it were a belt cinched too tightly. He’d visited the hospital but hadn’t been let into Geoffrey’s room. Only immediate family. Without introducing himself, to her relief, he breezed past the closed door. Standing in front of her now, he was dressed in a shirt entirely too small for his bulky frame. As she stared at it, she slowly realized it was much better suited to someone of Geoffrey’s body.

“How is he?” His strained voice cracked to the point of breaking.

She blinked several times, as if a mirage were speaking to her, the words coming in slow drones. “The same.” She reached for the desk chair and fussed with the swiveling until she steadied it. She sat.

“I know you don’t know who I am, Mrs. Stevenson. I’m Ty. Geoffrey gave me a key last weekend, so I’ve been…” He searched the apartment for something. “Yeah, I don’t know. I came here last night.” His voice evaporated.

“I see.”

They stared at one another and Carol could feel the seconds pricking her neck like persistent bee stings. Her hands trembled in her lap. Before she knew it, her legs had her standing. “I’m sorry I intruded here. I will see myself out.” She was descending the stairs and outside before she caught her breath. On the sidewalk, her heart pummeled her ribcage. Her lips quivered, her eyes twitched. She saw a park. She stumbled in that direction.

Towards the wood fence comprised of only a few posts and a few beams, she slowed. Beyond the oddly damp fence, grass sprouted in clumps here and there through the dark dirt; trees, their thin trunks with gangly pitches to them, still nurtured by their water bags. She walked through the opening at the fence’s corner and slumped on a bench, where the concrete sidewalk met the grass. Still with a view of Geoffrey’s apartment, she wondered if that man would leave. *How couldn’t I have known?*

She remembered sitting through all those basketball games, the girls he took to formal dances. *What sign had I missed? Or had he purposely hidden every clue from me?* She pictured those broad shoulders and that stunning silky smooth skin filling out her son's shirt.

A white man shuffled past her, and she flinched. He gazed at her and then turned away. Since he looked as if he'd slept in the wrinkly button down shirt he wore, he was probably leaving a night of drugs. But what was in that plastic bag? He stopped, turned, and crept towards her bench. She was glad she'd locked up her purse. The breeze cooled her neck and her hands trembled. Looming in front of her, he bit his lip like a child with something to say. His weak eyes told her he meant no harm, though she would've moved if she could've felt her legs. Why, today of all days, was she forced to deal with this?

"Uh, hello, Ms. Do you know anything about this park?"

She blinked, and as she did, she felt the panic in her recede. That soft tone, those sad bags under his eyes. This poor soul was too wounded to harm her. Though, as his question registered, she felt herself bristle. Did she look like someone who would know anything about this park? She took a deep breath and tried to ease her accelerated heartrate. "Excuse me?"

"This park. They've had signs up for a few weeks now, telling people to keep off the grass, and, well, I... I just wasn't sure if they had some sort of, you know, community watchdog group watching over the park to make sure nobody damages it." His gaze went in all directions. Geoffrey had that same look when he'd needed a ride to the mall.

She examined the park. The wrought iron light posts gleamed like they had just been installed. At her feet, trampled young grass. "What would somebody possibly do in a park in this condition, son? There's nothing here yet to damage." Still, this wonderfully open, virgin space was an improvement from the dilapidated homes that had pocked this corner when she was a child. She imagined Geoffrey sitting on that very bench, sketching, dreaming.

The plastic bag rustled as it swayed. The man's weary eyes floated on her. Why couldn't he see that she was in no mood for conversation?

"I...I don't know." Sadness oozed into his voice.

She followed his eyes to the ground, and there, on closer inspection, she noticed the white mesh underneath the little sprouts of grass. After clearing her throat, she asked, "How many people came together to make this happen?" She imagined Geoffrey canvassing the neighborhood, collecting signatures needed to get the shells cleared, the land designated. His sweat, that smile, her Geoffrey.

"Oh, I ah, I don't really know. They had a block party yesterday to dedicate it. The land had been cleared when I moved in a year and a half ago."

She counted the benches that lined the perimeter. She would've loved something like this as a child. A place to run free, the sun shining on her as she tackled her friends, rolling in the grass, no threat of approaching cars. Cars. *Oh, Geoffrey.*

"Are you okay, Ma'am?"

"I'm fine, it's just been a tremendously difficult week." She cleared her eyes. "You, you wouldn't happen to have a handkerchief, would you? A Kleenex, perhaps?" This public display to a total stranger embarrassed her.

"No, I'm sorry, I don't." His voice dipped. His hands patted his pockets.

"Thank you anyway." She pictured the fresh pack resting in the bottom of her purse.

"Well, Ma'am, I hope I'm not being rude, but what are you doing here at this hour if you're not watching the park? You don't look like you live around here."

That strange mix of compliment and insult frustrated her in a way she couldn't explain. Did Geoffrey look like a resident? Would she have said something like that before Geoffrey's accident? "No, I don't live here… I mean, I grew up… My son lives here. He was in an accident. He's in the hospital, and I needed fresh air." She made it sound so easy, so… voluntary. She wanted to chuckle at the absurdity of it all, this morning, this late hour. *Would Mason appreciate this story?*

"Fresh air, yeah, I know the feeling." Setting the bag down, he sat just short of her personal space, though she didn't move.

She could feel the warmth in that man. "My son was in a bicycle accident, hit by a car 6 days ago."

"Oh." His face's color disappeared, and his sympathy comforted her for a moment, although why she felt compelled to share these personal details with a complete stranger, she wasn't sure. Perhaps her honesty might compel him to go on his way and leave her in peace. He looked skyward and seemed to be catching his breath. "Sorry to hear that," he continued, his eyes floated towards her. "What… What happened? If… if you don't mind me asking."

"He apparently ran a stop sign on his bike and hit a car."

A little light returned to his eyes. "Is he going to be okay?"

She should have anticipated this logical follow-up but it still caught her by surprise. She took a deep breath and forced air over her tongue. "They don't know."

"I'm sorry." His hand lifted from his thigh, trembled a bit—was he thinking of reaching his hand to hers?—and collapsed again.

She leaned back, disappointed at the only sensible thing he could say, although it felt so hollow, so inadequate. When had being sorry every helped anyone? "Yes, I'm sorry, too."

"Some people are talking about the accident—your son. They're thinking the driver—I guess he is white." He paused and kicked dirt with his feet. Did he think she was blaming him or white people in general? He thrust his hands together. "Some are worried it could turn into another Grays Ferry riot."

Her jaw slacked. "The Grays Ferry riot?" She'd read about that deplorable display of violence that had cemented her reasons for leaving this neighborhood behind. "Those had something to do with white folks attacking a black family. What would that have to do with what happened to my son?"

He stared at her. He blinked, and in a soft voice said, "I don't know; all I know is that people are talking."

In the sky the sun was removing the purple and bathing the horizon in white. She had never noticed that the white came before the blue when the sun rose. She pictured Geoffrey, motionless in his hospital bed, listening to what this man was saying. *Of all people, you at the center of racial discontent. Return from whatever abyss keeps you at bay; summon your strength so that at the very least you can wake and dispel this negativity brewing on your behalf. Don't let this be your legacy.* When her mind lingered on "legacy," she closed her eyes.

"Are you all right, Miss?"

This man was too young to have grown children and therefore couldn't experience the breadth of what was disintegrating within her. She cupped her face in her hands. She breathed. She turned and opened her eyes. "May I ask what you have in there?"

He tensed. Apparently, she'd asked the wrong question. "It's ah, it's... well, it's a plant a friend gave me that has just started to sprout." His voice trailed into shame.

She fought the inclination to hug him like the mother she knew he needed. Like Geoffrey needed. Words raced to her mouth. "Son, why are you carrying around a plant at this hour?"

"Well..." A nervous chuckle. While glancing at his bag, he swished his jaw. "I know this sounds crazy, but I thought I would plant it in this park."

She pictured Geoffrey standing before her, years ago, in the kitchen, his eyes swollen from tears, while she asked him why he'd let his friends steal from the drug store, getting them all in trouble.

"I don't know, Mama, I just thought that was what friends did," Geoffrey stammered. She stood, a mix of anger, at the juvenile crime that would be forgotten quickly, and sadness, because it was the first time she'd seen her son fail. She had to watch the pain collect in him.

Now, sitting on that bench, she almost cried. Had she let him fail in all the right ways? Here and there, with the coming light, she noticed more trampled sections of the grass. Would it ever fill in? She thought about their own immaculate lawn. Had they ever enjoyed it? This grass, would anyone ever care what it looked like, or would they be content just to have it there? She imagined neighbors mingling, smiling, having conversations that backyard fences would have rendered impossible. *This is what you see, isn't it Geoffrey?* Imperfect beauty.

"Son, why are you planting something in this space?"

"Once it started sprouting, I guess I worried that I wouldn't be able to care for it properly, that maybe it would do better if it were out in the open." His voice saddened inappropriately for plant talk. He stared into nothing. "I guess it's easier to care for something if you're not the one responsible for it. Besides, I guess I wanted to add something to this neighborhood. I know it sounds crazy, but the thought just occurred to me when I couldn't sleep. I need to feel a part of something, you know?" He removed the plant from the bag. Three young, fragile leaves surrounded by dark soil. She looked at him, perhaps searching for comfort of her own, but his heavy eyes were fixed on his plant.

She'd hit a spot in him she didn't care to touch deeper. "Where were you thinking of putting it?"

"Uh, I hadn't gotten that far." He picked at the space between his teeth. As a boy, Geoffrey did this, when she had given him permission to select a toy. His eyes danced over the possibilities in front of him, reluctant to commit. "I guess I should put it out of the way, maybe..." He paused. "Uh, maybe in that corner over there, by that middle post of the fence?"

"Why there?" she asked. With his slumped shoulders, she felt he needed to be able to articulate it. Most of all, though, she wanted to smooth back the hair dropping in his eyes.

"Well, that way it can be in the park without people stepping on it. Tucked away, it could be something people would have to work to discover."

She chuckled before she could quell the urge. Should she apologize? "Sounds like a lot of thought for a plant." His eyes dipped and she felt the sting. This was obviously not about the plant. But she would not intrude on his wounds. "But a good plan, nonetheless." As he exhaled softly, the corners of his mouth raised. She scanned the area. There, near the neighbor's house, by the circuit breaker box, close enough to that young tree but not too close to get drowned in what will become its shade. She pointed in that direction. "How about over there?"

His eyes followed her finger and he nodded. Once he stood and turned, he extended his hand, as if assisting her. She stared at his hands, which just then she noticed were well manicured and smooth. "Oh no, son, I'll watch." The light in the sky brightened. "I don't suppose you brought something to dig with?" He examined the bag for the tool she knew wasn't there. He frowned. "Don't worry, this ground looks so fresh that I can't imagine you'll have a difficult time using your hands."

He strolled, and when he reached that corner, she gazed at Geoffrey's apartment. The light had gone out in the front window. Her chin slumped. Turning, she saw that he'd found the spot. Crouching, he cradled the potted plant. He glanced at Carol, who nodded.

After putting the pot to his side, he thrust his finger into the earth. He extracted chunks at a time. Then, turning his pot upside down, he freed his little plant. He eased it into the hole. Filling the dirt around it, he tapped the perimeter. He stared at it for a moment before standing and then dusting his hands. He backed away a few paces before walking towards her bench. Geoffrey would've approved, that much she knew. She smiled. When he got close enough, she said, "You might want to water it. Give it a good drink, especially the ground around it, but not a drowning, and then maybe return to water it again for the next few days. It will need a chance to acclimate to the surrounding soil."

"Thank you very much, Miss." His smile beamed. "You seem to know a lot about planting."

She turned this over in her mind. She thought of her mother. "My mother loved to garden, my mother and my sister both. Perhaps I picked up more than I remembered." She'd never understood why they'd enjoyed getting their hands dirty. For a moment, she regretted not working the earth with him.

Extending his hand, he said, "My name is Michael. Thank you, Miss…?"

She met his hand "Carol Jones." They shook, and as he held it his lips quivered and parted. She could almost see the breath being drawn towards his vocal cords. She knew better than anyone when someone teetered close to a confession but his lips closed. She gave him another moment, their eyes probing one another. She cleared her throat. "Now, about that water."

"Yes, well, thank you again. And… I am so sorry about your son." He looked towards the distant plant and she could have sworn his eyes were misting. "Well…" he studied his hands and his thumb worked the dirt into his palm, which he closed his fingers on. "Yeah." He nodded before leaving. Reaching the street, he hurried across. Was he really returning with that water? She felt some grit on her hand. Examining the dirt there now, she rubbed it between her fingers.

More light invaded the sky. *Geoffrey.* She wished the light in his apartment had come back on. It was all she could do to keep from running back, mounting the stairs and opening that front door. She breathed. Standing, she walked towards the street. Maybe she should stroll down her old block. A car's engine turned. Where would someone be going at this hour on a Sunday? She crossed.

After walking a few minutes, she had reached her block. Passing house after house, she noted that almost all of the homes had had the paint stripped from their facades; their brick, restored; their brick pointing, sharp. The sidewalks, free of trash, boasted concrete that appeared mostly freshly poured. Was that a restaurant on the corner? Cars, new or mostly new. And there it was. She slowed.

With her gritty fingers, she grazed the old red bricks. They prickled her fingertips. The mortar though was new; crisp, grayish; she wondered how much rain or snow it had seen. *Those steps. Didn't they used to turn sideways? Hmm.* That light by the door resembled one she'd wanted from Pottery Barn for the patio. That great big front window, now insulated and double hung, probably kept the cold out in ways she bet the aluminum framed one couldn't. She thought she heard cabinets opening and closing inside. *Was someone up?*

Behind her, a door opened. She turned. "Morning." The man dipped his head. His eyes lingered. "Carol Jones?" He stepped to the sidewalk.

Could that be? "Milton, is that you?" She crossed the houses between them. It had been decades.

"Carol Jones, what in the world are you doing back here, and at this hour?" He gave that laugh he always did when he had raced in front of her and Sherri to get water ice on those unbearable summer days. So long ago. How silly he'd always seemed to her, how unencumbered he'd appeared, constantly buoyed with that ridiculous smile, the kind that, for so long, she'd always associated with a lack of drive, for no one who ever tested themselves retained such a blasé attitude about what life demands. That smile, unchanged. A calm blanketed her.

"My son, he....Geoffrey, he's... in the hospital." She took a deep breath. "He's in the hospital and not doing so well." She looked at her hands, to the dirt between her fingers. "I needed some air so I thought I would...walk." She met his eyes. "You?"

"I have work to get done on a couple properties. Two tenants are moving in tomorrow. Figured I would get a jump while it was quiet out." She had no way of knowing that the house he was readying would welcome a family, one that would rent from him for three years before buying a house of their own a few blocks away. He had no way of knowing that this couple would recommend the area to their good friends, who would rent another house from Milton, and after two years, he would finally get his head above financial water long enough to tread. But at the moment, he felt defeated and this was not an emotion he would have admitted to the girl he used to play with when he was younger, the person whom he felt was just short of royalty, the person whom he never realized he had been trying to impress.

"You look well. And investments. Wow, I never thought I..." She felt her head spin: why had she never allowed herself to imagine that a person from this neighborhood, someone even raised steps from her, could become successful and remain here? Geoffrey obviously understood this, and yet he never challenged her obvious prejudice. Was that how he understood her, to be such a snob? She looked at the house that had been her home for 19 years, the home that her parents had first occupied the day after they were married, the one her father had said goodbye to before his last trip to the hospital and the one her mother had turned the lights off in before she went to bed that last night. Her voice fell. "My, this place has sure changed, hasn't it?" Her voice sounded thin.

His smile retreated. "It has indeed." He checked his watch.

The sun allowed more light into the sky. "I should probably get back to the hospital." She could not work the dirt that had settled into the fold of her knuckle. "Nice to see you, Milton. You take care." She hoped her voice didn't sound too clipped, but she wouldn't apologize.

"If you don't mind me asking, Carol, what happened to your son?"

She kicked a wrapper into the gutter. "He was in a bike accident on Monday."

"A bike…" His face fell in a way that expressed more concern than Carol would've ever imagined from a man she hadn't seen in decades. "I'm sorry. I hope he's okay." His voice wilted.

"So do I, Milton, so do I." The strangest thing suddenly crossed her lips. "You know, maybe we should've kept this house after all." He nodded, as if she had stated the obvious. Seeing the pity forming in his eyes, she recognized that he was likely humoring her, and she felt foolish. What was happening to her?

"You know, Carol…I'm not sure if I should tell you this, but some folks in the neighborhood organized a meeting to talk about the accident. They're meeting on Monday." She flinched, eyeing Milton. Thankfully, though, this information was pulling her together, providing a focus.

She felt her bearings return. "Do you have that information handy?"

"Yeah, give me a sec." He went through his door and returned quickly, clutching a piece of paper, which he handed to her.

"It's up the street, the new place on the corner. Some solid people opened it. I will be there, if that matters to you."

Her eyes scanned the spare details on the flyer. "Can I keep this, Milton?"

"Yeah, sure thing." She felt his gaze. Her eyes clung to the flyer. "Well, Carol, I have to get moving. You take care. Again, I'm sorry about your boy." She nodded as he walked towards his car.

She folded and tucked the paper into a pocket. Blue pierced the sky. Something churned in her, and her legs carried her quickly to the corner, to the left, and forward. Behind her, she heard a door open and remain. So she kept moving. A few blocks later, her phone vibrated. She checked the screen. *My plane just landed. I will be there soon.* Her fingers trembled over the keys. She stared at the screen, then closed her phone as she moved towards the hospital.

• • •

In the hospital lobby, she paused before her fuzzy reflection in the elevator doors. She felt raw. Fumbling for her phone, she dialed her husband. Muttering, he answered.

"Mason, Sherri has landed in Philly. She is on her way to the hospital now, apparently."

"Okay." Soft and exhausted, he paused. "Okay. On her way. She doesn't need a ride?"

"I suppose not."

"Okay, okay. I'm getting up and will be there soon."

Carol closed her phone and pressed the elevator call button.

From outside Geoffrey's room she heard the beeping and whirling. She let out the breath she hadn't realized she'd been holding since the elevator doors had opened. She slowed. Clenching her fists, she stepped through the doorway, then removed her coat and slung it over the chair.

At Geoffrey's bedside, she touched her son's shoulder. "I'm back, Geoffrey. Your Aunt Sherri is on her way, Son. She'll be here soon." She felt her throat constrict, her breathing labored. With the back of her hand, she caressed his cheek. "I went to your apartment, Geoff, just now. He was there, that man, whatever his name is. I…" Tears dropped from her face. "I… I just want you to come back to me, Geoffrey, to come back to us. Please." Even she could barely hear the last word she whimpered.

She remembered lifting him from his crib that one day and, after burping him, setting him on the carpet outside her bathroom so she could brush her teeth. A toddler who had not walked yet, was not supposed to for a few months yet, would stay put. Then, at the bathroom mirror, a toothbrush in her mouth, and then toothpaste dribbling down her mouth, she'd heard dull thuds, like a cardboard box tumbling down a flight of stairs. She rushed to the hall. There he was, standing, leaning against the wall, swaying a bit back and forth, his shirt brushing against the paint as he lurched forward. She had been about to chase after him, but held fast. He looked over his shoulder and giggled, then inched forward.

"Geoffrey..."

Something hit the floor. Carol looked as Sherri removed her hand from her luggage. Her lips parted for a moment, and with swift strides, circled the bed, touched Geoffrey's leg, and then reached for Carol. In her sister's embrace, Carol remained for several minutes.

"I'm sorry I couldn't get here sooner."

Carol pulled away. "You're here, that's all that matters." She suppressed her tears. "How was your flight?"

"Fine. Long, but fine. I was in San Francisco on business." Sherri stared at Geoff, her eyes misting.

"You get used to it, after a few days."

"Oh."

"Are you hungry? The cafeteria has some serviceable food, probably fresh coffee." She nodded. Carol guided her sister towards the door and down the hall to the elevator, for she knew the longer they stayed in that room, the more she would see Geoffrey through Sherri's fresh eyes and she could not acknowledge what she had become desensitized to just yet.

Into the room that someone had thought was a good idea to decorate in browns—the paint, the tile on the floor, the trim near the white tables—Sherri led Carol. Carol sat while Sherri set down her purse and then retrieved her wallet. With a trembling hand, she squeezed Carol's shoulder. "You still take your coffee black?" Carol nodded.

On the phone—offensively situated in the middle of the main wall—a man sounded exhausted. "Dude, yeah, she's good, she had a girl. Totally healthy. Yeah." He turned away when their eyes met.

In a corner, a man likely around retirement age hung his head over a steaming cup of coffee. A much younger woman was mouthing something as she rubbed his back. She was looking at the light in the ceiling.

Sherri placed two coffees on the table and took the chair next to Carol. "I really wish I could have been here sooner. I didn't ask for many details when Mason called, but, my god, Carol, just how bad is it?"

Carol clutched the coffee cup. "Bad." She sipped. Tears spilled from Sherri's eyes.

Minutes ticked by until the silence irritated Carol. "I was out getting fresh air earlier. I walked the neighborhood a bit, saw the old house." Her voice cracked. "Though it had been rehabbed, it still looked like I remembered it." She sipped her coffee and then thumbed the cup's insignia. "We should have kept that house, Sherri. You were right. I'm so sorry." Carol cried.

Sherri eyed her coffee, took a long sip, and then set it on the table. With her finger tips, she nudged it aside. "This isn't the time for that talk, Carol." She put her hands over her sister's and they both forced a smile. Once they'd finished their coffees, which they'd allowed to cool, they returned to Geoffrey's room and waited for Mason.

• • •

During the long night, though Sherri and Mason were nearby, Carol felt isolated. Her unsettled mind attempted to make sense of all that was coming apart around her. For how long had she allowed her distorted sense of her childhood to infect how she lived? And how much of this had she passed on to Geoffrey? And Geoffrey, her greatest accomplishment in life, being used by the people in this neighborhood as a bargaining chip to promote their agendas. How dare they? she thought. She kept imagining Milton's eyes, the extended hand with that meeting information, all that he was offering her, all that he was holding back. If she showed, would she too be used in a way? And would this help or hinder her son? She struggled to find comfort in the hard cushioned chair, failed to make adequate use of the small, thin blanket.

The next morning, she was startled awake by Mason's firm hand. "I'm going down for coffee, would you like some?"

Through a dry mouth, she managed: "Yes." Where was Sherri?

Left alone, she stretched, and in doing so, the paper in her pocket crinkled. She extracted it. She stood, unfolded the paper, and went to Geoffrey's bedside. She studied the blunt words. By the time Mason returned with Sherri in tow, Carol had the sheet memorized.

"What's in your hand," Sherri asked as she handed Carol the warm coffee.

"One of our old neighbors—do you remember that boy, Milton? He still lives on the block—he gave it to me. It's for a meeting the community is holding in order to discuss the accident." She looked at her husband, who raised an eyebrow.

Sherri sat while Mason went to the window. "What in the world could they be talking about?" Sherri asked. Mason shook his head.

"Apparently, people are making a race issue about the accident. It's in the papers too—the discontent, not the meeting." She set the paper on Geoffrey's legs and clutched the coffee. The thin cup was not guarding her fingers from the coffee's heat. "It's tonight, the meeting, and I plan to attend."

"And say what? You don't live there anymore." Mason asked, his voice a low, firm tone.

"I don't know yet, but I know one of us needs to represent our son." She stared at the cracked skin around her son's lips. Sherri placed a hand on her sister's shoulder.

After a few moments, Milton leaned forward. "By the way, the Henderson husband came by yesterday while I was at the house. He asked if we'd seen their sons' basketball in our backyard. Apparently, the ball was an important gift from an uncle… something. I had no idea what he was talking about but I said I would ask you. He seemed insistent and I assured him I'd ask." He looked at his fingernail, as if seeing it for the first time. "Any idea what he's talking about?"

She remembered the ball, tucked away in their basement. "I…" She imagined the look on their little faces as they received their ball back. She imagined their little hands fighting over that ball, one clutching it so closely he wouldn't let the other hold it. She pictured their glee and the return of a supposedly important item they believed lost. She looked at her helpless, inert son. She pictured herself going down those steps, finding that bin, heading out her front door and delivering the ball, with or without an explanation. Then she imagined it returning to her yard within a few days. How could she teach these children to treasure and protect something supposedly important? "I have no idea what they're talking about."

He nodded. "About this meeting, will you be fine if Sherri accompanies you? I don't know that I have it in me to occupy a room with a bunch of strangers, particularly those strangers, enduring their thoughts of my son."

"That's fine." She turned her head. "Sherri?" Sherri stood. "We'll be fine, but first, I'd like to take Sherri and head home, perhaps rest and then change into more presentable clothes."

Talk radio filled the silence on the drive home, and once there, Sherri retreated to the guest bedroom and slept. Left alone, Carol stood in her kitchen, staring at her neighbor's yard in the distance. The two children were throwing a football to one another. *So carefree.* In two days' time, alone again in her home, she would traipse to the basement, open that storage bin, retrieve the ball, and clutch it to her chest. Under the cover of the dawning light, she would step across her dewed lawn in her bare feet, hustling towards her back wall, where, standing for a moment, the ball held close, she would question what she was about to do, and, knowing that she would again find the ball in her yard, she would still foist the ball over the wall and, waiting, watch the ball roll to a part of the yard where the boys would find it easily. But, standing there in her kitchen, she felt her nerves revolt and her energy ebb. She knew she needed to collect herself for this meeting, and, somehow, walking into her bedroom and reaching her bed, she was able to sleep for a few hours. And, after waking and rousing Sherri, they would sit in her kitchen, make sandwiches, then take showers and then, dressed as if for a major trial, Carol would drive them back to the city, where, in their old neighborhood, they had trouble finding parking, a fact she wasn't sure was a good or bad sign.

The Meeting

As planned, Rose arrived first, reminded by those little yellow sticky notes: on the front door; on the refrigerator door, under her Florida magnet; on the milk carton, on the second shelf; in the middle of the bathroom mirror, which she had to tape up after her long morning shower. All had "leave at 5:30" in thick black marker. The momentum fueled by adrenaline she'd gathered as she removed each one, nodding to herself, willing herself out her front door and up the street—*you are doing right by your community*—dissipated as that nice couple had opened the door for her, their cautious smiles saying: I hope you know what you are doing.

Her own doubt nearly choking her, she surveyed the empty tables and chairs (half of which were turned away from her). Would it be out of line to ask if these were nailed to the floor? Still, she kept her concern as far from her throat as she could manage. She imagined Edgar staring at her with folded arms.

"We weren't sure what you had in mind, so we kept our normal dinner set-up." Erin's calm voice was like a fresh pot of coffee waiting to be poured.

"This will do just fine." In that moment, she felt her carefully laid plans evaporate, as she had imagined a room arranged like the community center. How foolish of her to not have assumed this room would remain like it would during business hours. Though why the positioning of the tables, the chairs would impact their discussion, she wasn't sure. She would likely admit that she was looking for anything and everything to assign blame to, should this fail tonight. Briefly, she wished she'd asked her nephew and his friends to stay and attend, but this would not be the introduction to the neighborhood she would want for them. Yet, perhaps his generation gravitated towards these moments in ways hers now avoided. She shook her head, hoping her tangled thoughts did not constrict all this moment could become for this neighborhood. Delivering her two weeks' notice to Lillian earlier still weighed on her.

That afternoon, walking to the Laundromat, the belief that Lillian had already betrayed her by courting that Mexican to replace her had propelled her. She would not be replaced; quitting first, she would leave on her own terms. This conviction guided her around the corner, lit her cigarette in front of the store, paced her by the front window, but crumbled when Lillian waved to her with that odd smile that Rose imagined people wore when they visited Disneyland. She needed to hate Lillian— *how dare she think of replacing her most loyal employee?* But maybe she hadn't given her boss a fair shake, and this rethinking stung as she stabbed her cigarette against the window sill.

Striding through the door, she had noted the six customers in various stages of their laundry. She had to resist going to them, encouraging them to better sort their loads, pay closer attention to the way they were folding their clothes. She knew she could make this store run smoothly, help this owner learn to speak to these customers, her neighbors. Now, of small consolation was the feeling that a few of these customers would take their business elsewhere, but, deep down, she realized that life would move forward without her. She had managed, somehow, after both Charlie and Edgar had left her, hadn't she? Yet, she had no idea that Lillian had entertained that Mexican woman's effort—from one immigrant to another. The idea of losing Rose was so far from her mind, but she wanted to appear receptive to a person who wanted to create her own opportunity in this country. Rose never knew that the perceived understanding between her and her boss was so strong that Lillian never felt the need to verbalize it. And like most things that remain unsaid, it got buried.

She would always regret quitting that job, the image of Lillian stammering as she processed Rose's notice returning to her in the quiet moments walking to her new post office, going to the kitchen for her second cup of coffee.

But now, standing in the restaurant, she felt shaken, as if she'd abandoned a friend she did not realize she'd even had. Counting the minutes until seven, she wished she could stop seeing that despair on Lillian's face. Then two people—a cheerful, though reserved couple she recognized from that block party over the weekend—meandered in. These white people nodded to them, and Rose smiled as they moved towards seats near the back among all the empty ones, as if they were gauging how far away from the blast's center was safe. Before she knew it, more people trickled in; then, soon, the room was about a quarter full, a mix of people she had known for years, people to whom she nodded when she passed on the street, and many she'd never seen before. She wondered how they'd heard of the meeting, and what this might mean about how many people would show. Mostly, she thought about missing these faces.

"Should we just hang back?" Erin asked. Rose flinched, for she'd done her best to dispel her authority here, though, clearly, this had failed.

Eyeing Erin, she said, "Wherever you're comfortable, baby." Fingering the necklace balled in her pocket, "Don't forget, this meeting is about all of us, so speak up when you feel the need." All these people so early, though as she eyed the clock, she recognized that perhaps this was at it should be. Donna entered, trailed by Keisha, whose wide eyes filled Rose with a touch of envy and sadness. They moved towards the front.

"Where do you want us?"

"This will do fine, I think." Rose motioned them to a high table by the bar. Keisha scrambled up the chair and kicked her feet a few times. Donna placed a hand on her shoulder and the legs slowed.

"Mama, look, it's Mr. Wilson!"

"Don't point, honey." But Keisha's little finger had already found Willis by the windows, wedged between two neighbors. He squirmed and scowled, eventually shifting his gaze to the floor. Her stomach tightened; at least she knew from which direction the trouble would come. She asked Erin for a glass of water.

As the minutes ticked by, seats filled. As 7:00 passed, they were left with standing room only. Black faces, white faces; some neither. Watches were checked, people nodded to, cans of soda opened. Every open space gradually disappeared. The voices quieted and eyes settled on Rose, and without checking the time, she understood that they'd waited long enough. Clearing her throat, she clasped her hands at her waist, hoping that locking them together would cease their shaking. Bracing for the storm gathered in front of her, she ached for a cigarette, and eased her shoulders back. If you do this too quickly, Edgar had warned, people won't trust you and you will lose your authority. She blanked her mind as best she could. Her eyes swept the crowd, and in the process, anticipating hate and anger, she encountered mostly receptive eyes. A little lightness found her, and she felt as if they'd already won. So this was what confidence felt like.

Overhead, the ceiling fans swooshed. Twice more she cleared her throat and waited for all the eyes to find her. With the attention of her community earned, she searched for her first word.

• • •

Carol and Sherri slipped through the side door and were thankful that two people stepped aside to reveal an empty corner in the back. Carol had hoped for a healthier breeze, but the open window was a godsend nonetheless. Did this place even *have* air conditioning? Her eyes swept the nice, clean bar and beautiful mirror stretching the breadth of the back wall. These folks spent good money on this place. More people filed in. Near the front, people began clogging the aisle between tables. Carol was sure she'd counted wrong when she'd reached sixty-three people. Would this tiny room handle all these voices? She was glad to see a smattering of people dressed appropriately in business attire, but was not encouraged by the folks in torn jeans and baseball hats. *How receptive would these people be to reason*? As she thought this, she fought against her snap judgments.

Near the open kitchen, removed from the crowd, an old black woman spoke with a woman and her child. *Was she in charge*? She questioned the wisdom to bring a child here. Behind the bar, a pretty white woman was working too hard to put things away, as if a health inspector might enter any minute. Clusters of people chatted. Given Geoffrey's assessment of the neighborhood's progress, Carol was not surprised by such a diverse mix of people. Perhaps this boded well, for just maybe the negativity would be marginalized. Although, given how young everyone seemed, she wondered if maybe they could use more maturity, more experience. *At 7:08, why hadn't things started?* A moment later, Milton entered from the other door.

Thankfully, the lighting in their corner was subdued enough to provide anonymity. The place was not big enough to hide, so what would she do if he said hello, identified her to the crowd? She was here to observe, perhaps guide, but not influence, for she did not want to become a target.

Gradually, voices dropped. The older woman's eyes roamed the crowd, encouraging an eerie peace in her wake. Carol stood up straight. "Thank you all for coming. For those of you who don't know me, I'm Ms. Rose. I organized this because, as a longtime resident of this neighborhood, I care what happens to it and in it. For a while, things weren't so good here. Streets were dirty, crime was high—people had lost interest, touch with their neighbors." She took a short breath. "But things have turned around. Some people think things didn't change for the good, and so when this accident happened last week, people felt themselves getting hot. 'This proves that people are trying to get rid of us,' these folks have been saying. But we can't let that negativity continue."

Murmurs rippled. This woman needed a pulpit.

"Now, before we get into this, I want to thank Mr. Tim and Ms. Erin for opening their business to us this evening." She nodded to the woman and man behind the bar, who smiled in a careful, reluctant way. Parts of the crowd ignored them. "Now, let's talk, and let's be civil. From what I've been hearing, some people, some who are probably in this room, think that white driver intentionally ran over that black man on that bike." Heads nodded and a couple people looked pleased. "I'm here to tell you that ain't so. It's terrible that that young man got hurt, but it was an accident."

"You there?" A scruffy man near the back of the crowd barked.

"No, but..."

"Then why should we listen to what you have to say?"

Milton stepped forward. "Show her some respect. We won't accomplish anything if we start snipping at one another. Let's hear what she has to say." Milton remained standing, and Carol felt the air thicken.

"Thank you, baby." Rose's warm smile could tame a jury. Holding Milton's gaze until tension eased, this woman should have been a lawyer. "Now listen, you might be upset about the way things have changed in this neighborhood, but don't let that anger infect something that has nothing to do with it. People start getting worked up, they invite other people to follow. Before you know it, we're getting violent." She paused, drew her hands together and dropped her voice. "That's good for no one."

The man who had barked leaned back, folded his arms, and frowned. She wondered just how many petulant little children made up this audience, and if there were more like him, she wondered what this meeting would accomplish. Though what she had hoped to see in action, she wasn't sure. She bristled, taking on the anger she knew her son would harbor in the midst of this conversation. Couldn't these people see they were fighting different battles? They were scrambling through the dark looking for a light switch that didn't exist.

An older black man stood. "Now Ms. Rose, we hear what you're saying, but hear us. These white people arrived, snatched our homes, our community from us. For those of us who couldn't afford to buy years ago and won't be able to buy any time soon, what happens to us? We know all too well. On top of that, nothing happens to that white driver, we read the message loud and clear. We don't matter." He smoothed out his tie as the veins in his neck and on the side of his head pulsed. He settled into his seat like a race car driver awaiting the green light. "I'm Ted, for those who don't know me."

"Let me tell you folks about respect." Heads turned toward a young man in a blue sweatshirt, who, briefly, reminded Carol of her client Darnell. He staggered to his feet and cracked his knuckles and then shook out his hands as he grimaced. "My boy, he's got Down syndrome. And right now, when he gets old enough for school, if this neighborhood don't continue to improve, my boy won't get the resources he needs to succeed. These schools don't have the right money. They need help, and like it or not, that help will come when all these people move in with their money." In the dim light his eyes steeled. "You talk about fair. What about my boy?"

The barker leaned forward. In a measured voice he asked, "Your uncle was Charles, right? You're Nathan?"

The man rolled this information around, perhaps sussing for the catch awaiting his answer. He didn't look happy. "That's right."

"He was a good man, Charles, and he stepped up—from what I recall—to help your mother raise you. Yep, a fine man, a man who had a good sense about things, people. You agree with that?"

"What's my uncle got to do with this?" His bravado waned.

"Your uncle appreciated things, like community, and he didn't walk around waiting for handouts. He knew that his people could care for their own, stand behind one another. Listen, Nathan, I'm sorry to hear about your boy, but… if you're waiting for these strangers to bail out your boy, you're looking for a handout."

"I..." Nathan looked like a floundering swimmer desperate for a life preserver or a strong hand. The barker bore his eyes into the young man, who withered with each second.

A woman stood and cocked her head. Carol braced. The surging wave of discontent crested. "Listen, his boy matters, so don't start no shit saying he doesn't. And who the fuck are you to bring up this man's uncle? That man ain't here, and you ain't his family. How the fuck you know what he would have thought about this community today?" She leaned forward, pointing to her chest. The people seated closest to her wisely shifted to afford her space. "My two sons matter too, and maybe the change in the neighborhood means they won't grow up to be like their fathers." She looked around, challenging someone to speak against her. She drew herself up and exhaled. "Now, Ms. Rose says she knows something about what happened, I'm going to trust her word. So let's shut up long enough to hear about what brought us here." She dropped to her seat and her body relaxed. "I'm Brenda, for y'all who don't know me." She sounded cheery, as if what had come before this last comment was needed and shouldn't be taken in any way confrontational.

The barker tensed his jaw. "Well, that's nice that you have his *back*, Brenda, but we can make change without things being taken from us. And since I don't know Ms. Rose, I'd like to hear how she knows what she claims to know." He adjusted his tie. The little girl standing by her mother cowered. Carol's blood pressure rose. The Brenda woman balled up her fist. Carol looked outside. A petite Asian woman peered in the window. Even in the dim light Carol felt the desperation in those eyes. The woman leaned towards the window, squinted, and then her face drooped. She left. *What was that about?*

"Why isn't anyone thinking of this black man on the bike?" Ted's voice climbed. "How can we turn our back on one of our own like this? What is wrong with you people?" Carol recognized that Geoffrey would take pride in being considered one of them, but she was not ready to align her child with this man's restricted world view. Perhaps most troubling was realizing by the nodding heads, the crossed arms, even the stiff backs, his ideas had legs. Given how those people were silent through most of this, she wondered what it would take to root out their anger too. And to counter it, where was all that youthful optimism Geoffrey had been so vocal about sensing? For this reason, she almost stepped forward, but Sherri touched her arm, shaking her head. For once, she chose to listen to her sister.

A white man in a suit stood in the middle of the room panning his gaze. "I'm Walter. Some of you know me. I've lived here for years, so I don't know if that makes me one of you or one of them, or whatever distinction some of you care to make. I live here and have loved living here, and I am a part of this community." He gulped and his eyes trained on the barker. "I don't know the man who was hit, but I know the driver. I can vouch for him. I've known him a while now. He's a good member of the community." He swiveled as he delivered those last few lines, his eyes meeting every seated person.

"Of course you're standing up for him." Ted slumped back as if the white man's voice had won the room. *How pathetic.* A sadness washed over that white man's face. *Why am I seeing this man and his concerns as infantile*? She thought of the squirrel they'd trapped and killed, the one that had been gnawing on their deck. She remembered a bit of remorse as the worker disposed of the animal. The next day, though she saw the little babe—or whatever young squirrels are called—the little thing that looked far too young and feeble to be scurrying around on its own in their yard. That deck had never seemed the same to her again. She leaned against the wall.

"I know him too, the driver." Milton said in a solid voice, slouching against the wall as he spoke. He looked at Walter and nodded. "And I also vouch for his character." The people in the crowd took turns between the two men, as Milton and the guy in the tie locked eyes. "He's my neighbor, in fact. He picks up trash when he sees it on the sidewalk, keeps the front of his house clean, doesn't throw loud parties, and brings over your mail if it's been mixed in with his. He's been here almost a year and a half, and I don't care what color his skin is." Milton leaned towards a table, and the people sitting there made space for his hands, which he placed on the tabletop. "Say what you want, about the accident, about the neighborhood changing. One has nothing to do with the other. You can be part of the problem—sitting here, griping about things beyond your control—or you can be part of the future here, make this change work for you somehow." He was waiting for some challenge to this stance, and he was clearly between waiting for the word and hoping it never came.

"Now, now, nobody is saying..." Ted's voice wavered. His anger, though it had been quelled, was in a holding pattern. He surveyed his neighbors, most of whom had sat back. The couple behind the bar exchanged worried looks. The woman by Ms. Rose clutched her child. The next moment,

Milton's eyes found Carol. "Are we just going to sit here and let them tell us to give up our neighborhood?" He stared, then his insistent, challenging eyes pleaded.

The voices swelled from various directions.

An older black man stood and pointed to Ted. "He's right! What are we doing here if not to help one of our own?"

"Fuck you, sit down," a voice from the crowd called out.

"You sit down; I'm standing up for my neighborhood, and fuck anyone who has a problem with that."

"Cut the language," a person from a different part of the room yelled.

Spinning around, he said to the air, "I am no child, so fuck you. I'm speaking for the people who can't, like that boy on the bike, like every boy that will be in a similar situation."

Carol watched as Rose raised her arm like a teacher who had long lost control of her class. Rose moved her lips, but her words found no voice.

Thrusting forward with strength she didn't realize she still possessed, Carol shouted, "How dare you all!" The room stilled. "That young man, whose person you continue to invoke, is my son, and I will not listen to a single one of you use his name to further your agendas." Carol swallowed hard and felt a bit dizzy. She reached for the nearest tabletop. "Now, I don't know whether this was an accident or not. Right now I'm too concerned with my son waking up. I can also tell you, that as a person who wanted to be part of solutions in life, he would despise being used in the way some of you are using him."

"You live in this neighborhood?" The barker asked.

"My husband and I don't, but..." She recognized that she might gain some traction by mentioning that she'd been raised here, but also understood that offering that truth might also work against her, as a person who "deserted" them.

"The suburbs then?"

"That's right."

"Must be nice." His fiery eyes dared her, but he clearly had no intention of releasing his hold on how he meant to use her son, even if Geoffrey too was "new."

Carol took a deep breath and clasped her hands. She knew how to handle a hostile witness. "But my son lives here. You, sir..." She caught the syllable on her tongue. Her rage was throttling her motivation, goosing her point. But what that was had eluded her. She didn't know the answer to the question the people in that room had: what do we do? She didn't know what they needed, what the neighborhood needed, but she knew what Geoffrey would want. The room in that moment was hers to control, to force them to hear her case. But now that she'd played the son card, she'd come up empty. To what truth would she speak? What argument was hers to make? She pictured her Geoffrey inert in his hospital bed. She locked eyes with Ms. Rose, whose body shielded the little girl. A moment later, that little girl's mother nudged the delicate woman aside. The energy in the room shifted towards that mother and Ms. Rose. Carol fought the urge to collapse. She kept telling herself that she'd failed, fell far short of whatever it was that she thought attending this meeting would accomplish. But as she felt pulled back, she resisted the notion that she really felt helpless, and perhaps this was emptying her in a way she had never experienced.

"Look, everyone, my daughter here saw the accident." Eyes shifted to that woman by Ms. Rose. "She says that man driving stopped, let her cross, waved to her, and then went. That man on the bike—no disrespect, ma'am—didn't stop. So you need to let this go. That woman in the corner, she and her family need your support and your prayers, not your anger."

The barker bolted up. "We're believing children now?!' The energy in the room deflated, yet the nodding heads that had usually accompanied his statements didn't surface. People in the audience shared looks and shrugs.

"Sir, my child says she saw it, she saw it. I plucked her from the crowd that day, so I know she was there. She knows better than to lie to me, and she knows better than to talk just to get people to hear her talk nonsense."

Voices erupted on either side, as attention diverted from the front and redirected to one another in the crowd. Entering the fray, Ms. Rose wedged between standing people, jabbing their fingers at one another. Behind her, Milton moved, reaching a hand towards her. The white folks behind the bar huddled closer, though the woman's hand moved towards the phone cradled near the cash register. Then the scream that seemed to linger long after the little girl, her fists balled, closed her mouth: "STOP!"

Her mother grabbed her by the shoulders and pulled her back.

"That man stopped for me!"

The barker rolled his eyes and sat, shaking his head. Other people who had been standing fell towards their seats. Cautiously, Ms. Rose returned to the front and placed a hand on the little girl's head.

"Let's all take a deep breath," Ms. Rose said. Carol trembled and Sherri guided her towards a chair, which a white person had just offered her. "Now, we want to use this situation to get this neighborhood together; not just to end this bitterness, but to make us solid so we can move forward, together."

More cursing and yelling followed, though the volume had been turned down, and in their words, perhaps enough of them realized that they would need a new vehicle for their understandable frustration and discomfort with the inevitable and dramatic change to the world around them. More and more, the comments spoke to feelings of looming displacement, an indifferent city hall, opportunistic people eyeing their homes as opportunities waiting to be snatched. In between, people repeated how much they wanted to be involved in what was already in this neighborhood and integrate, not disintegrate and start over. They *liked* where they'd chosen to live and wanted to figure out how to respect it better. The clock ticked. Eventually, the spent people trickled out. With precision, Ms. Rose seemed to know which comments to support, which to clarify, which to challenge, and which to leave hanging in the air. What a neighbor she would be. Never had Carol witnessed a person exhibiting such expert timing at understanding how to chip away at this boulder of an issue, whittling it down to a pebble that almost anyone present could have kicked down the street. None of this would help her son, but maybe, when he woke, he would have a better home to nurture him in his recovery. More than anything, this was all she could clutch.

As people left, the barker sulked. The little girl looked at Carol, who looked back. With a timid smile, her adorable braids drooped to her shoulders, she studied Carol. Carol imagined her witnessing her son's body sprawled on the asphalt, the blood leaving his body. She wondered if this image would stay in her young mind forever. Carol clutched Sherri's hand, which gripped tightly in return. *This* is how you address important issues, she imagined Geoffrey saying. How much of a fool she'd been to never validate this hope he'd always harbored for this place.

• • •

Rose knew she'd stemmed the tide of discontent to an approachable level when the room quieted and people left, carrying with them a relaxed attitude and a smile or two. People shook hands, introduced themselves, and avoided the sulking, angry man. She was half-tempted to go to him, ask his name, shake his hand, ask him where he lived, but she was spent. She did her best to keep her head up, a smile on her face. A few people mouthed a thank you on their way into the night. In that moment, she understood. This was why her son went to war, so he could stand up for something in the open. She'd heard this reason but never felt its meaning, not as she now did. She realized that, although her gesture paled in comparison to what Charlie risked and died for, this small step might make a big difference. If only this revelation blunted the pain. *Why did this wound feel so fresh now?* She could feel Edgar shaking his head, and she allowed a few tears to fall at the thought of him watching over her. *I hope you know what you're doing,* she could hear him mutter, a sly smile on his face. She'd done the right thing. Later, she'd wonder what had held Willis' tongue throughout the evening, and she wasn't sure if this boded well for things to come.

In the weeks to come, she packed her life into new, sturdy boxes and cleaned the house better than she had in years. After watching the movers cart off the last of her belongings, she would pan around the first floor. How quickly the remnants of her life—her family's life—in that house had been scrubbed. She would close her eyes, then sitting on a chair staving off the creeping emptiness circling her, she would wait for her nephew and his friends to arrive, to whom she would present her keys, along with a strong hug. The key ring carried a note: "be good neighbors." After stepping out that front door, she would never see her home again. She would spend the last of her days in Washington DC, in a house her cousins had opened to her—though she never felt at home under that roof, on that block, in that community. Although she would tell herself she'd done the right thing over and over again, she was not at peace. Without trying, her thoughts wondered about how Keisha had grown, how Brenda was fairing with her boys, how Milton was handling his houses, how that park had been maintained, and, lastly, whatever happened with Lillian. A phone call, a letter, an email would have answered any one of these questions, but, with every passing day away from that neighborhood, she felt a connection fade, one that she accepted losing, and in its absence, dead weight. Her neighborhood may not have "needed" her, but could they have used her there, just because? She carried this weight to her grave.

But before all of that, there were the eight people left in the room to tend to, two of whom approached her. How strong this woman must be to have shown her face tonight and speak up. She imagined her having a fine son, given the upbringing someone adorned in such a smart, well-tailored and laundered suit must have provided the boy. This realization stung as she thought of her Charlie. *Why were parents ever deprived of their children*? As the women neared, Rose wondered what she would say to this woman. Would she chastise Rose for not taking her son's side? Rose blinked and they were close enough to shake hands, which they did in a gentle, warm way.

"Thank you, Ms. Rose. This neighborhood is lucky to have a woman like you looking out for it. My son would enjoy your company." Rose almost hugged this woman but restrained herself. "I grew up here, but I ran when I could. But my Geoffrey, he returned here. He was… he *is*… pursuing an Urban Planning degree at Penn because he believes in communities like this, which was why he chose to live here." She stared at her hands. "If you find that man who was driving, you tell him that I don't fault him. Would you do that for me?"

Rose wanted to tell this woman that she understood her pain, but then she thought of how good it felt to let other people empathize from afar, not share in it. She also thought she should explain how she knew the young man who had been driving, but you could tell this woman was not looking to chit chat.

"I will, Mrs…?"

"Jones, Carol Jones."

Rose chewed on the name for a moment. It carried a hint of a memory, but it eluded her. "Nice to meet you, Mrs. Jones. I hope your boy gets better." Rose placed a hand on this woman's shoulder and squeezed a little. Carol placed a hand on Rose's hand and left it there for a beat. They both nodded, taking in one another's gaze, and then perhaps sensing that they had no words to share, Mrs. Jones and the other woman left.

"Did we do good, Ms. Rose?" In those little eyes, Rose saw Charlie's optimism, the one he held when he explained why he'd not only signed up for the army but would be eventually deployed overseas. She wanted to swim in that gaze. What good would it do her to say, well, we won't know for a while? Maybe so, maybe not. We might have even done some more harm? Rose wouldn't take that light from her. Now she understood that she was looking at a different kind of hope, that this young person needed something else out of the world, and who was Rose to tell her otherwise?

Basking in the girl's smile, Rose clutched the child's shoulder but met

Donna's eyes. "We did what we came to do, Keisha." Rose reached into her pocket and pulled out the gold chain with the cross. "Hold out your hand, young lady." Rose crouched down, slowly, hoping her stiff knees would hold.

Keisha lifted her hand.

"Now Rose." Donna's voice was controlled but firm in the way a good mother's should be.

"It's a gift, Donna. Let it do her some good."

Donna bit her lower lip and searched Rose's eyes for something. Meanwhile, Keisha's hand closed around the chain and cross.

"Thank you, Ms. Rose," Keisha said.

Rose let the warm feeling accompanying that hope, or maybe just an attitude of seeing the world not as it was but as it could be, envelop her. To the white couple still huddled behind the bar, she waved and nodded. They waved back, looking relieved. Outside, Rose crossed the street and walked the block and a half to the new park, where she smiled at whom she saw. That nice young man. He was staring at a corner of the park. She startled him as she approached. He smiled at her and then kept eyeing that corner. Without asking why, she put a hand on his shoulder. If she'd felt forward enough to ask what was on his obviously wearied mind, he might not share that in a couple days he would follow through with his resolve to let his father's car go, to donate it to a church—he'd seen a billboard advertising one that would haul it away for you. And this would lighten his burden, enough to rally him through his life for a little while, allow him to return to the groove of his job, his life. It would be years before the sting of the accident, however, would dull. In that time, as he would soon acknowledge, he had not and likely never would feel at peace in that home. In two years, he would be all too happy to sell the house, to an eager couple who wouldn't stop talking about how much they loved the charming neighborhood. But before all of that had a chance to pass, he felt a dim glimpse of hope, as if he wasn't sure where he was headed but it couldn't be any worse than where he'd been.

• • •

Relief. Carol and Sherri stepped through the door and into the fresh air. Milton had lingered near them as she'd thanked Ms. Rose, but they left before a word could pass between them. Warm words about her son would have been appropriate, but she'd shouldered all she could take for an evening, and perhaps genuine pleasantries that would lead nowhere—we should get together some time… or, here's my email, stay in touch. So they left. Carol waited until they were two blocks away before she collapsed to the sidewalk and sobbed until she ached.

The tears returned when, back at the hospital, she went limp in her husband's strong embrace. "Was it awful?" he whispered in her ear. She shook her head as she pulled away. "I need coffee, would you like some?" Again, Carol shook her head.

Her sister looked at her and smiled meekly. Carol stared outside. "If you don't mind, Mason, I will join you," Sherri said.

Soon a nurse entered and checked Geoffrey's vitals. Carol looked out the window, and as she did, she watched two young boys bouncing a basketball down the street. Before she could stop it, a smile formed on her face. She suppressed a sudden urge to laugh. She hunched a bit, and the nurse offered a concerned look. She smiled for him and then he left. Alone, she laughed, hard; and when she was done, she cried until her eyes stung. She was happy to have finished by the time Mason and Sherri eventually returned with their coffee. By that time, a calm had enveloped her, and she resented this feeling.

When she was the only one awake in the room that night, she sniffled and begged for tears that never came. The thin, stiff blanket covering her irritated more than it warmed. She strained her ears for a sound outside their room, but heard only silence. Where were the whispers of a passing conversation or the shuffling of feet? Even Mason's breathing was silent. Staring out the window she had trouble distinguishing the buildings, as her reflection seemed superimposed over everything. No matter where she turned, there it was. She thought she saw a tree swaying in the breeze, but it could have been a garbage bag blowing in the wind, for all she knew. She wondered how she could return to their huge house with its well-attended grounds, its immaculate interior, its stifling poshness, its sterile features for which they'd paid dearly. How would she interact with her neighbors when they waved from behind the wheels of their cars, called their "hellos" from their mailboxes? Most of all, she wanted to take a golf club to their back lawn and obliterate those fine, closely shorn lines.

Two days later, her son's eyes fluttered, and she steeled herself, for her tears had run their course.

Acknowledgments

This book would never have happened without the support of many, many individuals. First, I'd like to thank all those who read early drafts and offered useful feedback, especially my friends and peers at Queens University of Charlotte. A special nod to the Queens professors who mentored me through the bulk of this project: Fred Leebron, Naeem Murr, Ann Cummins, Jane Allison, Elizabeth Evans, and David Payne --Thanks to all of you for pushing me to be a better writer. I'd also like to thank previous writing teachers who had a huge impact on my approach to the craft: Mel Freilicher, Judith Vanderbok, and Lisa Zeidner. A shout out to my 5Writers peeps: Jennie, Darlene, Linda, Ron, and Emilia. Thanks to the continued support and encouragement of my family: the Windhausers, The Parks, and the Von Arxs. A nod to all my friends, who are always curious about what I'm working on—you'll finally be able to read the story you've been hearing about the past six years. I'd also like to thank every author who has written a book with which I have spent time: whether I enjoy your work or not, I learn from you—Keep writing.

Thanks to Fred Melhuish, Jr. and Michael Kelly, who answered my Septa questions.

Special thanks to Sonia for undertaking the task of helping me dot my i's and cross my t's in the final draft.

Thanks to Chris and Julianna for a great author pic.

Last, I'd like to thank Jared, who, in addition to his unwavering support of my work, never bats an eye when I'm holed up in the office, hunched in front of my computer, sacrificing time away from him/us, all in the name of pursuing my art. I love you very much.

BLACK ROSE
writing™

CPSIA information can be obtained at www.ICGtesting.com
Printed in the USA
BVOW08s1530120916

461037BV00013B/4/P